Readers love
ORDER OF THE
BLACK KNIGHTS

Gideon

"This was a strong start for a series that has the potential to be a step outside of the norm and I'm looking forward to seeing how it all plays out."

—My Fiction Nook

Matthias

"I am definitely a fan of this series and recommend it for sure!"

—Bayou Book Junkie

Vespar

"The romance, tension, adventure and mystery were awesome. This is a great read."

—MM Good Book Reviews

Jaeger

"This series just keeps getting better and better."

—Gay Book Reviews

By RK STAUNTON

ORDER OF THE BLACK KNIGHTS
By Ashe Barker: Gideon
By Alexis Duran: Matthias
By Thianna Durston: Vespar
By Evelise Archer: Jaeger
Gabriel

Published by DREAMSPINNER PRESS
www.dreamspinnerpress.com

GABRIEL

RK Staunton

Published by
DREAMSPINNER PRESS

5032 Capital Circle SW, Suite 2, PMB# 279, Tallahassee, FL 32305-7886 USA
www.dreamspinnerpress.com

Gabriel
© 2017 RK Staunton.

Cover Art
© 2017 Aaron Anderson.
aaronbydesign55@gmail.com
Cover content is for illustrative purposes only and any person depicted on the cover is a model.
Order of the Black Knights Cover Concept and Logo
© 2016 Thianna Durston.

ISBN: 978-1-63533-392-3
Digital ISBN: 978-1-63533-393-0
Library of Congress Control Number: 2016916567
Published April 2017
v. 1.0

Printed in the United States of America

This paper meets the requirements of
ANSI/NISO Z39.48-1992 (Permanence of Paper).

THE ORDER OF
THE BLACK KNIGHTS

EVERY CENTURY has seen its knights. But there are those who are never seen. They do what must be done, what has to be done—when nobody wants to get their hands dirty. They are called the Black Knights. First created in the 1100s by the wizard Moriel, these men seem cold and hard, and it is said that some have no soul. But for each knight, there is one who can bring out the man who waits inside. The question is whether or not he will kill the individual before he figures it out.

Through the ages, they've conquered and ruled and taken what they wanted. And they have adapted to modern times. Instead of being bullies for hire, they have taken their skills further—the Internet, the CIA, government infiltration, hacking, special ops, assassination, but each one of them has a need they don't understand—to squash, kill, or destroy.

If the Knight pardons an enemy, he will no longer be cursed. If not, he will continue to live the same life again and again, and each life will make him harder and more unyielding. And each life will make it less likely that he can be saved.

PROLOGUE

GABRIEL DIDN'T know whether to be amused or pissed that, in the end, it was a bullet that got him. He tried to laugh, but it came out as a gurgling wheeze that left him coughing and choking on his own blood. It wouldn't be long. He dropped his head back to rest on the wall of the building he was slumped against. The crack of his skull against the brick should have hurt, but he barely noticed. There was too much else hurting right then—his ribs, his chest. The bullets had left burning paths through him that hurt like a motherfucker. That would stop soon enough, though. He had already lost feeling in his feet.

There was a certain poetic justice to dying that way, he supposed. Like the old saying—you live by the sword, you die by the sword. He had certainly done plenty of living by a gat, though it wasn't his weapon of choice. He preferred subtler methods, poisons particularly, and he was the best man The Outfit had with them—maybe the best in the whole city of Chicago—certainly better than anyone Moran had. Any goon could use a gun. Subtlety took skill. He was the Shadow. He could slip in and out of almost anywhere, unseen and unnoticed, like a whiff of smoke.

He was dying that way too. On the main street off the alley where he sat, dozens of people swarmed by. Someone knocked—three times, then two, then three again. A door opened and closed. There was a speakeasy two alleys over, tucked in the basement of the Italian restaurant. Piano and sax drifted out, probably from the clip joint down the street. A couple of dames walked by, laughing and talking loudly. He could still vaguely see them, but his vision was dimming.

Not a damn one of them knew or cared he was there, bleeding to death in an alley filled with rotting garbage and smelling of puke and piss. He might die alone, but he could take comfort in the knowledge that his death would be avenged. No one messed with The Outfit and got away with it. Bugsy's goons may have gotten the drop on him, but there would be hell to pay when Capone got wind of it.

He curled his lips in a small, weak smile. His family had his back in this world and beyond. There might not be a drop of blood between them, but The Outfit was family, make no mistake. He was closer to them than he had ever been to his own blood.

He let his eyes slide closed as the numbness stole up his legs. It didn't surprise him much when the memories flashed in the reddish black space behind his eyelids. From the tenement fire that took his ma and pop when he was barely eight to when Franco Vassallo found him living on the streets, scraping by as a pickpocket and dodging the nuns and do-gooders, and took him to the Four Deuces. Torrio and Capone had been impressed with his quick hands and uncanny ability to disappear into a crowd—a ghost even then—and hired him as a delivery boy.

He progressed fast from deliveries to other sorts of errands and learned to use guns, knives, bombs, and anything else he needed as he went along. No longer a skinny orphan, the boy grew into a man. He had his first kill when he was barely eighteen, his first hit barely a year later, and over time, he became a skilled assassin and enforcer who protected The Outfit and its interests by any means necessary. There had been so many deaths... so much blood. He saw them all again.

Then the memories shifted and changed. They became older, much older, morphed through hundreds of years and showed things centuries before his own time—things he couldn't possibly be familiar with—and yet they were familiar and as real and intimate as the steel of the gun in his hand. They tunneled back, farther and faster, and finally converged on the moment some eight centuries earlier when he sold his soul to the devil.

Moriel.

Like the memories, the name was foreign yet familiar. Then the face came into focus in his memory. Oh yes. He knew that bastard.

"Moriel!" His shout choked off into a gurgling cough. He took the deepest breath he could, which at the moment really wasn't very deep, and tried again. "Moriel!"

A small, wizened man with a deeply lined face and intricately patterned midnight-blue robes appeared out of nowhere, stood over him, and peered down on his dying form. And Gabriel remembered.

THEY SAID he was lucky. After all, he had survived the fever that killed his parents—his father only hours before his birth and his mother moments after. Being only a bairn, it was a miracle the sickness hadn't taken him too. T'was only the Lord who could have saved him, they said. They gave him to the abbey when he was just hours old. The monks baptized him Gabriel, for surely he was to be a great messenger for God.

Gabriel snorted at the thought. He was a great messenger, all right. Great for running messages from the brothers to the blacksmith or the cobbler. Great for running messages between the brothers in the monastery. "Brother Anhelm, Brother Barnabas says would you please come and help him in the gardens?"

Great for running right into trouble. His knees still ached from spending the previous night kneeling on the frigid stone floor before the altar. Brother Fergus had caught him asleep in the gardens. As though his furious lecture on the sin of sloth wasn't enough, he also sentenced Gabriel to a night of prayer and contemplation.

It wasn't that Gabriel minded the night. Quite the opposite. The night was comforting. The quiet wrapped around him like a warm blanket. No one harped at him or ran him this way and that, or worse yet, punished him for something he had done wrong yet again. The steward gave him a thrashing last e'en, and that thought woke the soreness, spurring him to walk faster. The castle was still some ways off, and he had no desire to face another beating.

That year the monks had finally given up on trying to make him a scholar. He had a little Latin but no talent for manuscript illumination. No use for it either. Instead he now spent part of his days in the service of Lord Craeg, doing whatever his steward commanded. His contract had just begun, so he did not yet live in the castle, but only came for some hours during the day. The steward was still deciding whether Gabriel would be suitable for full-time service.

Gabriel rather hoped the steward would find him lacking. For though Lord Craeg was regarded as a kind and generous man, Gabriel had learned his steward was quick to anger and quicker to strike. The beating he was still feeling was proof of that. Not that he dared complain, even among the other servants. If word got back to the steward, it would only earn him another beating—if not worse. As the steward never failed to remind him, servants died all the time. No one would think twice if he fell into the fire while fetching food or met a bad end when he accompanied the steward to collect rents. There were outlaws about in the wood. Gabriel could disappear and no one would even spare a moment's thought about him.

Suddenly the busy hum of the village on market day—horses' hooves plodding through the muddy street, the furious honks of geese and lowing of cattle as people drove them to market, and the constant chatter of voices bartering and buying—gave way to a commotion up ahead.

Gabriel froze, and his stomach instantly turned to ice. An angry crowd could be dangerous too. A servant could all too easily be trampled or taken. No one would bother to save him. He was nothing—a foundling boy dependent on the goodness of the monks and Lord Craeg. His eyes darted around the edges of the crowded square as he searched desperately for a way around the crowd. But there was none to be found. His anxiety ratcheted a bit further, burning the back of his throat with acid, but he took a step toward the crowd in spite of it. The steward would beat him again if he were tardy, no matter the reason. If he couldn't go around the crowd, he would just have to go through it.

He plunged forward and pushed his way through the throngs of people and got a sharp elbow to the ribs for his trouble and then a bruised toe when a rather large woman drew back from some fright he couldn't see and tread heavily upon his foot. There was no apology. She didn't even acknowledge his presence. He didn't expect any different—not for a mere orphan servant, kept alive only by means of charity. He didn't own the clothes on his back or any morsel of food he had ever put in his mouth.

As he walked away, Gabriel let out a deep sigh. He would give anything if things could be different. He burned to leave and go somewhere where no one knew him and where he could make a name for himself on his own merits, not just on the circumstances of his birth. But he'd learned long before that such dreams were foolish. He would never be anything more than what he was—a nobody and an orphan.

He should count himself lucky he could at least read and write a bit. That was more education than most people got. The monks had not only given him a roof over his head, clothes on his back, and food in his belly. They gave him the tools to make a life for himself. Maybe the most he could hope for was to be little more than a servant—a scribe or clerk—but it would keep a roof over his head and food in his mouth. That was all a man had the right to ask for anyway. Anything more was frivolous foolishness. No matter how much he wanted it.

He had passed the worst of the crowd and could finally see the source of the commotion. A strange man stood on the back of a farmer's cart. He was dressed in robes much like those of the monks, but his were black—the color of darkest night in the chapel—and one would have to be blind or a fool to think the man a monk. His eyes were as black as his robes, and he fairly radiated power.

He was saying something about a king, about needing a new one—a king who had the people's best interests at heart. Was he mad? That was treason. It could get him killed. It could get them all killed. If the king got wind of that, anyone thought to be in league with him would be executed. Gabriel knew he should leave and make his way to the castle where the steward was expecting him. He was probably already late, but maybe if he hurried....

Yes, Gabriel knew he should leave, but he couldn't move. He was mesmerized by the dark stranger. He had never seen such power. It was like the man had a bolt of lightning coiled inside his robes. Nay, in his body. Maybe even in his soul.

"And who would be this new king?" asked Hugh the blacksmith, a burly bear of a man. His voice was distinctly mocking. "You?"

The dark stranger inclined his head slowly, regally. "Yes. My name is Moriel. And I am your new king."

The man—Moriel—reached up and drew back his hood. Fascinated, Gabriel pressed forward and wormed his way through the twenty or thirty people gathered around the wagon until he emerged at the front of the group. Up that close Gabriel could see the man's eyes weren't black as he had initially thought, but blue like Gabriel's own, though they were as deep and dark as Gabriel's were light. Though his robe appeared black from a distance in the thin light of the cloudy day, it was actually blue as well—a deep, rich blue infused with intricate patterns. This was no ordinary man. Those were noble's clothes. He would swear it. Only a wealthy man could afford such fine fabric and stitching. Gabriel had never seen the like, not even in the castle.

"How will you take the throne?" another man called out.

Moriel twisted his lips in the ghost of a smile. "I am a wizard. I cannot take the throne myself. I need fighting men. In return I will grant those men the power to do anything and have anything they desire. All they need do is help me."

"Will you take anyone?" Gabriel asked the question before he was even aware the words had left his mouth. He tried to swallow, but his mouth was dry as dirt. "Even if we have no training?" Even if I'm an orphan? That was the real question. It pressed hard against the forefront of his mind, but he didn't dare speak it aloud.

"Of course," Moriel said. "A lack of training is easily cured, but no amount of training can replace a loyal heart and a willing spirit."

"And what service would you require?" At that point Gabriel wasn't sure it mattered. It was his chance. He could leave and go somewhere where no one would know him and where he could be more than just a foundling. No one would know of his birth. He could buy land, build a castle of his own, have food and clothes and shelter, and never be beholden to anyone ever again.

No, not quite. He would still owe loyalty to Moriel, but at least that would be of his choice, not some accident of birth.

Moriel unrolled a scroll before his face. Gabriel blinked at the blank parchment, but before he could draw breath to question it, Moriel flicked a wand from the folds of his sleeve and tapped the parchment with it. Writing marched across the page like neat little soldiers. Gabriel leaned forward and tried to read it. The words were mostly familiar but made little sense. The print was old and stilted like the writing on the fragile scrolls Brother Anhelm copied into manuscripts.

Gabriel went on trying to puzzle out the words, but he was extremely grateful when a man behind him called out, "What's it say? I ain't no priest."

Gabriel glanced back to see the owner of the voice and had to bite his lip to keep from laughing. Red Godfrey, as he was known for both his red hair and the nearly constant red tinge to his beefy face from his love of drink, was certainly no priest. Gabriel doubted the man had ever seen the inside of the church in all the years of Gabriel's lifetime, save maybe for a wedding, a baptism, or a funeral. Still, he *knew what Godfrey meant. Like most of the people in the village, he could neither read nor write. Those skills were left to the priests, scribes, and the occasional noble.*

Moriel seemed to take his meaning. "It says that you agree to enter into my service. You will help me take the throne and take revenge on the clan who threw me out. You will become the greatest killers the land has ever seen. In return you will be gifted with great power."

Killers? Until that moment Gabriel was certain he needed to sign on. Already he was fighting the urge to reach out and mark his name on the scroll, but that one word brought him up short. Could he kill? He never had before. Living in the monastery, such a thing was unthinkable, but surely there were righteous reasons to kill as well. Even God had commanded his warriors to kill when taking the Holy Land. Everyone knew it was a different thing to kill in defense of one's king or home or country. That wasn't murder. That was an honorable duty. Wasn't that just what he would be doing if he joined Moriel on his quest? Killing in defense of his king? He could do that. He could be Moriel's loyal knight, just like the ones in the legends the traveling bards sometimes told.

He had lifted his hand to reach for the parchment when someone behind him asked, "And what would be the length of this time of service?" Gabriel let his hand drop back by his side and forced himself to wait sensibly for the answer.

Above him Moriel lifted an eyebrow. "You would wish for this to end, to lose the power I would grant you and go back to being just an ordinary man?"

Put that way, it sounded incredibly foolish. The man behind him stuttered. "Well, no, of course not, but...." People around him started to titter, amused by his humiliation.

Moriel sighed as if he found the whole ordeal incredibly tiresome. "I have no need for slaves. Just as one enters my service by his own choice, he may also leave by his own choice. It's a simple matter, really. All he need do is forgive an enemy."

Gabriel fought the urge to roll his eyes. Now Moriel sounded like Brother Barnabas, who was always preaching forgiveness of wrongs, as though that were the cure for everything. From what Gabriel could see, that wasn't the cure for anything. He was always supposed to forgive the people who wronged him, but it never changed anything. It never stopped them from doing it again. Moriel clearly knew that and didn't expect such frivolous forgiveness, if forgiving an enemy was the only way to break the bond. Gabriel might have signed up for that alone, just to be out from under that ridiculous expectation. To be free of that and to be given power—Gabriel could see no reason not to take hold of the opportunity with both hands.

But could he even enter into a contract? He was already bound to his master, a master who was probably furiously searching the castle for him. Except he hadn't entered into that contract himself. Though he was seventeen and nearly of age, Father Michael had entered into that contract on his behalf. What wages he was paid didn't go to him, but to the monastery in return for his upkeep and housing for all these years. No, that wasn't a contract he was bound to. It was merely one that had been forced upon him. This one would be different. It would be one entered freely. For the first time in his life, it would be something he did of his own choice, as his own man, and not at the guidance or direction of another.

"Who will be the first brave man to step up and stand up for the good of the people?" Moriel asked, holding out the parchment and a quill.

"I will," Gabriel said, far more boldly than he normally would, and he stepped forward and reached for the quill. When Moriel pressed it into his hand, a spark of energy arced between them and tingled over Gabriel's skin and down his spine. The force of it was so strong, Gabriel nearly took a step back, but he made himself stand firm. He took the quill and looked around for ink. Moriel had not offered any, and though it was certainly the tool of his trade, Gabriel wasn't allowed to carry it. The monks kept ink at the monastery, and the lord kept it in his study, but Gabriel wasn't allowed to handle it without supervision. Ink was expensive, and he was nothing but a clumsy boy who was likely to knock it over in his folly and waste it.

Seeing his confusion, Moriel replied, "The magic requires blood. You must cut yourself." Gabriel nodded. He had a small penknife for sharpening quills, which he kept in a pouch on his belt. He took it out, slid the cloth of his tunic off his shoulder, and made the mark without hesitation. It stung briefly where the blood welled, but Gabriel didn't mind. The slight pain made it all the more real. That was it. He could finally be free to be his own man, a man of power, not just a lowly orphan.

With that in mind, he touched the quill to his small wound and signed his name where Moriel pointed. He couldn't help but add a bit of a flourish, for he was proud of his ability to give a real signature, rather than make an X as most before him had.

The moment he finished writing and lifted the quill from the paper, power, the likes of which he had never known, flowed through his veins, sealed the small wound, and sang in his blood. Instinctively he stood taller, raised himself up to his full height—which put him a few inches above most men—and stared boldly back at the crowd, who watched him with varying amounts of skepticism.

Suddenly it occurred to Gabriel that such boldness might not be entirely appropriate in front of his new master. He turned toward Moriel and bowed respectfully. "My liege."

To his utter astonishment, Moriel reached out a hand to him. "Come, lad."

Gabriel took his hand and allowed Moriel to pull him onto the cart with more strength than a man with that many lines in his face rightly ought to possess. Once he caught his footing, he stepped a few paces behind Moriel. Power or no, what right did he have to stand shoulder to shoulder with the man who was to be his king? As the shock of his decision and that first incredible burst of power began to recede, he became aware of something else thrumming strongly in his blood—the fierce, driving urge to kill.

The steward's sneering face flashed into his mind. The need was so strong Gabriel nearly leapt down from the cart and raced to the castle. Gaining entrance would pose little problem. Everyone would simply think he was finally arriving for his duties, and when the steward took him away to beat him for his tardiness, as he undoubtedly would, Gabriel would turn and drive the penknife between his ribs. The blade probably wouldn't be sharp enough to kill, but it would give Gabriel the moment he needed to slip the much sharper and more dangerous knife from the steward's belt and end his life.

Perhaps the notion should have felt foreign to him, horrific even, for what should a young man raised with men of the cloth know of killing and death? No more than an hour prior, he would have known nothing. But it didn't seem strange at all. If anything, it felt right. That man was his enemy. He lived in a world of cruelty and lies, showing one face outside the castle and another within. That could not be allowed to continue. He must die.

So driven was Gabriel by that thought that his hand was already gripping the edge of the wagon in preparation for jumping down when Moriel laid a restraining hand on his shoulder and whispered in his ear, "Not yet, lad. The time will come, and soon, but there are things you must know first."

It was nearly impossible to make himself stop, but Gabriel had just sworn his service to Moriel. He didn't dare disobey. So he forced the compulsion down.

"You will get your chance," Moriel promised.

And he had. He spent several days traveling with Moriel on winding roads, through forest and countryside in places most people didn't dare pass for fear of being set upon by outlaws. No one bothered them. Gabriel wasn't particularly surprised. Who, save someone beset by madness, would try to steal from the likes of Moriel? He himself might not yet be so great a man, but he was learning quickly.

Moriel spent hours in the early morning of every day instructing him in ways to end a man's life more quietly and subtly than with a knife through the ribs. In the face of Moriel's subtle ways with plants and poisons, Gabriel's initial notion of using a knife seemed crude and almost childish. Why would he ever do something so obvious when there were so many other means at his disposal? An obvious weapon would do if he had no other choice, but it was dangerous to leave behind evidence of your work.

Deep in the night of the third day, he left Moriel's camp and went back to the castle. As he expected, it was locked up tight for the night, and most of the inhabitants had gone to bed. Even so, he had no difficulty getting in, for even before his few days of training with Moriel, Gabriel was quite skilled at slipping into the shadows and going unnoticed.

It took little time or effort to make his way to the steward's bedchamber. The man was sound asleep beneath piles of opulent coverings, mouth open and snoring loudly. Really it was almost too easy. Gabriel slipped a small vial of wolfsbane out of his pocket and uncorked it. He tipped it neatly into the man's gaping mouth and gently rubbed a hand on his throat to encourage him to swallow. The steward didn't even wake until the poison was already well into his system, and when he did, he was already choking and gasping for breath, unable to move, his eyes wide and helpless. He was dead within moments.

A thrill shot through Gabriel when the steward took his final breath. It was unlike anything he had ever experienced. It was true power.

Gabriel was about to slip away when Lord Craeg's son, Lucian, a slender, blond-haired, blue-eyed version of his father in both looks and temperament, emerged from his bedchamber. "What are you doing here?"

Gabriel knew at that moment that Lucian would have to die. When they found the steward dead in the morning, the boy would remember him. Then Gabriel himself would die within hours, and likely Moriel with him. Their attempt to take the throne would be over before it ever started.

"The steward kept me here to this hour, working on accounts as punishment for my absence these last days," Gabriel explained as he moved toward Lucian. "I'm to sleep in the barn. I apologize for disturbing your sleep." As he spoke he carefully guided Lucian back toward his bed.

"He has been asleep for hours," Lucian countered suspiciously.

Gabriel nodded. "He said he saw no need to lose sleep on account of my foolishness. Nor should you. Go back to sleep, young master."

At Gabriel's encouragement Lucian climbed back into bed and rolled onto his front. Gabriel drew the bedcovers up over him and then pressed one of the many opulent pillows over the boy's head. Lucian struggled and tried to throw Gabriel off. The two were roughly the same size, but although Lucian was older, Gabriel was far stronger, even before his newly added surge of power, because he was expected to do physical work that was far beneath a man of Lucian's class. It didn't take a great deal of effort to keep Lucian's head pressed firmly between the two pillows until his struggling stopped.

AND THEN the memory ended. Gabriel was once again about to draw his last breath in a dank and stinking alleyway. He glared up at Moriel, who stood over him with a distinctly smug expression on his face.

"Why?" Gabriel demanded. "I've lived many lifetimes since then and fulfilled the terms of your contract dozens of times over. Why continue this torture?" Now that the memories had returned, he knew he had lived countless lives since that day in that tiny village in northern England. Yet he had never really lived. Instead he had always lived in the shadows, forever driven by the urge to kill.

"Oh, but you haven't," Moriel replied in a voice so haughty that Gabriel would have punched that superior expression right off his face if he had the strength. "You haven't forgiven your One."

Gabriel could do nothing but stare. "Of course I have. How could I not? It's been centuries. I've forgiven many people."

"But not your One," Moriel insisted.

Before Gabriel could draw breath to ask who the hell that fated One was supposed to be, a flicker of Lord Craeg's son, the first man he ever killed of his own accord and not out of compulsion, flashed through his mind.

"Lucian?" he asked, shocked. "Lucian was the one who could've ended this?"

But Gabriel's dying body gave out before he got the answer.

CHAPTER ONE

THE MOMENT it began, Gabriel knew it would end in blood.

It was blazing hot, as most summer days were in the Middle East. The dirt beneath his feet was hard as a brick, baked by the raging sun and packed down by generations of use. It was a nameless rural village— one of dozens of such villages he had visited in the course of his duties. Although he didn't remember the names and would be hard-pressed to find them on the map, at one point he had known them all intimately— who called the shots, who held the power, and most of all, who knew everything there was to know about the happenings in the village and the surrounding areas. But the knowledge had long since faded.

But his mission was still startlingly clear. He was there to find and eliminate Abdul Naseem Ahmadi. Ahmadi was a thin man who resembled nothing so much as a stork. At home he preferred to wear traditional salwar kameez, *the long tunics and loose pants that were common to the region, but Gabriel had also occasionally seen him in Western clothes, particularly if he was meeting with a client from the West. The first time Gabriel met him some ten months before, he was quite surprised at how pedestrian Ahmadi looked. If he hadn't known better, he would've thought he was a professor of math or ancient literature in a university somewhere, not a very elite, highly sought- after bomb builder with ties to al Qaeda. He was also reclusive, extremely paranoid, and virtually impossible to get near.*

It took Gabriel, posing as an arms dealer and potential customer, six months to even get to meet him and then an additional ten months to build a relationship of trust—one he was about to violate without blinking an eye. Ahmadi had the blood of untold innocents on his hands. He purported to be a jihadist, but Gabriel had learned he was more of a pragmatist. Money talked. He sold to anyone prepared to meet his price—including terrorists—without regard to why they wanted his particular merchandise. That had signed his death warrant.

The meeting place was a low, flat-roofed, mud-brick house indistinguishable from any number of others surrounding it. It might have been Ahmadi's home, though Gabriel doubted it. More likely it was an anonymous meeting place.

Despite his reserve, Ahmadi was unfailingly courteous and hospitable. He met Gabriel at the door and invited him in with cheerful enthusiasm. As soon as they entered the house, he called for a woman to bring refreshments. She appeared through an inner door, behind which Gabriel could see at least two other women, slightly younger, gathered in what one of his foster fathers referred to as a coffee klatch. Gabriel exchanged polite greetings with her, and she disappeared again, presumably into the kitchen.

Gabriel and Ahmadi were soon settled on rug-covered cushions with a tray of tea and savories between them. They chatted about inconsequential things through the first cup of tea. His opportunity came when Ahmadi refilled their cups for a second time. Ahmadi turned away momentarily to speak to one of the women, and it took only the briefest sleight of hand for Gabriel to dump the finely powdered betel nut seeds he'd hidden in his sleeve into Ahmadi's cup. The powder dissolved quickly. Its dark brown color was virtually indistinguishable from the almond and cinnamon particles in the kahwah *tea.*

Ahmadi never even noticed. He turned back from his conversation, picked up the cup, and drank absently before he settled down to the real business of their meeting, or at least what he thought was the real business—the bomb Gabriel needed.

It seemed to take mere seconds for the poison to take effect, though in reality he knew it was more like ten minutes. First Ahmadi excused himself to the restroom as the nausea and vomiting started. He returned, pale and shaky, and suggested it would be best if Gabriel were to return at a later time. Gabriel readily agreed, but before he could rise to leave, Ahmadi stumbled over one of the cushions on the floor and landed sprawling in the middle of the rug, convulsing violently and vomiting blood—dark red blood that spewed over Gabriel's front and coated his hands until they seemed to be dripping a thick copper-tinged paint. Then the women ran in, frantic and flapping like frightened chickens. Heedless of the blood, the eldest one dropped to her knees by Ahmadi's side, touched his face, and started to scream. It was a horrid sound, ripped from the very depths of her soul. He stared at her blankly and felt nothing.

GABRIEL CAME awake with a start, bolting upright and struggling to breathe against the dark that wrapped around him like an inky blanket, heavy and smothering.

It hadn't happened like that. There was no blood. It wasn't nearly that dramatic. Ahmadi simply began to feel ill and asked Gabriel to leave. Gabriel was crossing the courtyard when he heard the women scream. He heard later that Ahmadi, who was known to have had occasional seizures as a child, died from a massive, unexpected seizure. No one save Gabriel himself and those who ordered his mission knew the seizure was helped along by a little-known poison and an undercover CIA agent with an in-depth knowledge of poisons and an intense need to kill.

Beneath the weight of the darkness, he could still feel it, thrumming hot in his blood, zipping like lightning over his bones—the desire to kill, to watch the life go out of his target's eyes, and most of all, to feel that incredible heady rush of power. It was like nothing he'd ever felt before or since, more addictive than any drug and twice as dangerous.

Gabriel fumbled for the light and switched on the lamp on the side table. It wasn't particularly bright, but it was enough to break the darkness. He wasn't in the desert. There were no more deserts, no more missions, no more lifeless bodies and grieving families. He hadn't let the darkness get him. He had walked away.

He rolled to his feet and padded into the adjoining bathroom. Automatically flipping the switch inside the doorway, he flooded the room with light. It was considerably brighter than the bedroom, and for a moment, the blaze hurt his eyes. He was grateful for that blinding moment because it grounded him in reality and chased away the nightmares and memories.

He pressed his bare feet hard against the floor and splayed his toes over the cool tile in a quiet house in Maryland where he could hear distant traffic outside his window. He was a world away from the heat and sand. He was no longer a CIA operations officer. He was just plain Gabriel Ingram, professor of security in the international studies department at Willingham University. There were no more ops, no more aliases, no more disguises, and most of all, no more blood and death and losing his soul.

To prove it he braced his hands on the counter on either side of the sink and stared into the large rectangular mirror hanging above it. He was black haired and tan skinned—attributes that had made it easy for him to blend in in the Middle East, where he had spent most of his career. But his angular face was clean-shaven. The beard he had habitually worn during his time overseas was gone and had been for the past several years.

The eyes that stared back at him were a striking light blue, his own natural color, not obscured by the brown contacts he typically wore when on assignment. His blue eyes had always been a liability. They were memorable and made him instantly identifiable. It had been safer to cover them.

He was a natural chameleon who could blend in just about anywhere. It was a trait that had stood him in good stead for years, until he began to lose himself. His own humanity and empathy were subsumed by the roles he played. That's when he knew he had to walk away, and he did.

He'd made a good life. He enjoyed his work and occasionally his students. The politics of academia had nothing on the life-and-death politics he had navigated for years. It was often tedious and sometimes maddening, but it was never deadly. He could live in peace without risking the darkness for himself or anyone else. He was out. He was safe, and he was never going back there ever again.

CHAPTER TWO

A RAPID knocking sound penetrated Lucas's consciousness and dragged him out of a sound sleep.

"Hey Luc, are you up?" His roommate, Eric, pushed open the door and stuck his head around the doorframe. "Don't you have class this morning? You better get a move on, man. You're going to be late."

Lucas, who had been sprawled on his stomach, pushed himself upright. "Huh? What're you talking about?" A glance at the clock on his bedside table provided the answer before Eric could say anything. Shit. How the hell was it already 7:00 a.m.? He would have sworn he had just fallen asleep moments ago, when he stumbled in shortly after 1:00 a.m., exhausted from an excruciatingly long shift on the suicide hotline where he volunteered twice a week.

He shoved the bedclothes back with a muttered oath, scrambled out of bed, and immediately tripped over his discarded sneakers and jeans, which were still scattered on the floor where he had blindly peeled out of them when he fell into bed. He swore again, yanked them irritably out of the way, and tossed them across the room.

Eric, who was already fully dressed in his customary tank top, plaid shirt, and jeans, shook his head. "Man, you have got to stop doing this. You need a better alarm clock or something?"

"I know. I know," Lucas said. He grabbed jeans and a clean hoodie from his closet, gathered the rest of his supplies, and pushed past Eric and into their shared bathroom. If he was lucky, he could take the fastest shower on record and make the bus to campus. If he ran.

Thankfully luck seemed to be smiling on Lucas that morning. He made the bus by a fraction of a second and collapsed into a seat as the bus driver began to pull away. He dropped his head back and closed his eyes. Eric was right. He had to stop. He wasn't a teenager anymore. He was nearly thirty, for crying out loud, a social worker and a graduate student.

Lucas's stomach let out a rumbling growl that drew him out of his thoughts and reminded him forcefully that he hadn't taken the time to eat that morning, nor at any other time in the past twelve hours. He'd been too busy to eat. Instead he frantically tried to do homework between calls and tried not to worry about Danny, the fifteen-year-old child he had to move to a group home the day before when his foster parents found a letter to a classmate that revealed Danny was gay. They asked for him to be moved to another placement. Danny took it in stride, but Lucas feared he wasn't nearly as nonchalant about it as he appeared. Lucas remembered vividly what it was like to be a fifteen-year-old boy who knew he was gay and was terrified of what would happen when people found out. And Danny had already faced rejection and abandonment.

His stomach growled again, which made two young girls—freshmen, unless he missed his guess—giggle. The back of his neck burned with mortification. He'd have to make a quick trip through the co-op before class and grab something. Maybe Professor Ingram would even be in the co-op that morning. That thought was enough to make him smile.

Gabriel Ingram was a professor in the international studies department. Lucas had never taken a class from him since he spent his time over in the social work building studying marriage and family therapy, but he knew Ingram's reputation for being tough, aloof, and something of an asshole. Personally Lucas thought the first two were rather obvious, but he had never once seen any indication of the latter. If anything Professor Ingram had gone out of his way to be nice to Lucas, inspiring any number of very hot and very inappropriate fantasies.

As much as he knew it was probably wrong, Lucas didn't seem to be able to stop his imagination or his libido. He couldn't help it that the man was the very definition of dark, mysterious, and handsome. Lucas shifted uncomfortably in his seat. Even thinking about him was enough to make Lucas's body stand up and take notice. What's more, he liked to think Professor Ingram had noticed him as well.

A month or two before, Lucas was in the co-op trying to scarf down what passed for a sandwich on his way to class. It was rainy and wet and he desperately wanted coffee, but he had settled for water and a sandwich instead, reasoning that food was probably a wiser choice. He had just finished the last of his sandwich and was guzzling what was left of the water when Ingram came by and put a hot cup of coffee on his table. Lucas looked up in shock, but before he could form words, Ingram shrugged them off.

"Looks like you could use it," he said and disappeared.

In the intervening weeks, Professor Ingram continued to appear with coffee at regular intervals on the two days a week that Lucas had morning classes. If he ever managed to make it to class without running late, Lucas hoped to convince Professor Ingram to have breakfast with him. He had tried watching for him around lunchtime, after his classes were over, and he wasn't about to give up. They were going to have to talk eventually. As much as Lucas enjoyed having a silent coffee benefactor, he really wanted to know what brought it on. Was Professor Ingram interested in him, as he hoped, or was it something else altogether?

And if Ingram was interested, why wouldn't he just come out and say it? Lucas had long suspected Ingram was gay, though he could not have specifically said why. They were both adults, well over the age of consent, and he wasn't in any of Ingram's classes. While it wasn't necessarily encouraged, there were any number of graduate students and professors who had personal relationships. There was absolutely nothing to stop them from getting to know each other if that was indeed what Ingram was initiating. But what if it wasn't?

Lucas was so engrossed in his thoughts that he was startled when the bus squealed to a stop in front of the student center. Where had the ride gone?

THE KID came barreling around the corner into the co-op like clockwork, a backpack slung over his shoulder with its zipper opened like the gaping maw of some boorish creature, flapping wide to reveal papers and books protruding from the top like masticated food. His hair was shower damp, and clumps of the bright blond locks were still dark and plastered to his head. His ragged sneakers were barely tied. The sheer level of absentminded disorganization should have been ridiculous. Normally Gabriel would have had contempt for the kid's clear incompetence.

But contempt was the very last emotion the kid raised in him. Gabriel had the oddest urge to smile, shake his head, put an arm around the younger man's shoulders, and guide him in the right direction. It was ludicrous, and Gabriel knew it. And though he couldn't think of the other man by any other name but "the kid," he was no child. He was perhaps five or ten years Gabriel's junior, but still very much a man.

And when he wasn't inspiring Gabriel to want to protect and coddle him, he inspired far more inappropriate thoughts. He was a student, and that alone made him off-limits, as far as Gabriel was concerned. He wouldn't risk his professional integrity or the life he had built for any fling, no matter how tempting. Still he couldn't resist the opportunity to do something—no matter how small—to soothe the urge to reach out. So he contented himself with buying the kid a cup of coffee a couple days a week.

It was a habit that started almost by accident one day a month or two before. Gabriel was in the co-op buying lunch when he noticed the kid slumped in a booth, scarfing down a sandwich like a starving man. It was a rainy day, but the kid carried nothing in the way of rain gear, not even an umbrella or jacket, just a hooded sweatshirt that clearly did little to stave off the damp. He looked cold, exhausted, and thoroughly miserable. On impulse Gabriel bought an extra coffee along with his own and set it on the kid's table when he passed by. The kid looked up at him with an expression that looked alternately stunned, confused, and grateful, and his bright blue eyes seemed full of more questions than Gabriel could ever begin to answer.

"You looked like you could use it," he said by way of explanation and walked away before the kid could ask questions he couldn't answer.

It was a onetime impulse, and that was what he meant for it to stay, but he found himself doing it again and again just to see those blue eyes light up. Now it was something of a tradition, a fun little game between the two of them that had become the highlight of his day on Tuesdays and Thursdays—one bright spot in his often-monotonous routine of classes and grading.

That morning he already had coffee waiting. He'd even learned to add sugar and creamer as the younger man preferred, though it was an abomination that destroyed perfectly good coffee. He glanced back over at the kid. He looked hassled and, frankly, starved. His face was pinched, and he looked over the food with clear wanting. Gabriel picked up a bagel and a muffin, added them to the coffee, and checked out. He met the kid halfway and pressed the coffee into his hand. He held out the bagel and the muffin. "Which do you want?"

The kid shot him a shocked look. He didn't offer any kind of explanation, just continued to hold out the food and wait.

"Muffin or bagel?" he asked when the kid still didn't answer, and held up each one in turn.

"Umm… muffin, I guess," the kid replied hesitantly. Gabriel passed him the muffin, took his own coffee and the bagel, and sat down at a small table to eat.

To his surprise the kid plopped down into a chair across from him. "Why are you doing this?"

He shrugged. "You look like you need it."

The kid didn't bother to argue. "I do," he agreed. "And I appreciate it. But why me? It's not as though I'm the only starving college student around here. You don't even know me."

Gabriel didn't know what to say to that. He was right. They didn't really know each other. But he knew who the kid was. It took very little research to find out he was a graduate student studying to be a therapist, of all things, and his name was Lucas Craig.

"I know who you are," Gabriel said finally.

The kid's eyes went impossibly wide. "You do?"

Gabriel chuckled. "Yes, Lucas, I do."

"How?" he spluttered, nearly choking on his muffin. He picked up his coffee and took a long swallow.

Gabriel's eyes went immediately and involuntarily to his neck and watched the long muscles work as he swallowed. But he tore himself away and turned his focus to the bagel in his hand.

"I'm a professor. You're a student. It wasn't that difficult. I assume you know who I am as well?"

"Of course I do, Professor Ingram. Who doesn't?" Lucas replied.

"Oh, I daresay there are any number of people who haven't a clue who I am, right on this campus, even," Gabriel said dryly. Lucas looked decidedly skeptical but didn't argue. "However, there are students who do indeed know who I am and who will be waiting on me for class in just a few moments, and presumably you have class to get to as well."

Lucas glanced at the clock on the wall above Gabriel's head. "Shit. I've got to go." He gathered up his coffee and the remnants of his muffin. "Thank you for this," he said and saluted with his coffee cup as he rushed away.

"No. Thank you," Gabriel murmured half to himself as he watched Lucas go. He gathered up the remains of his own breakfast at a much more sedate pace.

Though the thought saddened him, Gabriel knew the morning meetings had to stop. He was playing with fire, and not only because Lucas was a student. That obstacle wasn't entirely insurmountable, should he decide it was worth taking the chance. No, the true obstacle lay within himself, in the monsters that lived in his nightmares and the darkness that was a part of his very soul. There was a part of him that had been and always would be a deceiver and a murderer. Everything he had done was in the name of national security, but the blood was still on his hands, whatever the official record said.

Lucas didn't deserve to be painted with that. He was far too young and naïve. He might technically be of age, but the innocence fairly rolled off him in waves. Gabriel had no right to contaminate that with his own darkness. He needed to stay far, far away.

CHAPTER THREE

RUSHING ACROSS campus Lucas couldn't help but smile at how the stress of his crazy morning was abated by those few moments of coffee and conversation. It was the first time he'd ever gotten anything resembling conversation out of Professor Ingram. Of course, he still didn't have any answers, and that was frustrating. It was as though he were being intentionally cryptic. Rumor had it Ingram was once with the CIA, and if that were true, maybe being cryptic had become such a habit that he couldn't help himself. Lucas caught the heavy glass door of the social work building before it closed in his face. He hustled up the stairs and into his second-floor classroom.

At the very least, it seemed that Ingram liked him. He admitted he knew who Lucas was, so clearly he saw Lucas as more than some random kid. If he was just picking someone at random, why bother taking the time to find out who he was? Why would he even care? For whatever reason, it seemed Ingram had noticed Lucas as an individual. That alone was enough to warm Lucas's insides and make him want to giggle like a silly schoolgirl.

But he was getting ahead of himself. Just because Ingram noticed him didn't mean any romantic feelings existed. His interest could be completely professional—simply the concern of a professor who saw a student in need. Except he wasn't Ingram's student. They weren't even in the same department. Other than their chance meetings in the co-op and casually crossing paths on campus, they never saw each other. Ingram had no real reason to notice him—unless by some miracle he was as interested in Lucas as Lucas was in him.

Dr. O'Brien came in then, forcing him to pull his mind back to his ethics lecture. Not that he had to concentrate particularly hard, since he had been working as a social worker for nearly four years and he had heard it all before in numerous in-service workshops. But he made himself focus. He couldn't afford to get behind on his classes, not with everything else he had to do between his job and his volunteer work—no matter how tempting a fantasy the mysterious Professor Ingram might be.

Despite Lucas's determination to keep those thoughts at bay, they still popped up with alarming frequency any time his mind began to wander. And though that probably wasn't beneficial to the quality of his classwork, Lucas didn't really mind. If nothing else it made his classes fly by. Before he knew it, he was grabbing lunch and then boarding the bus that would take him to his office at Family and Children's Services. Since he had class, he only worked a half day. The other three days a week, he worked a full day, which allowed him to make nearly full-time hours for a decent paycheck. As usual the moment he walked in the door, chaos erupted around him. He got so busy, he forgot about everything else.

His afternoon was filled with call after call as he tried to find a suitable foster placement for Danny, with less than optimal results. It looked like he would be spending at least one more night in the temporary group home. Teenagers were notoriously hard to place and gay teenagers even harder. More than once Lucas wondered if he was making his job even harder by disclosing Danny's sexuality. He hadn't done that with Danny's previous foster placement since Danny had yet to come out—though Lucas strongly suspected—and that turned out to be a disaster. He was determined not to make that same mistake again. Danny needed someplace where he could be accepted as he was, not just a temporary stopover until someone found out again. If that meant it took longer between places, then that was how it had to be.

Lucas spent his last phone call of the afternoon explaining that to Danny. He continued to be nonchalant about the whole ordeal, but Lucas knew better. Beneath that couldn't-care-less attitude was a young man who longed for a place every bit as much as Lucas longed to find one for him. The phone call left Lucas more determined than ever to find the right placement.

By the time Lucas made it home, Eric was on his way out.

"You working tonight?" Lucas called through the open door of the bathroom where Eric was putting the finishing touches on his spiked hair. Even as he asked the question, Lucas could already guess the answer. Eric was wearing tight, worn jeans and an even tighter black T-shirt with the ends of the sleeves rolled up James Dean style, and black boots. It was his standard bartending outfit.

Eric put down the comb and crossed into the living room where Lucas had collapsed on the couch. "Yeah," he replied as he picked up his leather jacket from where it was draped over the back of the recliner and shrugged it on. "I'm at Sparks tonight, so don't worry about waiting up for me. I'll probably be really late. Who knows. If I'm lucky I might even find myself a man for the night."

Lucas rolled his eyes, but he knew there was a fairly high likelihood that actually would happen. Sparks was one of the most popular gay bars in the area, and it wasn't unusual at all for Eric to find someone to take him home on the nights he worked there. Eric thrived on the party atmosphere and was perfectly happy with one-night stands and short-term relationships that burned hot and fast and ended as quickly as they began. Lucas, on the other hand, had never fit into that fast-paced, high-adrenaline world. He needed stability and connection. Eric teased him about being an old man, and he teased Eric about being a manwhore, but neither would dare stand in the other's way.

"You'll be careful, right?" Lucas said automatically, out of long-established habit.

"Yes, Dad," Eric deadpanned. "Don't worry. I'll wrap it up." He patted his back pocket, where his wallet and, no doubt, several condoms were stored.

Lucas lazily flipped him the bird. "I don't mean just that, jackass. You know how things get during the school year. All kinds of new people coming in from who knows where. Just be safe. Okay? I'm not working tonight, so I'll be here."

"I won't get wasted when I'm working," Eric assured him. "I'll be fine. Now I've got to get out of here before I let you make me late too."

Lucas picked up an old burger wrapper from the coffee table—God knew how long that had been there—and threw it at him. But it arced far too wide. He could hear Eric still laughing even as he disappeared out the door.

He picked up the burger wrapper and tossed it in the trash. The apartment was bordering on a disaster area, and the majority of the mess was his. He'd been running flat out lately, careening from school to work to the hotline. He barely even saw Eric except in passing. How long had it been since the two of them had done anything together? Even just sitting down to watch a cheesy sitcom or a movie. Not since school started over a month before. That was unusual. They both led separate lives and had busy schedules, but they had been friends for more than a decade and typically tried to make time to do things together periodically. If he thought about it, Eric had probably tried to get him to do something and he'd been too busy to pay attention. He'd have to correct that, but he'd at least try to pick up some of the mess before he settled down to study.

THE CROWD was unexpectedly slow. Granted it was a weeknight, and Eric hadn't expected it to be as busy as it typically was on the weekend, but Sparks was one of the most popular bars around. It was a rare night that there wasn't a sizable crowd, even during the week. On the weekends it was generally so packed that even walking through the crowd on the dance floor took skill.

But there was only a moderate crowd of regulars scattered around tables and booths and spread across the dance floor. Eric sighed. It was nice not to be crazy busy, but a slow night put a big dent in his tips and an even bigger cramp in his plans to find someone to share his bed for the night.

A group of guys bustled through the door, jostling and laughing gregariously. Eric looked them over with a practiced eye. They were young, barely legal, he would bet. There were at least two couples in the group, still in that starry-eyed beginning stage where they could barely keep their hands off one another. There was a tall, dark-haired guy near the back with his hands shoved deeply in his pockets. He might be a possibility. One of the others said something, and he smiled shyly and slightly awkwardly. Yes, he might have been a definite possibility—on some other night. Eric wasn't in the mood for educating a timid virgin. He wanted someone experienced.

As though he heard his thoughts, Greg, a regular with thinning blond hair, a round face, and a noticeable paunch, turned and winked at him. Ew. No. Eric wanted experienced, not worn out. Greg was a nice enough guy, but everyone knew he'd been around more times than a washing machine.

One of the guys from the barely legal group sauntered up and ordered a round of several different brands of beer that took Eric a moment to fill. By the time he was done, Greg had apparently given up his feeble attempt at flirting and started talking to a guy who had come off the dance floor and leaned against the wall near him. Eric thanked whoever or whatever was listening for small mercies.

He wiped down the bar, pulled a couple of draft beers, and made a mojito for the guy who had been talking to Greg. It looked like he'd be going home alone after all. That was disappointing, but he mentally shrugged it off. There would be no shortage of eligible men that weekend, and he could always scratch his itch then.

He was making change for a bulky guy who ordered a double bourbon when his prospects suddenly did an abrupt reversal. An extremely hot Hispanic guy with slicked-back, ink-black hair and a tight T-shirt that clung to every curve sidled up to the bar.

Eric broke into his patented "sweet but slightly sexy" smile almost without thought. "What can I get for you, sweetheart?" he asked, leaning slightly on the bar.

"Well now, that depends," the man replied and flashed a sexy smile of his own. "What do you recommend?"

"Do you prefer sweet or strong?" Eric asked.

The man propped his arms on the bar and leaned over into Eric's space. "Maybe I like them sweet and strong."

Eric cocked his head to the side and studied the man, taking in his mysterious black eyes and full bottom lip. "In that case let's try you with a Drunken Caramel Apple."

He needed to gather the ingredients—dark rum, triple sec, and peach juice—so he very deliberately turned his back on the man. He was well aware the jeans complemented his ass to perfection. Might as well use them to his advantage. Then he lined up his ingredients on the bar along with a shiny green Granny Smith apple, filled a glass with ice and combined the various liquids into it, and added a bit of flourish just for show. From the amused expression the man was wearing, he knew exactly what Eric was doing. For the finishing touch, Eric sliced the apple and garnished the glass with it.

He set it down in front of the man with just a hint of exaggerated flair. "For you, sir."

The man smiled and took an experimental sip. "That's really good." It might've only been a comment on the drink, but it had the air of a compliment.

"Of course it is," Eric said with a saucy grin. "I've got skills."

As much as he would have liked to stand and talk with the mystery man, he did still have to work. So he moved up and down the bar, taking orders and mixing drinks. He expected the man to have disappeared by the time he made it back, but surprisingly, he was still there.

"If you like that, I'll make you an Unforgettable next," Eric told him.

"Unforgettable?" the man asked.

Eric nodded, passed a couple of Heinekens across the bar to another customer, and filled a glass with ice for a mixed drink. "Yep. Because it's unforgettable. You know, like me."

The man threw his head back and laughed. "So, Unforgettable, do you have another name?"

"Several," Eric said smoothly. "I'll tell you mine if you'll tell me yours."

"Damien," the man said. "Your turn?"

"Eric," he replied. "But I think I might prefer Unforgettable."

Damien grinned but didn't comment. The next time Eric came his way, he asked, "Have you ever done any modeling? I'm a photographer, and I've got to tell you, I think the camera would love you."

As pickup lines went, it wasn't terribly original. Eric had heard variations on the theme many times before. Usually he rolled his eyes and brushed it off, but he actually liked Damien. "Not really. I'm usually on the other side of the canvas. I'm an artist."

Rather than being deterred, Damien smiled broadly. "I knew there was a reason I liked you. You're a kindred spirit—a fellow creative soul."

Though he knew it was probably just another line, it warmed something in Eric's chest. It wasn't often that anyone acknowledged him as more than just a bartender. Lucas did. Sure. But Lucas always had.

"Maybe we could get together sometime and share our work," Damien went on. "I'd like to see your paintings, and I would love to show you my photographs."

Eric shrugged. "Maybe sometime." He wanted to share something all right, but it had more to do with swapping bodily fluids than with sharing his paintings. He didn't share his work with just anybody. His paintings were far more intimate in his mind than sex. Sex was just sex. It didn't necessarily have to mean anything and usually didn't. It could be fun, but mostly it was just fulfilling a need, like eating or breathing. His paintings, on the other hand, were like sharing his soul.

"I'd like that," Damien said.

"Maybe there are other things we could do first," Eric suggested pointedly.

"Yes, I believe there are," Damien agreed. "It's too bad we can't take this somewhere more private."

"I get off at one," Eric tossed back over his shoulder as he hustled away to take another order.

When he returned, Damien had disappeared, but Eric noticed there was a slip of paper tucked in the tip jar. When he fished it out, he realized it was a business card. On one side it read "Damien Castillo Photography," with an address just a few miles away. The address wasn't in a great part of town, but Eric didn't worry about that overmuch. He knew all about being a starving artist and having to take what you could afford. On the back Damien had written a phone number with the words *Call me later* scribbled beneath it. Smiling, Eric slipped the card into the pocket of his jeans. He would most certainly make that call.

The rest of his shift seemed to fly by. He thrummed with anticipation to the point where he barely noticed the crowd around him. One of the young guys had a try at making a pass at him, but Eric shut that down quickly. Some other night, maybe, but he was going to be otherwise occupied. Closing time couldn't come fast enough. When it finally did, Eric made short work of his cleaning and closing chores before he slipped into the back and found a quiet spot to call Damien.

He slid both his cell phone and Damien's business card out of his pocket, leaned against the wall to dial the number, and tucked the phone between his ear and shoulder when it started to ring.

"Talk to me," Damien said on the other end of the line.

Suddenly Eric nearly lost his nerve. He took a deep breath and swallowed hard. It wasn't as if he'd never done this before. "Hey, it's Eric from Sparks."

"Well hello, Unforgettable, I was hoping you'd call."

Eric could hear the smile in his voice, and it made him smile in return. "Yeah. I got your note." He could hear the heavy thump of bass in the background and hoped Damien hadn't gone on to another club. After working the bar all night, that was the last place he wanted to be. He had something more intimate in mind.

"Great. So why don't you come over?" Damien went on.

"Come over where?" Eric asked. "I can hear the music. Are you at a club?"

"No way, man," Damien told him. "Why would I still be out looking when I was hoping I had you to look forward to? That's just the radio. Me and a couple of my associates are just hanging out with some tunes. Don't worry. They'll get the message when you come over. They know to make themselves scarce when I'm looking for a private party."

"And are you looking for a private party?" he questioned slyly.

"I am if you are," Damien replied.

He definitely was. His body had gone on alert just from the sound of Damien's voice. "So where would this private party be happening?"

"The address is on my card," Damien explained. "It's not far."

Eric looked over the card again. "Adams Street. Yeah, I know where that is. Okay. I'm heading out now. Be there in a few."

"Looking forward to it," Damien replied.

Eric clicked off and returned the phone to his pocket. Waving good-bye to Q, the bouncer, he climbed into his car and headed in the direction of Adams Street, a side street into an older residential neighborhood. The houses looked worn, with peeling paint, overgrown bushes, and spotty, ragged lawns. The address on Damien's card led him to a small house tucked at the end of the street, a shoebox with peeling white paint. Three battered cars stood in the overgrown lawn. Eric sighed. Apparently Damien's friends hadn't gotten the hint yet. He climbed the steps and knocked on the door.

A thin African American man he didn't recognize opened the door. From behind him Damien called out, "Hey, Eric. Come in, man." The other man stepped aside to let him in and trailed him as he walked into a small living room. Damien was sprawled on one end of a worn beige sectional sofa that took up one entire wall of the room. A Hispanic man about his own age was sitting beside him.

"That's Jamaal," he said, gesturing to the African American man. "That's Julio." He nodded toward the Hispanic man. "This is Eric," he said to the two men. Eric opened his mouth to return the introductions and everything suddenly went dark.

CHAPTER FOUR

LUCAS JERKED awake and looked around blurrily. For a moment, he wasn't sure what had woken him, but then he realized he'd fallen asleep on the sofa with the lamp still on and his book in his lap. During the night, the book had fallen onto the floor. From the thin light coming in underneath the closed blinds, it was early morning. Ouch. He had a massive crick in his neck, but he gathered himself and sat up.

Pushing himself to his feet, Lucas wondered briefly why Eric hadn't woken him and told him to go to bed. A quick peek in Eric's bedroom on his way to the bathroom provided the answer. Eric hadn't come home last night. Hopefully he'd had a better night than Lucas.

Lucas visited the bathroom and then stumbled to the kitchen for coffee. A glance at the clock on the wall told him it was still early—nearly a full hour before the time he actually needed to get up. He had a momentary thought of trying to go back to bed, but he'd never get back to sleep. Might as well make coffee and make a start on the day. Maybe he could actually be on time for once.

He started the coffee to brew and went to take a shower. Since he didn't have classes, he'd be at the office all day. That meant he had to actually wear professional attire, which meant he needed to be sure he actually had something clean in his closet.

Thankfully he had remembered to send his clothes for dry cleaning and to pick them up. He put on his gray slacks and favorite blue shirt and selected a tie and went into the bathroom to tie it and do his hair. Once he was ready, Lucas headed back to the kitchen to make himself a cup of coffee and then hunted down his book bag so he could pack it. At the last minute, he added jeans and a T-shirt to change into. He was scheduled to work the hotline again that night and might not get a chance to come home and change. It was a long enough night on its own. Trying to get through it in a shirt and tie was bound to make it worse.

That done, Lucas realized abruptly that he actually had time for breakfast. That was such a rarity that he hadn't even considered it before. Was there even breakfast food in the house? He contemplated going to the co-op for breakfast, just on the off chance he might run into Professor Ingram again. It was a completely ridiculous idea. He had no reason to even go to campus. It would be completely out of his way and a total waste of time, but he was still tempted. Seeing Ingram never failed to brighten his day, even if he only saw him briefly. He might even manage to get more than just a passing glance. After all, he'd actually gotten a conversation the day before.

No. The trip would take far too long and would have him running late yet again. He would just have to wait to see Professor Ingram, no matter how tempting it might be.

With that decided, Lucas went into the kitchen to search for food. As he had feared, the provisions in their kitchen were pretty slim. He needed to get to the grocery store soon. Fortunately there was bread. He stuck a couple pieces in the toaster and leaned against the counter to wait.

He left a note for Eric, reminding him that he was working at the hotline that night. Then he anchored it to the table with a tube of Eric's paint so he would be sure not to miss it, grabbed his book bag, and hurried to the bus stop.

The day was so busy Lucas didn't have time to spare another thought for Eric or Professor Ingram. He barely had time to eat. Lunch was a soda and crackers from the vending machine while he called foster parents yet again, trying to find a placement for Danny. Dinner was a sandwich from a convenience store, scarfed down on the bus on the way to the hotline, and he swallowed a granola bar he found hidden in the depths of his book bag toward the end of his shift. By the time he made it home, he didn't have energy to do more than strip off his clothes and fall into bed, physically and emotionally exhausted. He was out before his head hit the pillow.

As was typical on days when he had worked the hotline the night before, Lucas woke up late. It was odd that Eric hadn't woken him, but he didn't have time to dwell on it. Eric must have left early. Lucas showered and dressed at speed, stuffed his feet into his sneakers without bothering to untie them, and ran for the bus.

On campus Lucas swung through the co-op for coffee. As he hoped, Professor Ingram was there waiting and pushed coffee and a muffin into his hands. "Take five minutes, breathe, and eat," he instructed as he guided Lucas into a convenient chair by means of hands on his shoulders.

Lucas was too startled to protest. Ingram rarely initiated conversation and had never even moved into his personal space, much less actually touched him. There was absolutely nothing untoward about the way Ingram touched him now. It was casual and should have been completely neutral, no more invasive than the touch of a doctor or any other professional, but it wasn't.

It was electric. Lucas would have sworn he could feel every cell in Ingram's hands. He was intensely aware of every subtle movement. It took both forever and no time at all to get to the table. Lucas cradled the coffee cup between his hands and tried to shake off his stupor.

Ingram glanced at his watch. "The point was to eat it, not stare at it," he said. "You don't have long. As much as I appreciate you not inhaling it like an uncouth heathen, it would probably be advisable to actually put it in your mouth."

Lucas blushed, took a bite of the muffin, and washed it down with coffee. That one bite was all it took for him to realize he was starving. He devoured the remainder of the muffin in moments. Too late he realized it was probably rude to scarf down food as though he hadn't eaten in days. He swallowed the still very hot coffee. The scalding heat chased away the last remnants of his disorientation and brought him back to reality. He put down his cup, intending to apologize for his lack of manners, but Ingram cut him off before he got the chance.

"We should both be heading to class right now," he said. "But I have to know. Why are you always rushing in at the last moment?"

Lucas winced. "Despite appearances I'm not a complete flake. I work three days a week as a social worker and go to class on the other two. I also volunteer three times a week at a suicide hotline. Those nights, which are typically the night before my class days, last until after midnight. I try to sneak in as much sleep as I can, and that usually means I'm running late."

"I never thought you were a flake," Ingram told him. "On the contrary, you seem to be more mature and focused than a lot of students I see. That's why I couldn't figure out how it was you always struggled so much with being on time. Now I see."

"You do?" Lucas asked curiously. "What do you see?"

"I see someone who is good at taking care of everyone but himself," Ingram replied.

Lucas shifted uncomfortably. That was undeniably true. He thrived on taking care of people. Though he had often been accused of it, he didn't have some sort of savior complex that compelled him to try to save everyone. But he thoroughly enjoyed taking care of people. He needed it like other people needed time alone or time outdoors. It was part of who he was.

Of course, as Professor Ingram had identified, the downside was that he wasn't always so great at taking care of himself. People had been preaching the virtues of self-care to him for years, but no matter how much he logically knew they were right, it just never seemed to stick. It was more than a little disconcerting that Ingram had figured that out. Lucas didn't like to think he was that transparent.

"Guilty," he replied lightly, shrugging. "There just don't seem to be enough hours in the day."

"I know that feeling," Ingram said honestly. "I think everyone does, and juggling graduate school and working in a demanding profession isn't easy, especially when you don't see yourself as a priority."

To his horror Lucas felt the tips of his ears start to burn and knew they were turning vividly red. He'd heard the same from any number of other people for years, but hearing it come from Professor Ingram made him feel like a scolded child. That made no sense at all. He was a virtual stranger. Why should his opinion be more important than those of friends and family he'd known for years? But Lucas certainly felt it in a way he didn't with other people. The words seemed to weigh heavily on his conscience.

That still made no sense. Lucas wouldn't deny he was fascinated by Ingram or that he was attracted to him. He might even say he respected him, and he had enjoyed many fantasies that featured him prominently, but that didn't explain why his few mildly disapproving words would make Lucas squirm like a naughty preschooler. What the hell was that about?

Before Lucas could come to any kind of conclusion, Professor Ingram interrupted his thoughts again. "You'd better go," he told him. A glance at the clock told Lucas he was right. He was going to have to run to make it to class on time.

"Yeah," Lucas agreed as he shrugged into his backpack. "Thanks for breakfast." He gathered up his debris, dumped it into the trash receptacle by the door, and headed for the social work building at a pace just short of a run.

AS GABRIEL watched Lucas go, he shook his head. Could it be any clearer that he needed to leave the kid alone? Not only was he a student and far too young, he was an innocent—a do-gooder. He didn't deserve to be sullied by the dark that was in Gabriel's soul.

Gabriel knew that from the moment he bought that first coffee, but he hadn't been able to resist. There was something about Lucas's happy-go-lucky nature that drew him like a magnet. No, happy-go-lucky wasn't right. Lucas wasn't airheaded. Nobody could work a suicide hotline and not know something about the darkness and demons that haunted people. He just didn't let it taint him. It hadn't left deep scars on his soul, and no one had the right to inflict that kind of darkness on him, least of all someone as damaged as Gabriel knew himself to be.

Gabriel knew he had to let it go. No matter how much he enjoyed them, there could be no more "accidental" breakfast meetings. The best thing he could do was walk away before they got in any deeper. Now he just had to man up and make himself do it.

CHAPTER FIVE

ERIC SURFACED into consciousness slowly, his awareness slogging up inch by inch, through waves of blackness. The first thing he noticed when his eyes opened was a winding crack snaking across a water-stained popcorn ceiling above his head. He blinked and tried to lift his hand to rub his eyes. But his hand felt heavy, and he heard the clink of metal near his ear. He was chained to the bed.

The events of the previous night came flooding back to him. He met a cute Mexican guy at the bar—Damien, that was his name—and went to meet up with him. He remembered calling him and going to his house, but then everything went black. What the hell happened? Where was he? What had the guy done to him? He glanced down at himself and realized with a wave of relief that he was still fully clothed in the shirt and pants he wore to the bar. It was unlikely he had been raped. A rapist probably wouldn't have bothered redressing him.

What was going on, then? And where was he?

It looked like some crappy hotel—not the house he had gone to. It was hard to tell in the faint, shadowy light. And where was Damien anyway? If he was with Damien, why was he chained to the bed? Granted, Eric knew plenty of people who were into kinky shit in bed. He wasn't opposed to it himself, but those were metal cuffs—the real things, like police used—not the leather ones that were commonly used in sex play. Why couldn't he remember?

Whatever had happened, he had to get out of there. If he had been gone as long as he thought he had, Lucas would be worried sick. He patted his pockets for his phone. At least he could let Lucas know he was okay, but the familiar shape of his phone was missing. He plunged his hands down inside the pockets and came up empty. Shit. That meant both his phone and ID were missing. The bastard had robbed him and left him chained to a bed. What the fuck was he going to do?

"You awake?" a female voice asked from somewhere over to his left.

Eric jerked, startled, causing the chains to rattle loudly in his ear. He turned instinctively toward the sound of the voice and immediately tried to scramble away at the sight of a young girl perched on the other bed with her knees drawn up to her chest. She was perhaps sixteen, though the provocative clothes and heavy makeup she wore were clearly designed to make her appear older. She had the sleek, long limbs of a colt or baby deer, skin the color of gleaming mahogany, and dozens of tiny braids spilling all over her head.

"Who are you? What are you doing here?" he demanded, though he dimly recognized he probably didn't have anything to fear from a girl who was both younger and smaller than himself.

"Chill, man," the girl told him. "It ain't me you need to be worried about. I'm stuck here, same as you." She held up her left wrist, showing that she too was chained. "Name's Monique, but they call me Chyna."

Eric pulled himself into a sitting position with his back against the headboard.

"They? Who are they?"

Monique shrugged. "The boss is Damien. The other two are Jamaal and Julio. You've got to watch out for Julio. He's quiet, but he's mean. I think they're some kind of gang or mob outfit or something."

Fresh terror washed over Eric. "What's that got to do with me? I'm just a bartender. I'm not into any of that shit."

Monique rolled her eyes. "You think I am? One minute I'm working my after-school job at the mall. Some guy comes up and gives me some spiel about being a model, and my dumb ass falls for it. Next thing I know, I'm waking up chained to a bed in a ratty hotel room in God knows where, same as you."

The terrifying reality slowly dawned on Eric. It wasn't a date gone wrong or even a mugging. He'd been kidnapped. As panic welled up inside him, he clawed at the handcuffs, to no avail. Then he jerked on the chain, but it wouldn't budge. "This can't be happening. I've got to get out of here." He snatched on the chain again, hard enough to make the bed bang against the wall.

"Will you shut up?" Monique hissed. "You're going to get us both in trouble, and believe me, you don't want that."

"I've got to get out of here," Eric snapped. At that moment nothing else mattered. He'd get Monique out too if he could, but one way or the other, he had to get out.

"You're wasting your time," Monique told him. "There is no getting out. Trust me, I've tried. It's useless. This is our life now. The best thing you can do is try to be good and not get hurt."

"Be good," Eric echoed, outraged. "Are you crazy? I'm not just going to stay here and take it. I have a life, and I've got to get back to it." Lucas was going to have a field day when he found out. He'd been warning Eric about the dangers of one-night stands for years, but Eric had always ignored his paranoid nonsense. Never again. He was changing his ways and turning over a new leaf as soon as he got out of there.

"Suit yourself," Monique replied, sounding resigned. "It's your funeral. You'll figure it out soon enough."

Before Eric could work out what she meant by that, the door slammed open, bounced hard off the wall, and Damien walked in. Eric breathed a sigh of relief. Good. Damien was back. Surely he could straighten out the whole horrible mess.

"Damien, what the hell, man? You gotta let me out of here."

Damien laughed. "Let you out? Why would I do that? Who do you think brought you here?" He reached out and patted Eric's cheek gently. "You're going to make me a whole lot of money."

CHAPTER SIX

THE HARSH bleeping of his alarm clock jolted Lucas awake the next morning. Blindly he put out a hand to silence it and dropped back onto his pillow with a groan. It couldn't be morning already. He'd only gotten to bed a few minutes before. There was no way it could have been six hours. He pushed up and forced his eyes open to glare at his alarm clock. The red digital numbers seemed to mock him. Lucas sighed, rolled over onto his back, and pushed back the bedcovers. He was really going to have to sit down and work out a better schedule. He might be just shy of thirty, but he was getting too old for it.

Lucas got to his feet, pulled out work clothes, and headed to the bathroom. It was only after he finished his shower and started to dress that he realized the apartment was eerily silent. The apartment was almost never silent. Eric even slept with the radio on. Lucas pulled on his pants and padded barefoot to Eric's room.

Knocking on the door, he called, "Hey, E, you awake?" When he received no answer, he pushed open the door and peered inside. Eric wasn't there, and his bed didn't look like it had been slept in. Had Eric even been home the night before?

When he came home from his shift on the hotline, Lucas had fallen into bed and gone immediately to sleep. He simply assumed Eric was home, but while Eric did have one-night stands fairly often, he rarely stayed the night and never more than one night. Eric wasn't the committed type.

Lucas went into the kitchen. Maybe Eric had left him a note. With their busy schedules, texts and notes were their most frequent means of communication, even if they did live in the same house. But the kitchen turned up nothing. The only note was the one Lucas had written to Eric two days before. It still waited in the middle of the table, exactly where Lucas left it.

From the looks of it, Eric hadn't read that note either. Did that mean he hadn't been home since the last time Lucas saw him as he was heading out to work two days earlier? That was odd. Eric wouldn't have just decided not to come home without letting him know. Unless he left a message Lucas had somehow missed? Lucas went back to his bedroom and disconnected his phone from the charger. No. There was nothing there.

He pulled on his shirt and punched Eric's number. It rang a few times and then went into voice mail. "Hey, man, where are you? Looks like you haven't been home in a while. Let me know what's up."

Lucas put the phone in his pants pocket and finished dressing. Eric's absence nagged at him a little, but he wasn't really worried. If Eric had hooked up with a guy for the night and forgot to let him know in the heat of the moment, he likely wouldn't be up yet. He would call when he got the message. Lucas gathered his things and caught the bus to his office, where he was promptly swamped by the crisis of the moment and forgot all about his errant roommate.

When Lucas finally managed to take a break for lunch sometime in midafternoon, he thought of Eric again. He checked his phone but found no new messages or texts from Eric. He called again, and the phone went straight to voice mail.

Great. Eric's phone was dead. Lucas sighed. Because he sometimes carried a work phone that required him to keep it charged at all times, Lucas had gotten in the habit of keeping his personal phone charged as well, but it was a habit Eric had never mastered. He'd probably be waiting at home by the time Lucas got there.

Late that night, after an interminably long shift at the hotline and an even longer bus ride, Lucas stepped through the door of his apartment, fully expecting to hear the radio blaring on the other side of the door and Eric—barefoot, shirtless, and covered in paint—behind a canvas in the middle of the living room. Instead it was stubbornly silent, and everything was still exactly as he left it that morning.

Lucas was really beginning to get worried. He had tried calling Eric a couple more times throughout the afternoon and gotten no response. He gave up on leaving voice mails. The three or four he left earlier in the day should be enough.

It wasn't like Eric. Sure, he was a little bit of a free spirit, but he just didn't drop out altogether. Lucas had barely gone more than a day or two without some sort of contact from Eric since they were in middle school. Something wasn't right.

Lucas tried his best to keep his panic at bay. Freaking out wouldn't do any good, and Eric would probably show up any minute with a shrug and a grin and some epic adventure to tell him about. Trouble just seemed to follow Eric that way.

He managed to hold on to that optimism until his phone rang a couple of hours later. When he answered, the voice on the other end said, "Hi, Lucas, it's Nathan. Have you heard from Eric?"

The lingering worry Lucas had been trying to ignore shot up into the stratosphere. Nathan was the manager at Sparks. "He's not there? I haven't seen him all day. I just assumed he had gone from wherever he was to work."

"No, he's not here," Nathan replied. "I thought maybe he was at home sick. I've tried calling him a few times, but it keeps going to voice mail. I thought maybe he was asleep and had turned his phone off or something."

"He's not here either." Lucas swallowed against a throat that had suddenly gone dry. "It doesn't look like he's been here all day. I haven't been able to get him either."

"That's weird," Nathan commented. "Some of the other guys, it wouldn't surprise me if they just disappeared. You know what it's like around here."

He did. A lot of their staff were older students, and the turnover was ridiculous. "That's not Eric, though," Lucas said.

"No, it's not," Nathan agreed. "That's why I was so surprised when he didn't show up."

"I am too," Lucas told him. "I don't know where he could be."

"Listen," Nathan began. Lucas could hear the noise rising in the background behind him. "I've got to go, but give me a ring if he shows up or you hear from him. Okay?"

"Sure. I'll do that if you will tell him to call me if he shows up there."

"You got it," Nathan said easily and hung up the phone.

Lucas put down his phone and paced the floor. Eric wouldn't have missed work, not voluntarily, and certainly not just to shack up with some guy. It was one of his pet peeves. He hated it when other guys blew off work for stupid things, and even if he had gotten sick or something, he would've called in. If Eric couldn't get to a phone, he was either hurt, which wasn't likely since the hospital hadn't contacted Lucas, or someone was preventing him from calling. The very thought turned Lucas's stomach to ice.

Lucas wanted to dismiss the thought as ridiculous. Why would someone kidnap Eric? His family didn't have any money. Anyone hoping for a ransom would be sorely disappointed. Besides, there had been no ransom demand. If that was what the kidnappers were after, wouldn't he have heard something? At the same time, Lucas had seen news stories on people who were found after having been kidnapped and held captive for years. It did happen. Not every kidnapper was after money. Could something like that have happened to Eric?

Lucas spent a restless night clutching the phone and praying Eric would call. Or text. Or something. Anything would do. He wouldn't even care where Eric was or who he was with, as long as he was alive and okay. Lucas didn't sleep much, and the few times he did manage to drift off were plagued by vague and horrible dreams of Eric trapped in dungeons and cages while Lucas was helpless to rescue him. By the time daylight broke outside his window, Lucas had come to one firm conclusion. Wherever Eric was and whatever might have happened, waiting was getting him nowhere. It was time to go to the authorities.

INSIDE THE police station, Lucas made his way up to the front desk. "I'd like to file a missing person report," he told the officer at the front desk, a stocky, middle-aged woman with short brown hair.

"Is this regarding an adult or a child?" she questioned.

"An adult," Lucas replied. "My roommate, Eric, is missing."

She made a notation on the notepad. "What's Eric's last name? How old is he?"

"Collier. He's twenty-seven."

"When was the last time you saw your roommate?" she asked.

"Three days ago when he left for work," Eric explained. "He's a bartender at Sparks. He told me he would be late and not to wait up for him, but that was three days ago, and no one has seen or heard from him since. He's not answering his phone, and that's not at all like him."

The officer nodded. She opened the file drawer and took out a form. "Fill this out and bring it back up. When you're done, I'll get an officer to take your report. We'll put it in the system, but I've got to tell you I wouldn't expect much, if I were you. Your roommate's probably just out partying somewhere and hasn't sobered up long enough to call. He'll probably show up on his own eventually."

Lucas shook his head. "No. You don't understand. Eric isn't like that. He wouldn't just disappear without contacting me. We've been friends for years. We're practically family."

"Okay, sir," she agreed, but her tone made it obvious she was simply trying to placate him. That irritated Lucas even more. What right did she have to be judging what Eric would or wouldn't do? She didn't know him. Just because he was a bartender at a gay bar didn't mean he would disappear without a word to anybody. Not every young gay man was some kind of flighty street kid, no matter how movies and TV shows liked to portray them.

She pushed the form and a pen in Lucas's direction. He barely restrained himself from snatching them out of her hand.

As he walked over and took a seat in a folding chair stationed against the wall, he tried to force himself to calm down and think rationally. He was a social worker. He knew how the system worked. Paperwork was a necessary evil. If it wasn't documented, it didn't happen. If he filled out the paperwork and they got it into the system, there would be an official record that Eric was missing. That was a good first step. At the very least, it was better than nothing.

Thus resolved, Lucas took up the pen the officer had provided and filled out the form. Thankfully the first part was simple. At least most of it was. The name, address, and description he could do in his sleep. Eric had been his best friend since eighth grade. He knew Eric's info almost as well as he knew his own. But he hesitated over the section that asked him to classify what type of missing person Eric was. Who knew there were different types?

He definitely wasn't a runaway or a voluntarily missing adult, no matter what anybody said.

If it were voluntary, he would've answered the phone by now, if for no other reason than to let Lucas know he was alive. There was no reason for Eric to hide from him. They had been sharing each other's secrets for years. Eric was the first person to whom Lucas hesitantly confessed that he thought he might be gay. Eric had, in turn, admitted that he thought he might be the same.

They stood by each other through the terrifying process of coming out to their families. Lucas's went relatively smoothly. His parents were open-minded by nature, and having been foster parents since before Lucas was even born, they had been exposed to a far more diverse population than most people in the small mountain town where they lived. They saw what could come of teenagers who were rejected by their parents for their sexuality, and swore never to do the same to one of their own. His coming out might have been a bit of a surprise, but they accepted him without question.

Eric wasn't so lucky. He was raised by his grandparents, mostly. His mom had taken off years earlier, and his dad was a long-haul truck driver who was rarely home. They were absolutely floored by Eric's admission. Lucas was with him that night for moral support, just as Eric was with him the day he came out to his parents, and he didn't think he would ever forget the looks on their faces. Shock didn't even begin to cover it.

If he and Eric had survived that together, there was nothing Eric needed to hide from him, and Eric knew that. Lucas was well aware of the lifestyle Eric lived, but he never judged Eric for it. The only thing Lucas ever did was urge Eric to be safe. If he had decided to shack up with his current man for a few days, he had absolutely no need to hide that from Lucas and had never done so in the past. If he was AWOL, it was because something was terribly wrong.

The bell above the door jingled and admitted a potbellied officer. Lucas turned his attention back to the form and quickly found the bottom section was quite a bit more challenging. He knew the make and model of Eric's car, but not the tag number. He knew the name of the bar where Eric worked, but not the address. He ran a quick search on his phone and filled it in. He had no idea how to access Eric's dental or medical records. Eric's grandparents had died when Lucas was still an undergrad—both of them within six months of each other—and God only knew where Eric's dad was. For that matter, who was Eric's next of kin?

They were like brothers, and he was probably the closest person Eric had, but legally, Eric's dad was probably his next of kin—not that Lucas had the foggiest idea where to find him. Eric and he exchanged phone calls sometimes, but that was all Lucas knew. Who should he put on the form? Lucas sighed and put down his own name. Eric would probably be home by the time his dad called again.

Picture? Lucas mentally slapped himself in the head. What kind of an idiot was he? Of course they needed a picture if they were going to look for him. Why in the world hadn't he thought to bring one with him? Not that he had a lot of experience dealing with that kind of thing. He'd had a few runaway kids, sure. That was part and parcel of a typical day in the foster care unit. But none of them had really been missing for more than a day, and it was pretty easy to figure out where they'd taken off to. It never incited the kind of panic he was feeling, not after the first few times, anyway.

This was different. This was Eric, and something was very clearly wrong. Having filled out as much of the form as he could, Lucas took it back to the desk. The officer reluctantly hauled herself out of her chair and picked up the form. She glanced over it and hollered in the direction of the potbellied officer who came in earlier. "Hey, Mike, this guy needs to give a statement. Says his roommate is missing."

The officer in question, whom Lucas privately dubbed Officer Potbelly, lumbered up and took the paper from the desk officer. He read over the form and glanced warily between Lucas and the desk officer with an expression that clearly said, "Are you kidding me?" He was professional enough to refrain from saying it or rolling his eyes, but Lucas would have bet money he was mentally doing both. "Right. Come with me, Mr.—" He glanced down at the paper. "—Craig."

Officer Potbelly gestured Lucas around the main counter. At the officer's direction, Lucas took a seat in the battered visitor's chair beside his desk, where he proceeded to have a nearly identical conversation to the one he had just had with the officer at the desk. Then the officer gave him a blank form and had him write out a statement detailing when he last saw Eric and what had happened in the days since, including why he thought Eric was in trouble. When Lucas handed the officer the form, the man read it over briefly and gave Lucas a distinctly paternal look.

"I've filed the report in the computer. It will go out to all the surrounding police stations, but I wouldn't worry too much about that, if I were you. In all likelihood your friend will come home on his own. This happens more often than you realize. People tend to be impulsive. They take off without thinking to let anyone know and then appear on their own a few days later. We'll let you know if we get anything, and you be sure to let us know when he comes home."

When, not *if.* If Lucas were in the mood to be charitable, which he definitely wasn't, the assurance of that statement might have comforted him. That might have been Officer Potbelly's intention. If it was, he was failing miserably. His smug arrogance only served to further irritate Lucas. He stifled the urge to scream.

"I'll do that," Lucas bit off through clenched teeth. He pushed up out of the chair, made his way out, and shoved through the glass entry doors.

DESPITE HIS immense frustration with the officers, Lucas still held some faint hope that the police would come up with something to help find Eric. Just because Officer Potbelly and his colleague didn't seem to take his concerns seriously, that didn't mean the surrounding police stations would be the same. Surely somebody would understand the reason for his concern?

He kept his phone charged and within reach at all times the next day as he waited anxiously for a call with an update. It never came. By midafternoon he could no longer concentrate on his work, so he gave up on waiting and called the police station, only to be told there was nothing to report. They urged him to be patient and reminded him to call them if Eric were to turn up. Lucas hung up the phone, torn between the urge to scream and the urge to cry.

In the end he did neither. Instead he poured all his nervous energy into his work. Miraculously he had finally found a placement for Danny. It was in a neighboring district, which meant Danny would have to change schools. But since Danny wasn't particularly invested at his current school, Lucas didn't think he would mind, especially if the placement turned out to be the great fit Lucas anticipated. Danny's new foster father was a single gay man who had a reputation for being great with teenage boys. He had agreed to the placement without a moment's hesitation. It was a time Lucas would normally be celebrating. If he weren't so damn worried.

The next day was even worse. It didn't help that he'd had almost no sleep. It was impossible to keep his mind on his classes when all he could think about was Eric. Every minute felt like hours, and every hour was agony. Unfortunately, being a social worker gave him far too much knowledge of the darker side of town.

Hundreds of possibilities plagued him. Gang fights and drug deals gone bad were unlikely. Lucas would have known if Eric were involved in anything like that. He was trained and he knew the signs. Still, anyone could end up in the wrong place at the wrong time, and anyone could have an accident.

Had Eric been in a car accident? The guys at Sparks said his car wasn't there. Wherever he was, Eric had been driving. Maybe he was in an accident and didn't remember who he was. But the hospital would have his ID. Somebody would've contacted Lucas. Unless—no, he wouldn't even think that.

Between his classes Lucas called the local hospitals anyway, but they had no one matching Eric's description. With all the new privacy laws, Lucas wasn't entirely sure they would've told him in any case, but it still amounted to a dead end. Another call to the police was no better. There were still no hits on his missing person report. Everywhere Lucas turned he only found another dead end. Eric couldn't have simply vanished off the face of the earth, could he? He had to be somewhere.

Frustrated and exhausted, Lucas would have liked nothing more than to go home and crawl in bed, but he didn't know if he could face the apartment again. It seemed so empty without Eric's constant chatter and the blaring radio that had driven Lucas crazy. How was anybody supposed to study with rock blaring at all hours? Eric always swore that music was essential to creativity. It was a constant and familiar argument. And the absence of it was a nagging reminder that Eric wasn't there.

Lucas bypassed his bus stop and wandered down the sidewalk with no idea of where he was going. He didn't care as long as it wasn't back to his apartment. The bus would be running for several hours yet. He could at least grab dinner before he went home. Not that he really felt like eating. His appetite had been nonexistent since he realized Eric was gone. He walked around aimlessly for a while and searched every face in every crowd, but Eric was nowhere to be found.

He should have been easy to spot. Eric's distinctive blond, dye-tipped locks usually stood out in any crowd. What color had Eric dyed his hair before he left? Blue? Red? Purple? Lucas had no idea. It was only a few days before. How could he not remember what color his best friend's hair was? Maybe it was green this week. No, that was last week, the night he wore the green sweater. Purple? Purple was one of Eric's favorites, but he always said he didn't like to wear it too often because it would lose the novelty and shock factor if he did. Dammit. It would be a lot easier if Eric didn't have the annoying habit of changing his hair color to suit his whim.

Ironically Lucas ended up at Sparks. That was the one place he knew Eric wasn't, but given it was the last place Eric was seen, Lucas felt drawn there. The atmosphere seemed unnaturally subdued. There was something palpably missing, a giant hole in the spirit of the place that everyone felt but no one acknowledged. It was both an irritant and a balm. It accentuated the ache of missing Eric and the worry over his well-being, but at least no one would dismiss him and pretend nothing was wrong.

He settled into a booth in the back corner, half-hidden in the shadow, and hoped it would conceal his presence and allow him to be left alone. He should have known better. Even though he didn't come out that frequently, all the regulars knew him through Eric, and practically every one of them sought him out at some point during the evening to ask after him.

Lucas didn't have any answers. Should he tell them that? Would it help? Maybe some of them knew something they weren't saying. At the same time, he was reluctant to say he didn't know. No matter how true it was, the words stuck in his throat. Admitting it, especially to people who knew Eric, made it even more real. In the end he told most of them he was expecting to get a phone call from Eric any day. It wasn't a lie, though expecting was probably the wrong word. Hoping was closer to true. Still, if he believed it long enough, maybe that would make it true.

Lucas tried to hold on to that thought through another restless night, but by morning, frustration had turned to anger, and he condemned himself as an idiot and a fool. Wishing for something to happen didn't make it true. He should know that. How many foster children had he seen over the years wish and beg and plead and cry and pray for their circumstances to be different, for their parents' addictions to be cured, for the ones who had abandoned them to come back? Wishing didn't make things happen. Commitment and work did. If he wanted to find Eric, he needed to do something, not just hope and wait on the police, but actively work on it.

But what could he do? What had the police done when one of his charges had made an attempt to run away? They checked with their friends, and they checked cell phone and social media accounts. Lucas had already checked with Eric's friends, and Eric had his cell with him when he disappeared. Lucas didn't have any way to access it, and he didn't know the passwords for Eric's social media accounts. With the schedule Lucas kept, he barely had time for sleep, much less social media.

What else? He could put up flyers, he supposed. Grasping that idea like a lifeline, he called in sick to work and spent a productive morning creating a flyer and taking it to the campus copy station to make as many copies as he could afford. Then he plastered them all over campus and all over town and left a stack at Sparks. That time of day, it was closed and empty save for the manager, but he promised to put them up and make sure they were circulated around as well.

The effort left Lucas feeling buoyed and hopeful. His appetite suddenly returned with a vengeance. By sheer habit Lucas made his way back to campus and to the co-op. He could've probably gotten better food in town at a restaurant, but the co-op was cheap and convenient.

Besides, part of him hoped he might run into Professor Ingram. Unfortunately he saw no sign of him. He was disappointed, but he probably shouldn't have been surprised. After all, Lucas had no idea of the professor's schedule except that he always seemed to be in the co-op early in the morning.

The disappointment only grew as the day went on and on. Although Lucas plastered the flyers everywhere he could think of, there were few calls and no new clues. By late afternoon Lucas felt like he wanted to crawl out of his skin. Nothing was happening. Eric was missing, and no one seemed to notice or care. The whole thing was insane. People didn't just disappear into thin air. Somebody had to know something. Eric had to be somewhere.

In desperation Lucas went to the library to research private detectives. He'd never known anyone who actually worked as a private detective, but they were always talking about them on television. The profession did exist, and a quick Internet search turned up three who were in the general area.

He walked outside to get a cell signal and called all three, but they turned out to be no more help than the police. One after another patiently listened to his story, named their fees, and found a way to quickly and quietly end the conversation when Lucas admitted he couldn't afford them. Lucas had to resist the urge to toss his phone onto the concrete and watch it shatter. His friend was missing. His friend could be hurt or worse. Didn't anybody care?

Lucas paced up and down the sidewalk in front of the library. He didn't know whether to punch something or burst into tears. Both urges seemed equally appealing. What the hell was he supposed to do? He couldn't just give up. Eric was out there somewhere, and someone had to find out what happened to him. Lucas might not know much about missing people, but even he knew the longer it went on, the lower the chances of them surviving. There had to be something he could do. He bought a soda out of the vending machine in the lobby while he considered.

The university was full of experts in every kind of academic discipline. Would somebody there know how to find people? They had their own police force, even, but Lucas didn't think they would be much help. Their jurisdiction only reached as far as the edge of campus. During Lucas's freshman year, campus police were unable to unlock cars for students who were parked in a lot across from the main campus because it was privately owned and outside their jurisdiction. If they were unwilling to intervene in something so minor, there was no way they would contradict the city cops. Especially since Eric wasn't currently a student, even if he was an alumnus.

Beyond that Lucas didn't know many people outside of the sociology and social services departments, but there were dozens of others. Could the answer he was seeking be right there?

He downed the last of his soda, tossed the can into the recycle bin, and went back to the computers to search through the faculty directory and carefully examine every professor's area of expertise. Most he could eliminate quickly. He doubted an English professor was going to be much help. Neither was the art professor who did pottery or the biologist who was experimenting with sustainable food supplies. The political science department seemed more promising. They taught classes in criminal justice, and they even had a major called international security. Surely someone familiar with the justice system would know something about how to locate a missing person, wouldn't they?

As he searched through the professors' specialties in political science, Lucas came to a biography in the middle of the page and stopped in his tracks. He was an idiot, a complete and total idiot. Professor Ingram was the university's security specialist. According to his CV, he really was a former CIA agent. If anyone would know how to go about looking for someone who was missing, he would. Why hadn't Lucas thought of that? He'd heard the rumors about Professor Ingram's former career. Of course. Who hadn't? But in his panic, it hadn't even occurred to him. He'd been too busy mooning after Ingram like a silly schoolboy.

For all he wanted to kick himself, Lucas was relieved. At least he didn't have to try to convince a total stranger to help him. Professor Ingram knew him. Lucas even liked to think they were friends of a sort. Professor Ingram would help him. He just had to.

CHAPTER SEVEN

GABRIEL SCRAWLED a final comment on the essay he was grading and dropped it into his Done pile. He eyed the stack of essays he still needed to grade. Had he been a superstitious man, he would have sworn the pile was growing larger despite the fact that he kept grading and removing essays.

Gabriel ran across the occasional student who was particularly insightful, and he enjoyed seeing the familiar material with fresh eyes. But that wasn't the case with his current class. They were mediocre at best, and grading their work was a tedious chore and nothing more. He sat back in his chair, rubbed his hands over his face, and debated going over to the co-op for a drink and a change of scenery.

Before he could decide, he was interrupted by a short, sharp knock at the door. He eyed the door suspiciously. It wasn't his scheduled time for office hours, and his colleagues rarely stopped by to talk. That wasn't something he welcomed, and they knew it.

"Enter," he barked. Almost before the word was out, the door was flung open, and Lucas stood before him.

"You have to help me," he said without preamble. "Eric has disappeared. Something horrible has happened, and nobody believes me."

Gabriel stared at him in shock. What in the hell was he doing there? It wasn't Lucas's normal class day. Embarrassing as it was to admit, he knew Lucas's schedule as well as he knew his own. What's more, Lucas had never come to his office or even to his building. He was surprised Lucas knew where his office was.

And who the hell was Eric?

Gabriel forced himself to stay calm and not give himself away. He had a reputation to uphold. "I see," he said coolly. "And just what is it you think I can do to help? I like you, kid, but I'm just a professor. I'm not the police. That's who you need to be having this conversation with, not me."

"Don't you think I have?" he asked, and the heat in his voice matched the coolness in Gabriel's, beat for beat. "I told you. No one is listening to me." He was nearly shouting, and his eyes flashed.

"Yes, I heard you," Gabriel replied, not the least fazed by the outburst. "So did most of the hall, most likely. If you insist on having this conversation, at least come in and close the door. The entire department need not be party to it."

Lucas glared at him but took a few steps forward and shoved the door closed behind him, stopping short of slamming it, which he clearly wanted to do.

"Have a seat," Gabriel told him, gesturing to the small visitor's chair near his desk. Lucas continued to glare, and Gabriel swallowed a smile. The kid had no idea. He was like a kitten puffed up at a tiger. Gabriel held his gaze, and eventually Lucas broke away and dropped into the chair. "Thank you. Now just what is it you're going on about? Who is Eric?

Lucas scrubbed his hands over his face and through his hair, making his blond locks scatter every which way in his wake. "He's my roommate. He disappeared almost a week ago, and no one has heard from him since. The police keep insisting he just took off. They say an adult has a right to disappear and not be found, and there's nothing they can do," Lucas said.

"They're right," Gabriel told him frankly. "Unless there is some evidence that your friend did not leave on his own, there's very little to be done."

"He did not just take off," Lucas insisted. "Who takes off without their stuff? His clothes are still at the house. His paints are there."

Contrary to what Lucas clearly believed, such a thing wasn't necessarily that unusual. Gabriel could think of several occasions when he had done just that. "Things can be replaced," Gabriel told him. "Perhaps it was simply easier to start over whenever he got to where he was going than it was to try to transport his things."

"He. Did. Not. Take. Off," Lucas bit out, frustration bleeding through every line of his body. "I know everyone thinks he's just some flaky gay club kid, but he isn't like that. I'm telling you he would not have left without telling someone. He would have told me."

"Even if you're right," Gabriel countered, "it remains to be seen just what exactly you think I can do about it. As I've said, I'm a teacher, not a police officer or a private detective."

"Don't play dumb with me," Lucas seethed as he leaned forward and braced his hands on the desk with far more menace than a sweet, hapless kid like him should have. "I know who you are."

That made the hair on the back of Gabriel's neck stand up, but he'd maintained his cover in situations far more difficult—most of them downright deadly—and didn't let it show. He calmly raised an eyebrow. "What is it that you think you know?"

"You're not just any teacher," Lucas said. "You may pretend like you're just another academic, but you're not. You're CIA."

The knot of muscles at the base of Gabriel's neck and in the pit of his stomach slowly relaxed. "I was, at one point in my life, a CIA case officer. That's hardly secret information." In fact it was clearly stated on his CV, including the one published on the university's website. The bland, generalized description that had been carefully crafted and approved before he left the agency gave no hint of what he had really done behind the scenes. "However, as you can plainly see, I'm now retired. I am, as I've told you several times, simply a teacher."

"That's bullshit," Lucas shot back. "You're CIA. You'll never be just a teacher."

"I'm afraid you're mistaken," Gabriel countered. "I don't know what gave you the idea that I was some sort of mythic superspy— though I am terribly flattered—but I can assure you I'm not. It's true that I was formerly in the service of the Central Intelligence Agency, but I served primarily in the capacity of a translator."

That was what his CV said, and it wasn't entirely untrue. He had served in the capacity of a translator for perhaps a year, until those higher up on the chain of command noticed that he not only spoke several Middle Eastern languages with the fluency of a native, but he could easily mimic minute inflections, gestures, expressions, and cultural innuendo with enough deftness to appear to *be* a native, rather than simply a fumbling American translator—though he could be that when the situation called for it. Then they quickly funneled him into more and more complex undercover missions, eventually including missions that didn't even officially exist—black ops, assassinations, and the like. That was the part of his life no one could know about, least of all a bighearted, innocent social worker.

"Unless you need documents translated from Farsi or Arabic to find your friend, I'm afraid I can't help you."

For a moment bleak disappointment swallowed the kid's features. It pained Gabriel to see it. Though he knew he couldn't tell Lucas any more about his past, he didn't like hurting him. The pain got worse when he saw the disappointment morph into white-hot anger. Gabriel knew then that he had likely broken their fragile relationship beyond repair. Maybe that was for the best.

"Fine," Lucas ground out. "Forget it. I never should've come here. You know, I never believed the things they said about you. All the whispers and the rumors. Everyone said you were a coldhearted ass. I never believed them. You've always been nice to me, but it turns out they were right. You are an ass. I thought you were different. I thought you were my friend, but I was so wrong." His voice cracked on the last word, swallowed by deep and shuddering sobs, and he crumpled.

Gabriel simply stared at him, and his resignation shattered. Shit. What was he supposed to do? He could handle the anger. Lucas was no more than a spitting kitten. Even the disappointment was regrettable, but necessary. He was prepared for that. But the kid was devastated, broken even, and Gabriel was the cause of it.

In the flash of a second, he was back in that crowded little house in the desert, watching the sobbing woman kneel over the body of her dead husband. Only this time he didn't have the luxury of being disconnected—a hardened operative who slipped on new identities with the ease of a new outfit and who could simply walk away and become someone else. This time it wasn't a target or an asset. This time it mattered. It was someone whom he—dare he say it—cared about, and he felt it deeply.

Guilt came crashing in on the heels of momentary shock and made him feel like the world's biggest asshole. He couldn't sit there like a gaping moron. He had to do something, but he had to tread carefully. He hadn't spent the last few years of his life vigilantly safeguarding that life to have the kid drag him back. He'd help if he could, but only peripherally. He couldn't risk anything that could arouse the black rage that once nearly swallowed him.

Gabriel took a deep breath to settle himself and then walked around the desk and placed a gentle hand in the middle of Lucas's heaving back. "It's going to be okay," he said in the calm, firm tone that had gotten him through hundreds of delicate situations with everything from jumpy new assets to irate arms dealers. "Take a couple deep breaths." He paused to give Lucas time to respond, and when Lucas only kept sobbing, he repeated sternly, "Breathe."

Lucas froze midsob and drew in a choked breath.

"That's it," Gabriel encouraged. "Again."

He coached Lucas until the hysterical sobbing had settled into wet sniffles and shaky breathing. "Better?" At Lucas's nod, he patted his back gently several times and then stepped away to retrieve the tissue box from the end table behind his desk. Despite what the rumors around campus said, Gabriel wasn't in the habit of *making* his students cry, but college students rivaled kindergartners when it came to a constant barrage of sniffling and coughing, particularly in the winter. Apparently no one carried handkerchiefs or tissues anymore.

He put the box on the desk in front of Lucas, who promptly took several and mopped his face. "Now," Gabriel continued when Lucas was done, "why don't you tell me a little bit more about what's going on? Then maybe we can figure out what to do next. What makes you think your friend hasn't just decided to go away for a few days?"

"I know him. He wouldn't just disappear," Lucas replied in a small, tremulous voice. He kept his eyes on his lap and looked thoroughly abashed. "He hasn't shown up for work either. He's a bartender at Sparks."

"I take it that's unusual?" Gabriel commented as he propped a hip on the edge of his desk.

"Very," Lucas said adamantly. "Eric never misses work, and even if he had, for some strange reason, just decided out of the blue to blow off work, he would have gotten in contact with me. I've called him and texted him over and over, and he's not answering. He wouldn't do that to me. Ever. We're practically brothers. We've been best friends since middle school."

"You've been to the police?"

Lucas nodded. "I did a missing person report, but they're not doing anything."

"Don't be so sure of that," Gabriel said. "A lot of investigative work goes on behind the scenes." That was true whether it was the CIA, the FBI, or a local police department. Much of their work went on unseen and was underappreciated, especially by outsiders who wanted things done yesterday. "I'm sure they're doing all they can."

Lucas snorted. "You wouldn't say that if you'd heard the detective I talked to. He's convinced that Eric is just some kid on a bender, holed up in a hotel room with his *girlfriend*." He spat out the word, rolling his eyes and encapsulating it in air quotes. "As if Eric would even have a girlfriend, much less be shacked up in some seedy hotel with one."

"Eric's gay, then," Gabriel commented.

"Does anyone work at Sparks who isn't?" Lucas asked dryly.

The kid had a point. You wouldn't catch many straight guys bartending at a gay bar. He had never been to Sparks himself, but he knew of it by reputation. It was quite popular on campus.

"That's a fair point," Gabriel conceded. "But prejudices aside, how do you know he hasn't just gone off with a boyfriend or hooked up with a guy?"

"Because he wouldn't ignore me," Lucas insisted. "I'm the closest thing to family he's got. He wouldn't ignore me unless he had no choice. No matter what he was doing or who he was with, he would have found some way to contact me. Just because he's young and gay and an artist doesn't mean he is a total flake."

"I know that," Gabriel said mildly. "Whatever prejudices you may have run into with the local police, you can rest assured they're not mine. I have traveled places many people have never even heard of and encountered things far more unusual than a young gay man."

Not to mention the fact that he had *been* a young gay man. When he was Lucas's age, he was a newly minted CIA agent going on his first missions, wide-eyed and thoroughly wet behind the ears. But he wasn't as innocent as this kid. He doubted he had ever been. Moving from place to place in foster care had aged him quickly, and if anything, Gabriel was grateful. It had given him survival skills that kept him alive.

The corner of Lucas's mouth turned up in a shaky, watery approximation of a smile. "That's exactly how the cops acted, like they thought Eric was some kind of foreign species because he's gay. Their whole response was pretty much, 'Son, you know how those people act.'"

Gabriel nodded.

"Please," Lucas went on. "No one is taking me seriously. Something terrible has happened. I know it has. And no one believes me. I need help."

The kid might be innocent, but he was deadly. There was no way Gabriel could possibly refuse his earnest expression, especially not when his eyes were red rimmed and his face was still tracked with tears. Gabriel sighed and mentally shook his head in exasperation. He was going to regret it. He knew he was. But he took a deep breath and committed himself.

"Okay," he told Lucas. "I'll help. I'm not sure what I can do, but I believe you, and I'll do what I can."

Lucas deflated before his eyes as the tension ran out of his body like air from a balloon. "Thank you," he said with utter sincerity.

"Don't thank me yet," Gabriel cautioned. "It remains to be seen whether I can actually do anything to help."

"You believe me," Lucas replied. "That's already more than anybody else has done. I had no idea what to do or where to go next, and no one even believed me."

"I believe you," Gabriel confirmed. He had no idea how anyone could see the sincerity in Lucas and not believe him. It was written in every line of his body. "As to what to do next, I would suggest checking in with the police and seeing if they have made any progress."

Lucas snorted. "Fat chance. I'd be surprised if my report didn't land in the trash can as soon as I walked out the door."

"It didn't," Gabriel assured him. "Or if it did, there's going to be hell to pay. They have a legal obligation to at least look into it, and however local yokel they may be, there are still politics involved. They don't want it to get around that they are refusing to look into cases involving the gay community. It would be a political and public-relations disaster. They do not want that coming down on their heads."

The kid had a surprisingly wicked and mischievous grin. "I hadn't even thought of that."

"They may not have either," Gabriel said, "but let's see if we can't enlighten them." He got to his feet and reached for the jacket hanging on the back of his chair. "Let's go. There's a bathroom down the hall where you can wash your face. Do you have a jacket somewhere?" Rain was blowing in from over the ocean and had turned the day overcast and chilly. Surely Lucas wasn't wandering around in nothing more than a battered T-shirt.

Lucas shook his head and looked sheepish. "Somewhere, maybe, but not where I can find it at the moment. I guess I haven't been exactly paying much attention to things like that lately."

Gabriel opened the bottom drawer of his desk, retrieved the hooded sweatshirt he kept there, and held it out in Lucas's direction.

"That's not necessary," Lucas protested. "I'm fine."

"Sure you are," Gabriel agreed. "Right up until the moment you catch pneumonia from the damp and chill."

"That's a complete myth," Lucas informed him. "You should know that. Pneumonia is an infection. It is caused by a type of bacteria or a virus. It has nothing to do with the weather."

"Tell me that after you've been on an all-night stakeout in the rain and woke up feeling like hell the next day," Gabriel said.

Lucas opened his mouth to argue, but Gabriel cut him off by holding up a hand and raising his eyebrows. "Just put on the damn shirt." He could see Lucas wanted to resist, to make his point anyway, but he held his tongue and put out his hand.

"Fine. Give it here."

Gabriel passed the shirt over, and Lucas snatched it briskly over his head and shouldered into it. Since Gabriel was both broader and several inches taller than Lucas, it swallowed him to the tops of his thighs and the ends of his hands. It made him look even more like an innocent kid.

There was nothing childlike about the way Lucas glared while he pushed up the sleeves, though. "Happy now?"

Gabriel nodded. "Thrilled."

Another day it might have been fun to tease him more, but they needed to get going. Hopefully finding out what was going on with the investigation would ease Lucas's mind, and Gabriel wouldn't have to get further involved. Kidnapping was the FBI's territory. He was a spy, not a detective.

Gabriel opened the door and nodded Lucas through it. They walked down the hall in silence. Lucas disappeared briefly into the small unisex restroom as they passed it and came out looking considerably more steady and with his eyes clearer. That took a weight off Gabriel. It had shaken him more than he liked to admit to see Lucas that upset.

Gabriel stepped ahead to guide Lucas in the direction of his car. He strode quickly through the faculty parking lot at the back of the building to his usual parking space where his sleek black Aston Martin coupe sat. It was his one indulgence when he left the agency. Since he'd spent most of his career going from one undercover assignment to another, living off the agency's dime, he had years of paychecks sitting untouched. And after years of traveling in nondescript agency cars, the last thing he had wanted was another cookie-cutter ride. But he didn't have to worry about blending in anymore. He could do as he pleased.

When he realized Lucas was no longer moving behind him, Gabriel glanced back to see that he had stopped and was staring at the car.

"Surprised?" Gabriel asked.

"A little," Lucas admitted.

"Why? It doesn't seem like the type of thing I would drive?"

"It doesn't seem like the type of thing any professor would drive," Lucas replied. "Or anything I've ever ridden in either. I'm a little afraid to get near it for fear I'll break something I can't afford to pay for."

"You think I'd drive something like this without having great insurance?" Gabriel said easily. He chuckled. "I have it covered. Trust me." Lucas still looked a little wary, but he opened the passenger side door and slid into the car. "Buckle up," Gabriel prompted as he automatically buckled his seat belt, started up the car, and pulled out.

Lucas blushed but promptly fastened himself in. "Sorry. I guess I've gotten too used to riding the bus."

"No worries," Gabriel said. Lucas sat quietly after that, and Gabriel didn't make any attempt to engage him. He was thankful for the quiet because he needed to figure out the best way to handle the situation. He wouldn't let the cops give Lucas the runaround, but he'd be a friend—quiet and supportive, but nothing more. That should be easy enough. He could do that.

GABRIEL HAD been in and out of any number of law enforcement agencies in his time, and he knew that many rural police forces operated on a shoestring budget, so the inconspicuous storefront office only identified by the sign above the door and the scattering of police cars parked out front didn't surprise him. He pushed open the glass entrance door, making the bell above it tinkle, and ushered Lucas in before him.

The middle-aged female officer at the front desk looked up and smiled at him. "How can I help you gentlemen?"

Gabriel looked to Lucas and gave him the opportunity to take the lead, but one glance was enough to know he wasn't going to. Lucas looked equal parts frustrated and terrified.

Gabriel stepped up to the desk. "My friend came in a few days ago and made a missing person report. We were wondering about the progress of that investigation."

The officer smiled politely. "Let me check." Then, as though neither Gabriel nor Lucas were standing there at all, she turned to the man seated at the desk behind her and yelled, "Hey, Mike, these folks want to know about that missing person report."

The other officer, a balding man with a significant paunch, heaved a heavy sigh, levered himself out of his chair, and came around the counter to meet them with clear reluctance.

Unlike the woman, who had all but ignored Lucas, this officer focused entirely on him and never even acknowledged that Gabriel was in the room. "It's like I told you, son," he said. "I put in the report, but nothing has come of it. Your friend probably just decided to move on."

Out of the corner of his eye, Gabriel could see Lucas clench his hands into fists. Before the kid could lose control and explode, he broke in. "I see. And have you followed up on the report any further, perhaps checking out his last known location or talking to his coworkers?"

It was perfectly clear from the man's expression that he had done no such thing. In fact, if Gabriel had to guess, he would say the idea of entering a gay bar even in the course of an investigation horrified him. But all the cop said was "I told you. Nothing came of it."

At that point Lucas turned a furious shade of red and the muscles in his jaw stood out like steel bands.

"I see. Thank you for your time," Gabriel said quickly. Then he hustled Lucas out the door before he gave in to temptation and ended up charged with assaulting a police officer. Not that Gabriel would have blamed him. The cop was clearly incompetent.

They made it out of the building and to the parking spaces on the street before Lucas exploded. "See? I told you. They're not even fucking trying. They don't care at all. Eric could be dead for all they care. He hasn't even tried to look anywhere. I know you saw that."

"Of course I did," Gabriel told him evenly.

"Then why didn't you say something?" Lucas demanded. "I thought you were going to do something about it. What happened to reminding them they didn't want to bring the wrath of the gay community down on their heads?"

"It wouldn't have mattered," Gabriel explained. "That kind of threat is only effective to someone who understands the power of media and a social movement. That man doesn't. He honestly believes he's right and would have stubbornly gone on believing and acting accordingly no matter what I said."

"So now what do we do?" Lucas asked.

That was the million-dollar question. The obvious answer was to do some investigating, prove Eric was not simply a person who was voluntarily missing, and turn it over to the state police for investigation. That would connect Lucas to the right people for the job, and Gabriel could go back to his quiet life as a professor.

The only problem with that scenario was that Gabriel would have to pull out some of his old skills and old contacts. It meant getting entangled far more than he had ever intended and walking way too close to that place he had promised he was never going to again.

Lucas hadn't even moved. His eyes were trained on Gabriel as he waited for him to have some kind of answer, some kind of direction, some kind of hope. It was beyond Gabriel how the kid could think someone like him could give him any of that, but it was just as clear that he did. He was practically vibrating with anticipation. If Gabriel gave in to his fears and refused to continue, there wasn't a doubt in his mind it would crush the kid. Almost certainly it would put the very scars on his soul that Gabriel had been trying so hard to avoid.

On the other hand, if he gave in, he would risk his own soul again. Could he go back into that world, even slightly, and come out unscathed? That shadow world had a pull on him. The thirst for the kill was strong, and it would only get stronger.

But it wasn't as though he would actually have to go undercover. It was a simple investigation, mostly watching and observing, nothing more than gathering intel, really. It wasn't all that different from the academic research he still did on a regular basis for his papers and articles... although that research didn't usually require him to interview witnesses or stake out locations. Maybe he could do it after all. He would have to be very careful, but as long as he didn't have to go undercover or let himself fall into old habits, he could handle it.

Lucas was still watching him.

"Now we do what the police should be doing," he replied. "Where was the last place Eric was seen before he disappeared?"

"Sparks," Lucas said. "He left there after his shift, like normal."

"Then that's where we start."

CHAPTER EIGHT

IT WAS still a couple hours before opening, and Sparks was deserted. Besides Gabriel's car there were only two vehicles in the small parking lot. Lucas recognized them both as belonging to Nathan, the manager, and Beau, one of the bartenders. He strode up to the staff entrance. Gabriel flanked him like a brooding bodyguard. He rapped on the door, and a moment later, Nathan appeared and peered out the small window at the top of the door. He saw Lucas and backed away. There was a faint series of clicks as he unlocked the door and flung it open.

"What's happened?" Nathan asked without bothering with introductions or preamble. "Is it Eric? Have you found him?"

Stepping through the door, Lucas shook his head. "Not yet, but that is what we're here about. This is Gabriel. He's helping me look for Eric."

Nathan peered at Gabriel suspiciously. "You a cop?"

Gabriel laughed. "Not at all. I'm a professor at Lucas's school. He came to me for help."

The answer came so quickly that Lucas almost blinked. Gabriel helpfully left out any mention that he was a former CIA operative who probably knew more about such things than all of the local police force combined.

"We were hoping you might have the security footage from the night Eric disappeared," Gabriel went on. "It might be able to tell us something."

"Sure," Nathan replied, having apparently decided to trust them. "I kept them in case the cops came looking for them, but nobody ever came." He went over to a cluttered metal desk tucked into the corner of the room and pulled out a couple of DVDs in clear plastic cases.

"That's because the local idiots think he just ran off," Lucas told him bitterly. "I filed a missing person report, but they're not doing anything because of course everyone knows a young gay guy is probably just shacked up somewhere."

"Is that something Eric would do?" Gabriel asked. It was all Lucas could do to keep from turning around and glaring at him. He had already told Gabriel there was no way Eric would do something like that, not for so long. Did Gabriel think he was lying?

"Would he go off and hook up with somebody? Sure," Nathan replied. "But not for this long and not without checking in. A couple of hours, maybe, but not a week. He's never missed a shift without calling in, and before you ask, no, he doesn't call in often. He'd done it on occasion, but no more than any other guy around here and a lot less than some. Eric is one of my most reliable guys." He passed the DVDs over to Lucas. "Let me know if you find something. Okay? I'm worried about him too."

"Will do," Lucas promised. "Thanks, Nathan."

In the car, Lucas passed the DVDs over to Gabriel. "What now?" he asked.

"Now we watch the video and see what it tells us," Gabriel replied.

"I don't understand," Lucas said. "How is a video from before he left work going to help? We know he was fine when he left there. Nathan already told me that the first time I came looking for Eric."

"Yes, but now we'll know whether or not the video verifies that information," Gabriel explained.

"Of course it does," Lucas insisted. "Why would Nathan lie to me? You heard him. He's as worried about Eric as I am."

"You're probably right," Gabriel agreed. "But it never hurts to double-check. Besides, that's not the only thing the video can tell us. It can also tell us who Eric was with that night, whether there was anyone who looks suspicious in the bar or someone who might have been paying close attention to him. It might even tell us who he left with or which direction he went when he left, which would at least give us some idea of where to search."

"Oh," Lucas said quietly. He felt like an idiot. Nathan had had the security footage the entire time. He could've looked at it days before. "I guess I should've thought of that."

"Why would you?" Gabriel asked. "Do you have any sort of law enforcement or investigative experience?"

"No," Lucas admitted. "I know child-abuse investigations from my capacity as a social worker, but that's really all. And I don't usually work on the investigative end of things. I'm not in the intake department. My cases are all kids who are already in foster care."

"So how could you have possibly known what things to look for in this sort of investigation?"

Lucas shrugged. "I don't know. It just seems like something that should've been obvious. I should've known. I should've done something."

"That's just guilt talking. You couldn't possibly have known anything about this or done anything about it before it happened, unless you have psychic abilities you haven't told me about yet."

Lucas smiled. "Nope. No unusual abilities here. Not even many particularly good usual abilities."

"Then let the guilt go," Gabriel told him firmly. "Beating yourself up unnecessarily isn't going to do anything to help us find Eric, so why bother wasting time on it."

He made a good point, but that didn't change the way Lucas felt. He wished it were as easy as just letting it go. Eric was his friend. He had to do something.

"The real question," Gabriel went on, "is why the police hadn't thought to check the footage. You may not have the investigative experience to know this was something you should do, but they certainly should have. This should have been one of the first leads they pursued. If you have to blame somebody, blame them, not yourself."

Unfortunately that only served to make Lucas angry all over again. He brooded on that anger until they arrived at Gabriel's house. Then he followed Gabriel through the foyer and down a short hallway into a large, open living room where Gabriel put the DVD into his player.

The television screen on the wall filled with grainy images from several cameras. One pointed directly over the bar. Two others showed various angles of the dance floor. Still others showed the entrance and the parking lot.

"You said Eric is a bartender, right?" Gabriel asked. Lucas nodded. Gabriel pulled up the view of the bar and made it fill the screen. "What time did Eric's shift start?"

"Usually around six," Lucas replied. "He works closing."

Gabriel zoomed the recording ahead until around that time. They saw Eric come in and chat casually with several people as he prepared to begin work. "Any of these people look familiar?"

"Yes," Lucas said. "They're mostly staff and regulars. It won't get busy until later."

As he had predicted, the first couple hours of the tape were really slow. There was only a scattering of people on the dance floor, some of whom occasionally drifted back and forth to the bar, and one man whom Lucas knew to be a regular who parked himself on a barstool and never moved. No one seemed to be paying particular attention to Eric at all. If anything Eric looked bored.

Lucas couldn't blame him. He was pretty bored himself. He had to get up and move around just to keep his mind on what he was doing. Gabriel, of course, had no such problems. He sat still as a statue and scrutinized every second of the tape. If the sheer mind-numbing sameness of it bothered him, it didn't show.

Finally, about three hours in, things began to pick up. The bar got significantly busier and more crowded. That made watching the tape more interesting, but it also made it much harder to keep an eye on everyone in the room and watch for suspicious activity. Not that Lucas would've known what constituted suspicious activity. So far it all looked like normal club activity to him.

That was until one particular Hispanic guy came up to the bar. At first he flirted a little and ordered a drink. Though the video didn't have sound, the nature of the conversation was pretty obvious. That much was normal, but then he didn't move away from the bar like most people did. He stayed and kept talking to Eric for quite some time. Eventually he ordered a second drink and kept chatting periodically with Eric while he drank it.

Even when Eric moved away to serve other customers, the man's eyes never left him. He watched every move Eric made. Finally the guy pushed up off the bar and started to move away. But then he stopped, pulled what appeared to be a business card out of his pocket, wrote something on the back of it, wrapped it in money, and stuck it in the tip jar.

Gabriel paused the video. "Do you know this guy?"

Lucas shook his head. "I've never seen him before. Eric's never talked to me about him either. And trust me, that is the type of guy Eric would have talked about."

"You're sure about that?"

"Absolutely," Lucas insisted. "This guy is just Eric's type. Hot, confident, and a strong bad-boy vibe. Eric always goes for the bad boys. Trust me. If he had met this guy before, I would have been hearing about it for days."

As if to lend credence to Lucas's words, on the screen Eric came back over to where the guy had been and looked around for him. Then he caught sight of the card in the tip jar, immediately fished it out, read it, and pocketed it. The camera briefly caught sight of his face, and where previously he had looked friendly and professional, if not particularly excited, he suddenly looked like he had won the lottery. The smile never left his face throughout the remainder of his shift.

After a while Gabriel began to fast-forward through some things when it was clear no one else took a particular interest in Eric. He slowed down when they saw the man who had been talking to Eric exiting the building. He was flanked by two other men, both younger—one Hispanic and the other African American. Lucas didn't recognize them either. The parking-lot security camera showed them getting into a large, late-model sedan, though it was too far away to be sure of any of the details. In the dark the make and model were not identifiable, and the tag was barely visible. Getting the number was absolutely impossible. The best they could do was make out the direction they left out of the parking lot.

"Interesting," Gabriel murmured. "Now let's see what your friend does." He fast-forwarded the video to the end of Eric's shift, and they watched Eric total his cash drawer, make up his deposit, and slip it into the bank bag under the counter. Then he wiped down the bar and pulled his phone and the business card out of his pocket. Eric flipped the card over and dialed a number. He took the phone between his ear and his shoulder and disappeared into the employee area behind the bar where there were no cameras.

That was when they needed the damn sound. It was several minutes before Eric came into camera range again, and when he did, his phone was tucked back in his pocket. Lucas swore from sheer frustration. They could've been talking about anything. Trust Eric to go and have the conversation where nobody could see a thing.

Eric smiled and waved to Nathan and the bouncer and casually strode out the door. The cameras showed that he climbed in his car and drove off in the same direction the other man's car had gone. Then he quite literally disappeared.

Gabriel switched off the recording. "If I had to guess, I would say Eric probably arranged to meet the man he was talking to earlier. Does that sound like something he would do?"

Lucas groaned and dropped his head into his hands. "Unfortunately yes. Eric as much as told me he was looking for a hookup for the night when he left that day. If he thought he had a chance of making it into that man's bed, he would have gone."

"Even though the man was a stranger?"

"Yes," Lucas said. That was incredibly embarrassing to admit, even though it wasn't the kind of lifestyle Lucas chose for himself. "To be perfectly honest, the fact that he was a stranger probably made it more exciting for Eric. He loves that kind of thing." Lucas hated saying that. It made that cop's theory that Eric was just shacking up with somebody seem all the more plausible. Gabriel was likely to think he was only leading him on a wild goose chase.

"I know this looks bad, but you have to believe me. Eric might have done that for the night, but he wouldn't have done it for this long, not without contacting anybody."

"You don't have to convince me, kid. I believe you," Gabriel said. "It's not as though that's an unheard-of thing for young guys to do. Besides, it's not my job to judge. I'm just interested in helping you find him."

"Thanks," Lucas said quietly. For someone who owned a reputation for being an asshole, Gabriel had been remarkably understanding—at least once he agreed to help. "What do we do now?"

Every time they turned around, he looked to Gabriel to tell him what to do next. He knew it was probably annoying, but he just didn't know what else to do.

If Gabriel was annoyed, it didn't show. "I'm going to get a screenshot of the guy we think Eric went to meet and take it back to the bar to see if anyone can identify him." He ejected the DVD, took it into his office, and appeared a few minutes later with a printout of several pictures of the Hispanic man. A second sheet showed his companions and their car. "I'm going to run these back and see if anyone can identify them," he told Lucas. "I'll be as quick as I can, and when I get back, we'll see about doing something for dinner."

"I could help with that," Lucas put in quietly. "I can cook. I'm not exactly a gourmet chef or anything, but I'm pretty sure I could put together something edible." He didn't often have the time or the opportunity to cook, given his crazy schedule. But he enjoyed doing it when he could, and maybe it might make him feel a little less helpless.

"Sure, kid, that'd be great," Gabriel replied easily. "Help yourself. Anything in the kitchen is fair game. If you need something that's not there, call or text me, and I'll pick it up while I'm out."

"I'm sure I can manage." Lucas headed into the kitchen.

IN THE car Gabriel let his head drop back against the seat and took a few minutes to just breathe. What the hell had happened to his life? Over the course of less than a day, he'd gone from quietly grading papers in his office to unofficially investigating a potential kidnapping. The whole day was a blur, and as though that weren't enough, he had seriously underestimated how difficult it was to be around Lucas so much.

Gabriel couldn't deny he was attracted to him. There had always been a mysterious pull drawing him toward Lucas like a tractor beam in the sci-fi shows he liked to watch as a kid. Being in close quarters with Lucas for the last several hours was seriously overwhelming. He was hyperaware of Lucas's every move and heard every tiny movement, every indrawn breath. And his scent—Lucas's unique scent permeated everything. Gabriel couldn't help but wonder what it would be like in more intimate circumstances. Would he carry Lucas's scent on him for hours and even days afterward?

Gabriel shifted uncomfortably in his seat. He was rock-hard and had been for quite some time. What was it about Lucas? Why was being around him so consuming?

He realized abruptly that Lucas's presence had even eclipsed the ever-present hum of his need to kill. He hadn't noticed it at all since Lucas walked into his office, and he only thought of it because it returned with a vengeance once he was alone in the car. Nothing short of successfully taking down a target had ever quieted that need. But he hadn't even had time to go to the gun range to take the edge off in weeks. By rights he should be so preoccupied he couldn't think straight, not so distracted that he didn't even notice it. What the fuck was that about?

The whole situation gnawed at him. He hated puzzles he couldn't solve. Lucas was one variable he couldn't figure out.

He could, however, do his best to figure out what happened to Lucas's friend, and the sooner he did that, the sooner he and Lucas could go back to normal. They could resume their casual chats in the co-op, and Gabriel could go back to maintaining a safe distance.

With that in mind, Gabriel put the car in gear and headed back toward town. As soon as someone at the bar identified the guy, he could retrieve Eric, and it would all be over.

He really should've known better. Investigations were rarely simple. Witnesses were iffy at the best of times, assuming you got lucky enough to get witnesses at all. In his haste Gabriel had forgotten that very few people were as observant as he was. No one inside Sparks had a clue. A few of them said they had seen the guy from time to time. He wasn't a regular, but he'd come in once or twice in the past few months. Not one of them knew his name.

That sent alarm bells off all over Gabriel's brain. People routinely introduced themselves, even in a casual place like a bar. They at least gave a first name, even if it was an alias. The fact that no one knew the guy's name said he was deliberately trying to stay in the shadows. And that meant he had a reason to. He had something to hide. Whatever he was up to, it wasn't good.

Dammit. As much as Gabriel hated to admit it, most of the evidence was telling him Lucas had been right from the start. Something had gone terribly wrong, and someone needed to find out where Eric was.

Gabriel just wished that someone didn't have to be him. But the local police weren't doing the job, and until he had some concrete proof, the state police wouldn't get involved. And the feds couldn't intervene unless what was going on fell under federal jurisdiction. It all came back to proving Eric was in danger. There was no way around it.

For a long moment, Gabriel could do nothing more than stare at the picture in his hand and swear vehemently. He was a college professor. He didn't deal in shadows and secrets anymore.

Gabriel scrubbed his free hand through his hair and took a deep breath. Okay, enough of that. How could he identify the man in the picture? For the briefest of seconds, Gabriel missed his old job, his old life. At the agency he had analysts and technicians he could call on. It was so routine he never gave it a thought. He wasn't at Langley, but he did still keep in contact with one guy....

Moose could make the identification. Gabriel didn't have the slightest doubt. Myles Hadley, a.k.a. Moose, was one of the most talented analysts Gabriel had ever known. He had personally seen Moose enlarge and identify images that were hardly bigger than stray pixels. Moose left the CIA a couple of years before Gabriel to take work in the private sector. He now owned and operated his own business and did contract work for the government, the military, and a select few private clients, primarily powerful men with big money and even bigger secrets. Gabriel hadn't spoken to Moose in some time, but he knew that, if he called, Moose would be there.

If he called....

Making that phone call would take him one step back into the life he swore he would never go back to. If he made the call, would he be able to stay away? Or would the pull of that life, dangerous drudgery though it was, be too much? Would the agency get wind he was sniffing around and try to seduce him back in? Could he even afford to take the chance?

On the other hand, how could he even consider not using all the resources at his disposal? Eric was clearly in trouble—though what kind of trouble remained to be seen. It would be unconscionable for Gabriel not to try to get Eric out of it because of his own insecurities. For Lucas the choice would be clear. He wouldn't hesitate to sacrifice himself for the sake of someone else.

But Gabriel was nothing like Lucas, despite whatever delusions Lucas might be laboring under. He had far too healthy a sense of self-preservation to throw himself under the bus like that for someone else. Gabriel learned very early on to rely on himself and only himself. Other people might come through every once in a while, but most of the time they just let you fall on your face in the mud, and there was no one there to pick you up but yourself.

But sometimes you had to use your resources, and he trusted Moose as much as he trusted anybody. If he had to involve someone, Moose would be the best person.

Resigning himself, Gabriel took a deep breath, pulled out a cell phone from the glove box, and dialed a number from memory. He spoke briefly to a receptionist who connected him through, and a moment later, Moose's familiar booming voice answered.

"Moose, it's Shadow," Gabriel said without preamble, giving the call sign and nickname he'd been known by at the Agency.

"Shadow, how are you doing, man? I heard you had gone civilian and fallen off the map. Nobody's heard from you in so long there have even been a few rumors that you died," Moose replied.

"I'm still alive and well," Gabriel told him. "I'm working on something, and I need your help."

"Never said I believed the rumors," Moose went on, unfazed. "I've known you too long. Nobody gets close to the Shadow."

If he only knew.... Hell, Moose might not believe it even if he did. Gabriel had owned that reputation for most of his life, especially during the time he was working as an operative. Nothing touched him. Not in years. Until Lucas.

"Anyway," Moose continued, breaking into his thoughts, "what can I do for you?"

"I'm tracking a missing person, a local kid who went to work and seemingly disappeared into thin air," Gabriel explained. "I've got a photo of the last person he was seen with, but no one seems to know who this guy is. I need you to run facial recognition and tell me who this guy is and why he's trying so damn hard to hide. I can't get a handle on him, but I've got a really bad feeling about this."

Moose gave a low whistle. "Whoever he is, if he's tripping your radar, it can't be good."

"That's what I'm afraid of," Gabriel admitted.

"How did you get involved in this, anyway?" Moose asked. "Last I heard you had gotten out of the game completely and taken a teaching job or some such."

"You heard right. I'm out of the game for good. This is a favor for a friend and nothing else. I wouldn't be involved at all, but the local LEOs don't know their ass from a hole in the ground. They're assuming this kid ran voluntarily just because he is gay, and you know I can't stand by and let that happen."

Moose murmured in agreement. He didn't say anything. He didn't have to. Gabriel had spent the majority of his career in places that could politely be called "not gay friendly," and he had no tolerance for the casual violence that was all too often perpetrated against gay people. He had blown his cover more than once in his early years and gotten into more than a few bar fights. Everyone who knew him well—and Moose did—knew that.

"What are you sending me?" Moose said abruptly, and Gabriel couldn't help but smile. Moose was a good guy, and he had managed to navigate the murky world of the CIA without being tainted by it. Gabriel admired the talent and wished he had a bit more of it.

"I've got a DVD copy of the security footage from the last night the victim worked. I'll send you stills of him and the target so you'll know who you're looking for."

"So you're gonna make this easy for me, then," Moose teased.

Only Moose would call identifying a completely random individual from security footage easy, but he did have a point. Moose had done far more difficult things. "I aim to please," Gabriel shot back. "Where do you want it sent?" He fumbled around until he found a scrap of paper and pen to scribble down the address Moose rattled off. "Got it. I'll get it out first thing. Thanks, Moose."

They ended the call. Once Moose was in business mode, he had little time for small talk—a quick discussion of the details of price and payment for his services, and he was gone. Moose was nothing if not professional. It was one of the reasons the two of them got along so well.

Gabriel put his phone away, started the car, and headed toward home. Despite not having made any real progress, he still felt a slight sense of satisfaction at having the next steps clearly in front of him. He just hoped he wouldn't live to regret his decision. Either way it was too late to worry about it, and he had far more pressing matters of concern. Mainly what he was going to do about Lucas.

They would need to work together to find Eric. Okay, maybe not need. They could manage by phone without actually physically being together, but Gabriel was no fool.

Lucas might be innocent, but he was determined. Gabriel knew there was no way in hell he would convince Lucas to let him investigate on his own. If he thought he had the slightest chance, he would have tried. It would certainly be easier without the distraction of Lucas's presence.

He had made a career out of reading people, learning them nearly as well as they knew themselves, figuring out how to get close to them, what would motivate them, and sometimes how to eliminate them. The flip side was knowing what wouldn't work. There was no point in spending days, and sometimes weeks, working on a tactic that was doomed to fail. To do so would have been foolish at best and suicidal at worst, so Gabriel had gotten extremely good at knowing which road to take.

Any distraction, no matter how slight, could be dangerous, and Gabriel's attraction to Lucas had the potential to be all-consuming if he let it. If he couldn't go ahead without Lucas, he would have to minimize the time they were together. He needed to put the distance back between them and communicate with Lucas on neutral ground— like in the co-op rather than in his office, and certainly not in his home.

What the hell was he thinking when he brought the kid home with him in the first place? He never invited people into his home. Colleagues who had worked with him for the entire time he'd been at the university had no idea where he lived. Gabriel always maintained his home, wherever it might be, as a sanctuary, the one private place that was his alone. So why had he violated that? It wasn't a conscious decision. At the time, it just seemed the next logical step was to get somewhere where he would be able to view the video footage, because he was confident it would give him some clue that would enable him to find Eric, and it would all be over. He had been so sure of it that he hadn't bothered to think beyond it or consider other possibilities. That was stupid and potentially deadly. Had he been out of the field so long that he had lost his touch? Tunnel vision was a rookie mistake. He was acting like a damn green kid fresh from The Farm. Already his hormones were fucking with his judgment.

Okay. The first order of business was to get Lucas back to his own apartment. He'd left Lucas in his house and given a near stranger free rein of his domain. What's more, he took Lucas up on his offer to make dinner, as though they were on a goddamned date. What was he? A fuckin' twelve-year-old schoolboy? He was damn sure behaving like one.

First thing in the morning, he would head to the gun range. Then he would find someone to share his bed for the night. If his sex drive was screwing with his judgment, it had clearly been way too long. Gabriel took a deep breath to settle himself. He had a plan. First he would get Lucas home. It was just excess testosterone. He'd been dealing with that since puberty. He knew how to handle it. Everything would be fine.

CHAPTER NINE

EVERYTHING WAS fine. At least that's what Lucas told himself. It didn't matter that Gabriel had been gone a long time. It didn't mean anything bad had happened.

In fact maybe it was good. Maybe one of the guys at the bar had identified the stranger and Gabriel had already found Eric. Maybe when he did return, he'd have Eric with him, and the three of them could enjoy dinner together. That wouldn't be nearly as romantic as the "just the two of them" dinner Lucas had planned, but if Eric was safe, he wouldn't care.

He could always find a way to get Gabriel alone some other time. Some other time might even be better. He wouldn't be in school forever, and it would probably be a lot easier to convince Gabriel to go out with him if he were not a student. He knew perfectly well Gabriel thought of him as a kid. Gabriel *called* him a kid more often than not, but Lucas figured that was because he was a student, and Gabriel thought of all the students as kids. Lucas's grandmother had been a teacher, and she persisted in referring to her former students as "her kids" even after they were adults with children of their own. He often did the same with the foster children he worked with, so he could hardly fault Gabriel for that.

Lucas wiped his hands on a dish towel for what felt like the hundredth time in the last few minutes and forced himself to stop pacing. He had made a path back and forth in front of the kitchen cabinets as he listened for Gabriel's car to pull in the drive. He wished he had his MP3 player, or at the very least could turn on a radio. But there wasn't one anywhere he could see, and he didn't want to snoop.

Actually that wasn't entirely true. Lucas would've loved to go searching. He was desperately curious for anything that might give him the least bit of insight into Gabriel. He was a complete mystery, but snooping seemed insufferably rude.

Gabriel had been nothing but kind to him. If he were really the asshole the rumor mill on campus made him out to be, he would have tossed Lucas out of his office after his outburst. Lucas wouldn't have blamed him. After all, they had only met for coffee and muffins a few times. It wasn't as though he had any claim on Gabriel, however much he might wish that were different.

He still cringed at his audacity. He should count himself lucky Gabriel had actually agreed to help. As if that weren't enough, Gabriel had actually allowed him into his home.

For some professors that wouldn't have been unusual. Some of them routinely invited certain students into their homes, usually their TAs or students they were working closely with. Gabriel wasn't one of them. From all Lucas had heard, Gabriel was intensely private. He didn't even seem to socialize with the other professors. Allowing Lucas into his home was a rare courtesy, and Lucas had no intention of abusing that.

There was a TV in plain sight—the one they used to watch the DVDs earlier, but one look at all the buttons on the remote convinced Lucas it was out of his league. It looked like something that would power the space station. There was no way he would chance accidentally wrecking something by fooling around with it. With his luck it would probably take more than he made in a month to repair. It was safer to keep his hands to himself. Unfortunately that meant dealing with the quiet, and the quiet was driving him slowly mad.

Suddenly he heard the car pulling into the driveway. A quick peek through the window on the door assured him it was Gabriel. He stepped away from the door to give Gabriel enough room to get into the house. He would not pounce on him and demand information. He would not.

But his resolve lasted about as long as it took Gabriel to close the door behind him. "Did you find him?"

Gabriel shook his head. "Not yet. No one at the bar recognized the guy either. A few people remembered seeing him come in before, but no one knew his name, not even the bouncers or bartenders."

"No one," Lucas echoed incredulously. "How could no one have ever even heard his name?"

"It's not that hard to pull off if you don't want your name to be found out," Gabriel said grimly. "It's just not something most people bother trying to hide. If this man was, he was doing it deliberately."

Lucas's heart sank. Even he knew enough to know that if a guy was deliberately hiding his identity, it couldn't mean anything good. There was a slim possibility he might have been looking for anonymous sex, but in Lucas's experience, even the guys who hit on him for an anonymous hookup would give him a name. It might not be their real name. In all likelihood it probably wasn't, but it was still a name. He swallowed hard against the rush of fear and grief that rose in his throat and threatened to choke him. He couldn't think about that. Gabriel would know what to do. They would find Eric. Everything would be fine.

"I made dinner," he said weakly as he gestured toward the lidded dish in the center of the table and the two place settings on either side of it.

"I see that." Gabriel gave him a small smile. "Thank you." He moved past Lucas to pick up the two glasses from the table. "What would you like to drink? I'm afraid I don't have that much to offer. There's water, milk, juice, and beer."

Lucas had noticed as much himself as he was exploring the refrigerator for dinner ingredients. "Water is fine." Gabriel looked like he was about to reach for a beer, but at the last minute, changed his mind and filled both glasses with water from the filter pitcher in the refrigerator. Before Gabriel could try to juggle them both, Lucas snagged one of the glasses and settled himself at the table.

Gabriel joined him. "What have we here?" he asked as he lifted the lid from the dish between them.

"It's nothing fancy," Lucas said. "I'm not much of a fancy cook, but my mom insisted that all us kids learn how to cook a few basic dishes. It's just a plain shepherd's pie—meat, potatoes, and cheese." He had used real potatoes instead of the boxed kind he usually did, but that was only because Gabriel didn't have any of the boxed kind. It took a little extra time, but he hadn't minded. Anything to keep him busy.

A sudden bright smile spread across Gabriel's face.

"I take it you like shepherd's pie?"

"I do," he confirmed. "It's a particular favorite of mine, in fact, but I haven't had it in a long time. I don't usually take the time to cook it for myself."

Gabriel's clear approval spread like a bubble in Lucas's chest and made it impossible for him not to smile back. "I'm glad you like it. Consider it a thank-you for all your help. It's not nearly enough, but maybe it's something."

"No one should be ignored and left out in the cold like your friend has been by the police here. I'm just doing what they should have done," Gabriel said, tucking into his food with enthusiasm.

"All the same, you could've blown me off just like they did. I'm grateful you didn't." It wasn't exactly an apology for his earlier display, but Lucas hoped it made up for it at least a little.

"Even I'm not that much of an asshole," Gabriel murmured self-deprecatingly.

"So if no one recognized the pictures, what do we do now?" Lucas asked. He tried to be polite, but he was dying to know. How were they ever supposed to find Eric if no one knew who that man was?

"I've been in touch with a contact who's good with images and facial recognition," Gabriel told him. "I'm going to scan the footage we got from the bar and the stills I printed out to him first thing in the morning. He's agreed to take a look at them and see if he can identify our mystery man."

Instantly Lucas felt his body relax. Thank God. The relief in knowing Gabriel not only knew what to do next but had already taken steps in that direction was overwhelming. In the wake of that relief, Lucas found he was suddenly starving. He dug into his dinner with more enthusiasm than he'd had for any meal since the whole horrible ordeal began.

It was a quiet meal but not uncomfortable. Gabriel was taciturn at the best of times. Lucas noticed that even when they first began their informal coffee dates. Usually Lucas would've tried to draw him out by making small talk or telling casual stories, but as much as he enjoyed that, it didn't feel right. It had been a long day. Maybe they both needed the quiet to recuperate.

To Lucas's surprise it was Gabriel who eventually broke the silence. "As much as I've enjoyed dinner, I shouldn't have kept you here so late. I'm sure you have other things that need to be done."

Lucas shrugged dismissively. "I doubt I would have done them, anyway. I haven't been able to concentrate on anything since Eric disappeared. It seems like all I do is pace the floor and worry about him."

He just couldn't get his mind on class or work. He was too preoccupied with his worry for Eric to get anything done, even when he tried to show up. He was being irresponsible, especially when it came to his work. There were other people counting on him—children and families who needed him to get his head out of his ass and get his act together. Sure, he had plenty of sick leave, and other workers could cover for him if an emergency came up, but it wasn't fair to anyone, especially the kids. He was the one who knew them. They trusted him, not whatever random worker was assigned to cover for him. But he was barely sleeping. He was beyond exhausted and quite literally worried sick. He didn't have room for anything else.

But he knew it had to stop eventually. His grades were already suffering, and if he wasn't careful, he'd lose the scholarship that made it possible for him to attend school and not work full-time. Eric wouldn't want him to do that. He just didn't know how he was supposed to keep functioning when his mind kept wanting to imagine all the horrible things that could be happening to Eric.

Suddenly his appetite disappeared, and he pushed the plate away.

"If you're done I can take you back home now," Gabriel said.

"There's no rush," Lucas told him. "It's not like there's anyone there waiting up for me." He said it dryly, trying to be casual, but his voice cracked, and he found himself—to his horror—fighting back tears.

"You don't know that," Gabriel said. "Eric could be waiting for you there now."

Lucas could tell Gabriel was trying to be positive, and he appreciated the effort, but that didn't make it true. He shook his head. "He's not home. He would have let me know if he were. And even if he hadn't, if he showed up at the bar for work, someone there would've let me know. Nothing's changed."

To his credit Gabriel didn't try to argue. "Probably not," he agreed. "But it still won't hurt for you to be there, just in case he does come home."

That was undoubtedly true. Lucas had been telling himself that for days. But sitting around in that lonely, empty apartment with reminders of Eric all around him was making him crazy. If he hadn't gotten out of the house, he would have lost his mind. Of course his display in Gabriel's office probably counted as losing his mind, but it had gotten something done at least.

Lucas didn't want to go back, but there was no way he could tell Gabriel that. Besides, if he didn't go back, where would he go? It wasn't like he had anywhere else he could stay. There were a few friends he could probably call who would let him crash on their couch for a night or two, but he would have to explain the whole ordeal over again, and he wanted to do that even less than he wanted to go home.

Abruptly Lucas realized he should at least attempt to get in touch with Eric's dad. He had no idea where he was, but Eric probably had a contact number somewhere in his room, and Mr. Collier deserved to know his son was missing. It seemed needless to worry Eric's dad when he first went to the police station, but it was becoming abundantly clear that finding Eric wasn't going to be a quick or easy thing. He swore vehemently inside his head at the thought of making that phone call. It was going to be horrible.

His expression must have given him away because Gabriel suddenly asked, "What's wrong?"

"I need to call Eric's dad."

Gabriel arched an eyebrow. "You haven't told him?"

Lucas dropped his head. "No. I don't really know how to get in touch with him. He's a long-haul truck driver, so he could be anywhere. And to be honest, I kind of kept hoping I wouldn't need to make that call… that Eric would show back up and everything would be fine."

"That's understandable," Gabriel replied. "But he needs to know. I'm not an expert on parent-child relationships, or any other relationships, for that matter, but surely he has a right to know his son is missing."

"I know," Lucas admitted, and even to his own ears, his voice sounded terribly small.

"Does Eric have any contact information for his dad?" Gabriel asked.

"Probably," Lucas admitted. "I know he talks to him sometimes, at least a couple times a month."

"Where would he likely keep this information?" Gabriel questioned. He spoke quietly, mildly, as though they were discussing nothing more emotional than what to have for dinner. Yet his voice was firm, and it compelled Lucas to answer, no matter how much he didn't want to have the conversation.

"Either in his room or in his wallet," Lucas said. He was restless, so he gathered their plates, took them to the sink, and filled it with water with the ease of long practice. His parents insisted all the kids take turns washing dishes after dinner. They never bothered to install a dishwasher. Though he would deny it to his parents even to this day, Lucas found something comforting and stabilizing in that long-established habit. Unfortunately busying himself didn't distract Gabriel from the conversation in the slightest.

"We'll just have to hope it's in his room. If it isn't, there are other ways of tracking him down. I'm assuming you do know his father's name."

Lucas nodded. "Frank Collier."

"Do you know whether he works for a trucking company or is an independent contractor?"

"I think he works for a company," Lucas said as he rinsed a dish and slotted it into the drainer on the counter beside the sink. "I'm not sure which one, though."

Gabriel got up and retrieved a dish towel, picked up the plate to dry it, and put it away. "Do you remember anything about his uniform or his truck that might be identifiable?"

Lucas passed over the next dish to dry. In the exchange his hand briefly brushed Gabriel's, which sent a spark like static electricity over his skin. He couldn't stop his reflexive jerk or the sharp indrawn breath that accompanied it. He swallowed hard and sternly ordered his body to behave. "I think maybe there was a tree or something. It was dark green, whatever it was."

If Gabriel noticed Lucas's reaction, he didn't show it. "Good. If you can't find his information at the apartment, that will at least give us someplace to start. But before we can know that, we've got to get you home."

Lucas looked down at the sink and realized with a start he had washed the last of the dishes. They had finished the chore mechanically, without him even noticing. He drained the sink, wiped it out, and then dried his hands on a towel. Finding himself without anything else to do, he cleared his throat. "Just let me get my bag."

The drive back to the apartment was quiet, and the knots in his stomach grew larger with every passing mile. How was he going to face Eric's dad? He should have called him days before, when he first discovered Eric was missing. But even the police hadn't believed him, and if Eric had really been hanging out with a guy somewhere, he would have killed Lucas for involving his dad.

Though Lucas had absolutely no doubt Mr. Collier loved Eric and tried his best to accept Eric's sexuality, he and Eric managed their relationship by keeping each other at a safe distance. As much as Mr. Collier tried, he really didn't understand, and any time Lucas saw them together, they very pointedly avoided any subject even potentially related to Eric's sexuality—boyfriends, relationships, dating, or anything of the sort. But Lucas had to involve him.

It was more than calling Eric's dad, though. Lucas's anxiety had begun before that even occurred to him. He just didn't want to go home. If he were perfectly honest, he was scared of being there alone. Which was ridiculous. He'd stayed there alone plenty of times. It wasn't unusual for Eric to stay away overnight, and Lucas had been alone there for the last few days since Eric disappeared. He'd been fine. What was different?

Okay. Maybe he hadn't exactly been fine. He'd been worried nearly out of his mind and spent most of the time watching mindless TV or playing computer games on his laptop to distract himself, all the while racking his brain for any possible place Eric might have gone that he hadn't thought of and trying not to let his nerves make him physically sick.

Knowing Gabriel was there and would know what to do had proven to be an incredible comfort. They might not know much more than they knew when they started, but at least they had some direction and Lucas was no longer solely responsible for figuring out what to do. Having found some comfort, he wasn't at all keen on giving it up again. Not that he could say so. Gabriel already thought of him as a kid. Behaving like a clingy toddler wouldn't help him change that impression.

The trip was over far too soon. Long before Lucas was ready, Gabriel parked his car on the street in front of the duplex Lucas had shared with Eric for the past eight years, and Lucas steeled himself, got out of the car, and crossed the small yard. He breathed a sigh of relief when he realized Gabriel had followed him. He paused on the stoop, reluctant to open the door.

Gabriel stopped slightly behind and to the left of him. Though the space was big enough for both of them, it required standing very close together. The heat of Gabriel's body soaked into Lucas's back and cut through his overwhelming anxiety like a blade. Every nerve in his body came involuntarily to attention. Lucas swallowed, wet his lips with the tip of his tongue, and did his best to ignore it. He turned sideways to allow Gabriel to step up onto the stoop with him so they stood face-to-face. "Thank you for your help," he said and then immediately winced at how lame and weak he sounded.

"Like I said, someone needed to," Gabriel said simply. He stuck his hands in his pockets and subtly shifted his weight from foot to foot. "I'm glad you felt comfortable to come to me."

Felt comfortable? That was clearly an exaggerated kindness on Gabriel's part. Lucas had been out of his mind with desperation. Terrified was more like it.

"I'll call you tomorrow," Gabriel went on, and Lucas nodded. He forced himself to unlock the door and push it open, and he felt more than saw Gabriel turn to go down the steps.

"Wait."

Gabriel froze midstep and immediately turned back to look at him.

"Do you even have my number?" he asked as he stopped in the open doorway and turned back to face Gabriel.

Gabriel's face shifted from confused to blank and back again. He took his phone from his pocket and thumbed through the contacts. "No," he said after a moment, "I don't guess I do."

"It will be hard for you to call me, then," Lucas teased, and he smiled despite his anxiety.

Gabriel jogged up the steps, and they traded phones and added their information to one another's contacts. "Sorry. I wasn't trying to blow you off."

"I know," Lucas said. He passed back Gabriel's phone and pocketed his own. "Now you can call me tomorrow."

"And I will," Gabriel promised.

Lucas stepped back. He meant to say good-bye and close the door, but his hand closed over Gabriel's wrist before his mind was even consciously aware of what his body was doing. "Don't go," he heard himself say, sounding like nothing so much as a child begging a parent to stay with them after a nightmare. "I can't do this alone."

He hadn't meant to say that out loud. Yes, he was terrified. He couldn't remember the last time he even spoke to Eric's father beyond the briefest of pleasantries when he answered the phone. And it was going to be hard enough to go into Eric's room to find the number. He hadn't set foot in Eric's room since Eric had been gone. He wasn't looking forward to doing that alone. But he wasn't supposed to say so out loud.

"Okay," Gabriel agreed quietly. "I can stay long enough for you to make the phone call. I know that won't be easy."

Lucas let out a breath he wasn't aware he was holding. "Thank you," he said and stepped back to allow Gabriel in the door.

WHAT THE hell am I doing? I'm supposed to be distancing myself, not coming into his apartment. I don't need to be getting any closer than I already am.

Even as Gabriel ranted at himself, his feet never stopped moving. What else was he supposed to do with Lucas standing there looking white as a sheet? It was plain as sin the kid was only moments away from falling apart again.

There was a time when he would have walked away from a scene like that. Hell. He had walked away from more than one scene of sobbing family members as they knelt over their dead or dying relatives. It was why he had chosen to leave the agency. But he wasn't that soulless spook anymore, and he didn't have to act like it. For once he could act like a decent, compassionate human being. Plans and good intentions be damned.

He stepped over to Lucas and touched him lightly on the shoulder. "Are you okay?"

"Yeah," Lucas replied. "It's just…." He gathered himself. "I haven't been in Eric's room since all this happened. I don't know if I can go in there by myself."

"It's fine. I don't mind sticking around," Gabriel said, and he meant it.

Lucas closed his eyes, and Gabriel could see him gathering his courage. He fixed his eyes on the small hallway that led off the cluttered living room where they were standing, and he began to move toward it with the distinct air of a man on a mission. Gabriel made sure to stay close. He honestly wouldn't have been surprised if the kid broke into tears. It had been a hell of a long day, and Lucas had already broken down once. Gabriel had had enough dealings with panicked assets to know it didn't take much to throw them into another meltdown.

Three rooms opened off the hallway to the left, away from the living room. Gabriel guessed there were two bedrooms with a bathroom in between. Lucas moved swiftly past the first two doors and came to a stop in front of the third. Then he took another shaky, deep breath and reached for the doorknob.

Gabriel reached around him and opened the door, and for a moment, there was nothing but stunned silence. Lucas stared at the door, and Gabriel waited, trying to give him time to adjust. But when Lucas still didn't move, Gabriel gently moved him aside and went into the room. Lucas followed.

It was an average-sized bedroom, painted a bland off-white—no different than hundreds of thousands of others in apartments and rental homes across the country. It was occupied by a full bed, dresser, and night table in a matching dark wood like cherry or perhaps mahogany. It was only in the hastily made-up and slightly rumpled bed coverings that Eric's personality showed through. They were a lush, deep purple that immediately made Gabriel think of *The Arabian Nights* or a similar Middle Eastern fantasy. All it needed was a wispy lavender canopy, and it would've been right at home on a movie set. A long dresser with a mirror sat against the wall nearest Gabriel, and a rainbow of temporary hair dyes were scattered across the top, along with a tub of some hair product, a brush, and a comb. A stack of canvases was propped carefully against the wall next to the small nightstand.

"Where do you think his dad's information might be?"

Stepping hesitantly around him, Lucas shrugged. "Could be anywhere."

"Where do you suggest we start?"

Lucas didn't answer. He went over and opened the dresser drawers. Gabriel stepped inside and closed the door. He found a bulletin board on the wall behind it. It was filled with photographs and myriad paper odds and ends. Long used to taking in details thoroughly and at speed, it only took a quick once-over for Gabriel to isolate the likely possibilities on the board. A second sweep told him there was nothing valuable to be found there.

He lingered over the pictures and went back to one that had a prominent place in the center. Two young boys, both blonde and leggy, stood by a small pond. The one to the right had his arm looped over the other's shoulders while his compatriot held a string of fish that hung between them. It took him a moment to realize the boy holding the fish was Lucas. His hair was shorter and lighter, the golden blond highlighted by the sun. His skinny, coltish build hadn't taken on the breadth at the shoulder and chest that Lucas had developed.

"Is this the two of you?" he asked.

Lucas twisted around from where he was searching through the nightstand to look. "Yeah. That's Eric's grandparents' pond." Abruptly Lucas's face crumpled, and his eyes filled. "That was the summer we came out—to each other and eventually to our families." He swiped at his eyes. "Do you think we're going to find him?"

"Yes," Gabriel said with absolute conviction. There wasn't a doubt in his mind they would find Eric. The real question, which thankfully didn't appear to have occurred to Lucas, was whether or not they would find him alive. The longer it went on, the slimmer that chance became.

They were already past the critical first forty-eight-hour window. Gabriel had seen people located in far more dire circumstances, but those people, more often than not, were trained military personnel, not wet-behind-the-ears kids only a few years out of college. But until they could determine who Eric was with, there was no point speculating. They didn't even have concrete evidence that Eric hadn't just hooked up with the guy from the bar or someone he met afterward. But his gut said that wasn't the case.

"Any luck?" he asked Lucas.

Lucas shook his head and turned back to his search. He shuffled through a drawer and came up with a folded piece of paper that looked to have been torn from a notebook. Gabriel watched as Lucas unfolded it and smoothed it out against the edge of the table, and then read it. "Wait a minute. Jackpot. Here it is."

"Good. Now you can give him a call. Who knows? Maybe he has heard from Eric."

"Maybe," Lucas replied, though the way the color drained from his face made it clear he expected the call to be less than pleasant. Abruptly he thrust the paper at Gabriel and bolted for the door. As the distinct sounds of Lucas emptying his stomach penetrated the thin wall between the bedroom and bathroom, Gabriel winced in sympathy but didn't follow. He doubted Lucas would appreciate the audience. Instead he went to stand in the doorway and leaned his shoulders against the frame where he would be clearly visible when Lucas reappeared.

Lucas eventually emerged—pale, sweaty, and more than a little shaky.

"Are you okay?" Gabriel asked quietly.

"I'll live," Lucas said. He reached to take the note out of Gabriel's hands.

"I can call him," Gabriel offered. "I don't mind, particularly if it's this upsetting to you."

Lucas managed a small smile but shook his head. "Thanks," he said with surprising conviction, "but I need to do this myself. It will be better coming from me and not a stranger." He took the paper from Gabriel and crossed the living area into the kitchen.

Gabriel didn't bother to follow. Lucas clearly wanted privacy. Instead Gabriel moved into the living room and stationed himself far enough away to give privacy, but close enough to be within easy reach if Lucas needed him.

From his position he couldn't hear exactly what was being said, but he could hear the murmur of Lucas's voice. It hadn't reached that high-pitched note of genuine distress. That was a good sign, at least. It was hard for Gabriel to imagine what it must be like to be in Mr. Collier's shoes. Unless he had, by some miracle, heard from Eric, it would be a shattering and life-changing phone call.

Gabriel was usually tasked with quick and quiet elimination. He never had to clean up the aftermath or even consider how some of the sudden disappearances he caused might affect their families. His targets might have been evil bastards, but they were also sons, daughters, fathers, mothers, husbands, and wives. Not that he could ever afford to acknowledge that. Functioning successfully in such an environment meant not thinking beyond the operation and the particular assignment. An operative might be forced to get to know a target, to learn their habits and earn their trust, but to think of it as anything more than strategy would lead to suicide or insanity. It was awkward and uncomfortable to bump up against that reality outside the familiar confines of an operation—like a suit jacket too tight across the shoulders.

Gabriel shrugged involuntarily and suddenly became aware the kitchen had gone silent. He waited a beat and then moved to go check on Lucas, but Lucas stumbled through the doorway before he had a chance. Gabriel hadn't taken more than a few steps when Lucas plowed into him and clutched blindly at his shirtfront. He was crying silently but with enough force to make his shoulders shake.

More out of instinct than conscious thought, Gabriel wrapped an arm around him and held tight and gently cupped Lucas's head with his other hand. Then he let him cry. It would've been pointless to do otherwise. He very much doubted Lucas could carry on a conversation in that state, even if he wanted to. Instead Gabriel held him until the worst of the storm had passed. When Lucas returned to more normal crying, Gabriel guided them to the sofa and shoved assorted junk out of the way so he could take a seat. He pulled Lucas down with him and settled Lucas on his lap with his head turned in to his shoulder.

Sometime later Lucas finally stirred and tried to sit up. Gabriel helped him but made no attempt to remove him from his lap. Lucas scrubbed his hands over his face and wiped away the worst of the mess. Then he took several deep and very shaky breaths.

"Ready to tell me what happened?" Gabriel asked mildly. "Was Eric's father angry with you?" It would hardly be the first time Gabriel had known someone to lash out because they were afraid. A wave of startling and fierce protectiveness swept through Gabriel at the thought of someone making Lucas the target of that anger.

Without looking up, Lucas shook his head. "No, not really. He said some things, but he didn't mean them. I knew that as soon as they made it out of his mouth, and he apologized in the end."

"What, then?" Gabriel dropped his arms when Lucas sat up. He didn't want Lucas to feel trapped or constrained, but his tearstained face made it almost impossible not to touch him. He clenched his fists over the itch in his palms.

"Nothing. Everything." His voice sounded raw and utterly exhausted. "Stress more than anything. It just…. It makes it real, you know? I mean, of course I know it's real. I've seen the video. I filed the police report. But this, hearing his dad like that, it just makes it really real."

Gabriel murmured in the affirmative. That peculiar sense of unreality had accompanied every black-ops mission he had ever been assigned. Inevitably, after the mission was over, some small thing would happen that would contract the bubble and suddenly make everything real. It didn't surprise him that Lucas was experiencing the same. It had been a wrenching day for him. The stress and adrenaline alone would wreak havoc with his system.

"You're practically dead on your feet," he told Lucas. "You should get some sleep."

Lucas snorted. "Like that's going to happen. I've barely slept since this whole mess started. I lie awake and stare at the ceiling. I can't stop thinking about where Eric might be and what he might be going through. The few times I do manage to drift off, the slightest noise wakes me up. Every groan and creak sounds like footsteps. My nerves are practically grated to shreds."

If Lucas wasn't sleeping, that had probably contributed to his volatile reactions. Most people couldn't go very long without sleep, but Gabriel needed very little. It was yet another of those things that made him not quite normal. "Is there anyone you could stay with for the night?"

"Not really," Lucas replied.

"No one?" Gabriel pressed. "You're a college student. Surely you have a friend or classmate who would let you crash on their couch."

"I'm a graduate student," Lucas corrected. "That's different than undergrads who routinely crash on each other's couches. Most of the other students in my cohort are married with families of their own. Not only that. I'm a gay man in a program that's more than 80 percent female. Even if I had classmates I knew well, which I don't, I seriously doubt their husbands would agree to a random man sleeping on the sofa."

"What about the guys at the bar?" Gabriel suggested. "You seemed to know them pretty well."

"Enough to say hi, maybe, but they're Eric's friends, not mine. Besides, they'll be at the bar all night. I'd still be alone. That's not going to help any more than being alone here," Lucas countered.

Gabriel rubbed a hand across the back of his neck. "You make it sound like you don't have any friends. I can't believe that. There must be someone."

Gabriel had always been a loner, but he liked it that way. Keeping to himself relieved him of having to deal with irritating social niceties. He could handle them for a cover or an official university function, but he found them to be a waste of time. They were meaningless and got in the way of getting things done. But Lucas wasn't him. Lucas was genuinely nice and friendly, and he cared about people. A guy like him should be a social butterfly in the middle of a large circle of other goody-goody types like himself. He shouldn't be alone.

"Pathetic, isn't it?" Lucas said. "I work all the time. I barely even spent any time with Eric lately, and we live in the same house. I've been so wrapped up in trying to finish school and do well so I can keep my grant and working so I can pay the bills and volunteering so I can build up different types of work experience that I haven't had any time for myself, or even to socialize with my friends. It's a recipe for burnout. I'm training to be a therapist. I know isolation is dangerous, and I did it anyway." His laugh sounded dry and brittle. "Some therapist I am. Physician, heal your freaking self."

His tone was bleak and bitter and wrong. It was a tone Gabriel had heard from veteran agents who were worn and tired, drained beyond caring. It should never come out of the mouth of someone like Lucas. Gabriel knew what he needed to do, and he knew he was going to regret it. He took a deep breath and took the plunge.

"Go get your things."

Lucas's head snapped around, and he stared in wide-eyed disbelief. "What? Why?"

"You can stay with me. Just for a few days, until we hear from Moose."

Lucas continued to gape. "You're serious."

"You make it sound like I'm doing something monumental," Gabriel said. "I'm merely acting in my own best interest. You're going to persist in wanting to pursue this with me until we locate Eric, but if you don't get some sleep, you're going to be insufferable and impossible to deal with. Clearly staying here alone isn't allowing you to get the sleep you need. If you're with me, I can ensure that you get sufficient rest. That also ensures that you won't continue to be sleep-deprived and driving me mad. So you see, it's entirely selfish on my part."

Lucas bit his lip. His eyes lit with amusement and he appeared to be trying to hold back laughter. He obviously didn't believe Gabriel at all. "If you say so," he said lightly. Then he slid off Gabriel's lap and disappeared into his bedroom.

Gabriel wasn't surprised Lucas didn't believe him. He didn't believe it himself. How the hell was he going to cope with the kid living in his house?

Gabriel pushed to his feet and paced around the room. He scrubbed his fingers through his hair and tried to think it through. He had never used it, but he did have a guest room. It was fully furnished and had an attached bath. Fortunately it was also on the opposite side of the house from Gabriel's bedroom and office. They wouldn't necessarily have to be up under each other. The house was large enough for them to both have their own space. What's more, he and Lucas had class the next day. They would be separate all day. They would only be together for meals and when they worked on finding Eric. That wasn't much different than what they normally did.

He could handle that. It would be fine.

CHAPTER TEN

GABRIEL'S CONFIDENCE held out for perhaps a further twenty-four hours. The first night was no trouble at all. They had both had a beastly day and were so exhausted they fell into their respective beds with only the briefest necessary conversation. It was unquestionably odd to find Lucas perched at his kitchen island in pajamas the following morning, but it wasn't totally unpleasant.

It wasn't all that different from their quick, casual breakfasts in the co-op, except he had time to ensure Lucas actually ate properly, rather than bolting it down at breakneck speed and rushing off to class. They rode to campus together, but the rest of the day passed much the same as it usually did. They went off to class and shifted into their normal routines. Then Gabriel went home alone. Lucas insisted on taking the bus to work. Afterward he planned to do a shift at the suicide hotline to make up for his absences of late. Gabriel argued against that, but he lost.

It was completely irrational, but Gabriel would have preferred to keep Lucas with him. Lucas, however, pointed out that there was no reason to disrupt their lives any more than they already had until they knew something more. He was right, and Gabriel knew it, but that didn't make it any easier to let Lucas go off alone—which was absolutely ridiculous. Lucas had been living on his own for years. There was no reason to think he was in any more danger today than he was yesterday, but Gabriel's protective streak wasn't concerned with logic. Why should it be? From the first time Gabriel saw Lucas rushing into the co-op, frazzled and half-starved, he had felt an irrational, bone-deep protectiveness, and the more time they spent around each other, the stronger it seemed to get.

Gabriel took a deep breath and let it out slowly. It wouldn't be much longer. Moose should get back to him any time. Then Lucas could go back to his own house.

He strode into his bedroom, stripped out of his work clothes, and dressed in dark jeans, boots, and a fitted black T-shirt. It was a good night to hit the gun range. Lucas was gone for the night, so he might as well take advantage of the time alone to burn off some of his own stress.

He went into the walk-in closet and pushed aside the row of neatly hung shirts to access the gun safe concealed behind a panel in the back wall. Then he pressed the hidden lever and typed in the security code with practiced ease. He had a small pistol tucked away beneath papers and odds and ends in the bottom drawer of his nightstand, but that was solely for quick access. Most of his things lived here—a couple of heavier handguns, his good knife, and assorted mesh bags and stoppered glass bottles that held his uncommon herbs and poisons.

He hadn't needed those in years and hoped to never need them again, but they were the tools of his unique trade, and he hadn't been able to give them up. Some of them were exceedingly rare and therefore very valuable. They were his savings account. They could be liquidated for a significant amount of money if he ever needed it. At least that's what he told himself. Maybe deep down they were an odd kind of security blanket too.

But the poisons were not what he wanted. They were only useful for a quick and quiet kill. He needed noise and aggression, something to bleed the heat and the pulsing demand for violence out of his system. He picked up the Desert Eagle 44 Mag and pocketed the appropriate ammo. The gun was heavy and solid with a sizable kick. That should be perfect. And if he got a mind to play with anything else, the range always had a selection of popular guns available to rent.

Just over two hours later, Gabriel came back through the door feeling relaxed and refreshed. It wasn't the fantastic euphoria that followed a kill, but it felt good. Or at least it had. He was barely back home two minutes when the relaxation gave way to restlessness. Lucas's presence was everywhere. Looking around, Gabriel couldn't pinpoint exactly what made it feel that way. It wasn't like Lucas had clutter strewn everywhere, at least not outside of the guest room where he was staying. If anything, Lucas had clearly made an effort to be respectful of Gabriel's space.

The only visible signs of his presence in the common rooms of the house were his breakfast dishes drying in the drainer in the kitchen. But

Gabriel could feel him everywhere. He'd hardly noticed it earlier, but it was all over and nearly smothering—like an invisible cloud of static electricity that set his nerves on edge and made the hairs on his arms and neck stand on end. And that wasn't the only thing that stood at attention.

What the hell? It was hard enough fighting the constant attraction when Lucas was around, but he couldn't even be alone in his own home without getting a raging hard-on? What kind of bullshit was that? He'd done enough wrong in his life that he wouldn't be particularly surprised if fate decided to punish him, but this wasn't punishment. It was torture. Why the hell had he ever agreed to let Lucas stay? He remembered Lucas crying in his arms and his fierce need to protect him, and that image did nothing at all to abate his erection. He adjusted himself in his jeans and hoped for some relief, but when none came, he gave in to the inevitable and slipped into his bathroom.

Gabriel shucked his clothes at speed, turned the shower on hot, and stepped in. He groaned as the hot water poured over him. In his mind he held Lucas in his arms and felt the heat as his smaller body trembled against him. He imagined it was not from tears but from need.

Like hot silk over hard bone, he fantasized Lucas's skin against his own and the unique presence that was undeniably Lucas. He barely had to touch himself. He used the soap to lather his hand and fisted his cock a handful of times. Lost in a mix of memory and imagination, his body went tight a split second before his release exploded out of him.

Gabriel leaned forward and braced his hands against the wall. He let the water wash over him while he caught his breath. Then he picked up the soap, quickly washed off, and turned the water to cold to school his body back into submission. A lingering sense of guilt nagged at the back of his mind. But his guilty fantasy was as close as Gabriel was ever going to get to Lucas, and God help him, he wanted to enjoy it.

CHAPTER ELEVEN

IT WAS nearing 1:00 a.m. when Lucas slipped the key Gabriel had given him into the lock and crept into Gabriel's house. Aside from the single porch light that was thoughtfully left on for him, the house was dark and silent. He didn't want to disturb Gabriel any more than absolutely necessary, so he stumbled in the darkness until he found the floor lamp that stood sentry by the massive sectional in the great room. The lamp bathed the area around it in a soft yellow light. In Lucas's exhausted state, he thought he'd never seen anything so welcoming.

He left the light burning behind him, made a beeline for the bedroom Gabriel was letting him use, closed the door behind him, and snapped on the bedroom light. The room was both larger and far more elegantly appointed than his own bedroom back in his apartment. A sleek black queen-size bed dominated the room, its heavy coverings a rich burgundy with gold accents.

It should've felt strange and different, and it *was* a world away from his own messy room and the familiar striped comforter that sagged off the end of his bed. It felt like staying in a fancy hotel but without the impersonal atmosphere. He felt infinitely safer there than he had in his own home ever since he discovered Eric was missing.

It was Gabriel, not the room or even the house that made him feel safer. Without even trying, Gabriel made him believe everything was going to be okay.

Lucas stripped down to his boxers and slid between the cool sheets. He was so tired that he hurt, but his mind refused to shut off and let him rest. What was it about Gabriel that made him feel so safe? He supposed it was partly because Gabriel actually believed him. More than that, Gabriel knew what to do and didn't expect Lucas to handle everything and make all the decisions. It probably didn't hurt that he was dead sexy.

The image of Gabriel holding him after his phone call with Eric's dad had haunted him all day. It should've been phenomenally embarrassing. Lucas had sobbed like a heartbroken preschooler, but what he remembered was the touch of Gabriel's arms around him, holding him tight, and the feeling like nothing in the world could possibly reach him.

He remembered the heat of Gabriel's body against his own. What would it be like to feel that heat without shirts in the way? Without pants? To press against him body to body, skin to skin? What would it be like to run his hands over Gabriel's chest or have Gabriel's hands on him? Would he be as demanding, as forceful, as take-charge in bed as he seemed to be otherwise? Or would he be gentle and tender and take things soft and easy? Lucas's thoughts strung his body tight as wire. It only took a few fast, hard strokes to bring release.

He didn't have the energy to get out of bed and make it into the bathroom, so he cleaned up as best he could with tissues from the box on the side table. Suddenly he could barely keep his eyes open. His last conscious thought before he slid into sleep was that maybe one day he'd have the chance to find out for real.

CHAPTER TWELVE

ON SATURDAY morning Gabriel's private cell phone—the burn phone—rang. He recognized Moose's number and thumbed the answer button. "Shadow," he answered automatically, although Moose probably knew his real name. In fact he suspected Moose was probably the one who sanitized his discharge papers and created the CV that allowed him to obtain his current employment, but old habits died hard.

"Got the package you sent me," Moose told him. "Don't know what you got yourself caught up in, Shadow, but I got to tell you, it ain't good."

Gabriel's heart sank. If Moose said it wasn't good, that likely meant it was only a couple steps below an international crisis. His gift for understatement was legendary. "What is it?" Gabriel asked.

"Looks like your boy spent most of the night chatting up a gangbanger by the name of Damien Castillo."

Gabriel breathed a sigh of relief. "A gangbanger. That's all. Hell, Moose, I thought you were going to tell me I had uncovered a terrorist cell or something. A small-time hood is nothing."

"Except Castillo ain't exactly your average street thug," Moose broke in. "He's got a rap sheet as long as my arm, and he's on a watch list for suspected human trafficking. Word is his gang is a subsidiary of MS-13. He's bad news, and if he's got your boy, the kid is in way over his head."

"Shit." Gabriel sank slowly back into his chair. Though he had suspected it was more than a simple case of a runaway kid—despite what the local LEOs believed—he never suspected it ran so deep. Human trafficking was big business. It fed prostitution rings that were to modern gangs what bootlegging was to the mobsters of the '20s and '30s. And MS-13 owned a reputation for being ruthless and violent.

In an instant Gabriel's body was on high alert. Time was always of the essence in a missing-person case, but Eric's just became even more so. They had to get him out now, if he was even still alive. *Please let him still be alive.*

If Eric's disappearance worried Lucas, finding out his best friend was dead would crush him. Gabriel couldn't imagine having to relay that news. He was prepared to hunt down and take out anything or anyone who dared hurt Lucas. That thought brought him up short. Again.

"Shadow, you there?" Moore asked, drawing him abruptly out of his thoughts.

"Yeah, I'm here," Gabriel said. "Just trying to figure out what the fuck to do next. Any idea where they went?"

"Castillo left after a couple hours," Moose replied. "He and two other males, one Hispanic and one African American, drove off in a dark-colored late-model sedan. Maybe an older-model Caddy."

"Tell me you got a plate."

"Sorry, man, no can do. The security cameras aren't particularly good quality. I can see them get into the car and pull out, but I can't get enough detail to see the plate."

"And Eric?"

"The inside cameras show him cleaning up after his shift, and he makes a call to someone on his cell. Then he leaves through the back entrance and heads out in the same direction Castillo and his crew went. If I had to guess, I'd say he was headed out to meet Castillo somewhere."

Gabriel concurred. For the fuck-all good it did. They still didn't know shit. Correction—they knew Eric was in a shitload of trouble. Fuck. That was exactly the kind of dark, convoluted underworld garbage he needed to stay the hell away from. One wrong move and he could end up right back in the abyss, right back in that dark rage he'd spent the last few years crawling out of by tooth and nail.

But he couldn't walk away—not when he knew what those bastards were doing. They were preying on vulnerable kids. Maybe Lucas's friend wasn't technically a minor, but Gabriel would bet his ass most of them were. He couldn't let that go, and Lucas wouldn't stand for it if he did. Just what the fuck was he supposed to do?

Gabriel didn't realize he'd spoken aloud until Moose replied, "How about you start with telling me exactly what it is that's going on here?"

And so he told him everything—how he met Lucas, their breakfast dates and tentative fledgling friendship, and how that all shifted when Lucas showed up in his office and dissolved into hysterics. He told him about the asshole cops and this kid, Eric, who everybody seemed to be content to let slip through the cracks except for Lucas. Lucas, who was so fierce and so determined that he made Gabriel believe it himself.

"And he was right," Gabriel insisted. "This proves it. He's been right from the start. This investigation should've started a week ago, but not a damn soul could be bothered to listen and take the time to look for a missing gay kid."

"And that pisses me off as much as it does you," Moose assured him, "but you're a civilian, Shadow. The best thing you can do right now is to take care of your boy and turn this over to the appropriate authorities."

Gabriel sniffed. "Yes. Because they've been so very helpful thus far."

"I'm not talking about some dumbass local LEOs," Moose retorted. "You've got evidence that this kid was last seen with a known gang member and suspected human trafficker. That not only kicks him up into the high-risk category, the human-trafficking connection makes it a federal case. I've got a contact with connections to the FBI human-trafficking task force—Levi Parrish. He was at Quantico when we were at The Farm. He's a few years older than us. Hooked up with the feds after a stint in the military. We had acquaintances in common. Worked with him a few times since, on kidnapping cases. He's a good guy. He'll do right by the kid. Last I heard he was either in Baltimore or DC. I'll get you an appointment."

Though the part of Gabriel that was and would probably always be a cynical spook automatically resisted the idea of working with anyone else, particularly someone he didn't know, most of him was relieved. He trusted Moose implicitly, and if Moose said Parrish was a good guy, he was. "Yeah, okay. Thanks, Moose. I owe you one."

"Fuck that," Moose shot back. "As tempting as it might be to have you owing me a favor, I want these bastards as bad as you do. They need taking down, hard, and I mean to have a hand in doing it. You just worry about taking care of your boy. I mean it, Shadow. Don't let him out of your sight. If these motherfuckers get wind that he's poking around in what happened to his friend, he's a dead man. They'll kill him without a second thought. If he means anything at all to you, keep him close."

"I'm on that," Gabriel told him. "He's not going anywhere alone. You just let me know as soon as you can get that appointment and we'll both be there."

"Roger that," Moose said and clicked off.

Gabriel went into the guest room and found Lucas seated cross-legged in the middle of the bed with a mess of books and papers spread out in a semicircle around him. "Get your keys," he said without preamble. "We're going over to your apartment to get the rest of your things."

Lucas jerked his head up, and Gabriel could see his body go into high alert and brace for the worst. "What happened?"

"That was my contact, Moose, on the phone," Gabriel said. "He identified the man Eric was last seen with at the bar. His name is Damien Castillo. He and his two buddies are affiliated with MS-13."

"And that's bad?" Lucas asked.

"It's certainly not good," Gabriel told him. "It means we're not talking about small-time thugs here. This group may be small, but they have connections to a very large and very dangerous network. They're involved in any number of illegal rackets, including suspected human trafficking. It means that not only is Eric in danger, you might be too."

"Me?" Lucas squeaked, wide-eyed. "What have I got to do with anything?"

Aside from getting me into this mess. "Plenty. First of all, if they find out we're looking into this, you might as well paint a target on your back. They'll come for you, and they will kill you. Secondly, from what you've told me, you are Eric's closest friend. Essentially family." Lucas nodded. "That means even if they don't know what we're doing, you're still in danger. If Eric doesn't cooperate, they might come after you to ensure his cooperation. Make no mistake. These men are ruthless and have no qualms about killing anyone who gets in their way. They'd take you out with no more thought than swatting a fly."

All the color drained from Lucas's face, and his expression of confusion and apprehension morphed into one more akin to terror. Good. He needed to be scared. They were playing with the big boys, and he damn well needed to know it.

"If they're that dangerous, shouldn't we go to the police?" he asked.

Gabriel wasn't sure whether to be annoyed or impressed. Even clearly scared out of his mind, Lucas was still thinking logically. That was a good sign—or it would've been, if the kid weren't arguing with him. "We will, but this is bigger than a local case now. Moose has a contact with the FBI he's going to try to get us an appointment with, and in the meantime, we just need to lie low and keep you safe."

And he had to figure out how to do that without losing his soul in the process.

CHAPTER THIRTEEN

THREE DAYS later, on what should've been an ordinary Tuesday morning, Lucas found himself trailing Gabriel through the door of the Baltimore FBI field office and wondering what in the hell had happened to his life. He thought his life was crazy when he was running between classes and work and volunteering. But when Eric disappeared, crazy took on a whole new meaning. And since Gabriel got that phone call over the weekend, it seemed to have gotten even crazier.

Eric was mixed up in a human-trafficking racket run by a dangerous gang. And he, who should be doing nothing more than juggling paperwork and placements and trying to keep his head above water with his graduate work, had a meeting with an agent from an FBI task force. What the hell?

It was the kind of thing that happened in the movies or a spy novel. It didn't happen to ordinary people like him. Yet there he was, holding out his ID for the guard at the security checkpoint and stepping through the metal detector.

"We have an appointment with Agent Parrish," he heard Gabriel say to the guard in response to something Lucas hadn't heard. The guard fiddled with his laptop, and a moment later, the printer behind him started up. When it finished he handed printed ID badges to both of them. Lucas examined his as he peeled off the backing and stuck it to his shirt. It was clearly marked Visitor with the date, his name, a black-and-white copy of his ID photo, the time, and the agent he was there to see. Anyone could tell at a glance who he was and why he was there. It was above and beyond the routine security Lucas was used to.

The guard made a brief phone call and waved them to the side to wait. A few minutes later, a large African American man with shoulders like a linebacker and short, neatly cropped salt-and-pepper hair and beard strode up to them. "Professor Ingram?" He offered a hand to Gabriel. "Agent Levi Parrish." The agent's presence alone made Lucas want to take a step back, but Gabriel met his eyes squarely and shook his hand. Then Gabriel laid his free hand lightly in the center of Lucas's back and nudged him forward.

"This is Lucas Craig," Gabriel said. "He's the one who initially alerted us to this situation."

"Mr. Craig." Agent Parrish stepped forward to shake his hand. "We can talk in my office." He ushered them into the elevator on the opposite side of the lobby and pressed a button. When the doors opened again, they stepped into a busy, crowded office area with desks scattered across the wide-open floor. Other offices lined the walls. Agent Parrish opened the door to one of those and gestured them inside.

There was only one metal visitor's chair in front of the large desk that dominated most of the room. Neither Lucas nor Gabriel moved to take it. Agent Parrish shut the door and propped one hip on the edge of his desk. "Why don't you tell me what's going on? Moose said you thought you might have stumbled on something connected to human trafficking? But I'd like to hear it from you."

Gabriel caught Lucas's eye with a slight nod and an expression Lucas read without difficulty. *Tell him*, it said. *Tell him everything.* And so Lucas did. He told him. He described every gut-wrenching moment since Eric disappeared. Had it really been over a week since he had seen his friend? Had it really only been a week with all that had gone on? Agent Parrish listened without comment. There was none of the skepticism or judgment Lucas felt from the police. Lucas began to hope that maybe, just maybe Agent Parris would believe him—right up until about thirty seconds after he finished speaking.

"I see," Agent Parrish said, sounding carefully neutral. "And what is it that makes you think your friend is involved with human trafficking? What makes you think he didn't just decide to leave on his own?"

Anger raced through Lucas. He wouldn't do it again. He wouldn't justify himself to yet another law enforcement officer. Dammit. He would've turned and stomped out were it not for Gabriel standing between him and the door. He swallowed hard and tried to formulate an answer to Agent Parrish's question, but before he could, Gabriel pulled a sheet of paper from his jacket and dropped it on Agent Parrish's desk. It was a screenshot of the man from the video. Agent Parrish glanced down at it and his eyes went round.

"That was the last man his roommate was seen with," Gabriel told him quietly.

Agent Parrish swore vehemently under his breath. "I knew Castillo would surface again sooner or later, but I hoped we could get to him before he got anybody else. Your friend isn't his usual target, but there were rumors he might be trying to expand his market. I didn't expect it to be to men, but it's not unheard of."

"My friend has a name," Lucas said through gritted teeth. "He has a dad. He has friends. He has a life. He's not just some random expendable gay kid, and I'm fucking tired of people acting like he is."

Agent Parrish looked shocked. "Of course he does. I couldn't care less about his sexual orientation or his skin color or anything else. He's a victim, and you have my word that I will do everything in my power to get him out of there."

Lucas took a deep breath and rocked back on his heels. "That probably wasn't entirely called for," he admitted. "At least it wasn't all directed at you. The local law enforcement has been less than helpful, and when you started asking the same things…."

Parrish nodded. "Don't sweat it. If that's the worst I have to deal with today, it'll be a very good day. Have there been any more sightings of Castillo since he was seen with your friend?"

He directed the question to Lucas, but it was Gabriel who replied. "Not that I can tell. He hasn't been back to the bar, at least. No one there recognized him, which tells me it was a quick in and out. That surprised me, to be honest. It's a target-rich environment, being a college town. I would've thought he'd keep fishing in a big pool of young people—male and female. If that's what he's after, why only take one?"

"Two things," Parrish replied. "A single missing person is less likely to attract attention. It's more easily dismissed. One person disappearing can be written off as that person deciding to leave town. More than one makes it look less like a coincidence. It's also much easier to move one person than it is to move several. These guys like to move quickly to keep their victims disoriented. They favor a fast snatch and grab and a quick getaway. Taking a single victim facilitates that. It's much harder to try to escape if you don't know where you are and don't know anyone."

"Wait a minute," Lucas blurted. "So you're telling me everything I've been doing looking for Eric is useless. He's probably not even in the same town anymore?"

"He was probably out of town within a few hours of leaving with Castillo," Parrish told him. "By this point I would be shocked if they're even in the state. They cross state and jurisdictional lines frequently and deliberately. The more law enforcement agencies you can involve in an investigation, the more complicated it becomes. We're not exactly good with communicating with one another, and perps like Castillo play on that. They're counting on the fact that we won't connect the dots, or that even if we do, we'll be too distracted by jurisdictional pissing contests to do anything about it until they're long gone." He shook his head and looked rueful, but Lucas noticed something like understanding passed between Agent Parrish and Gabriel.

That got Lucas's hackles up again. He was damn tired of being left out of the loop. He might not have the experience Gabriel and Agent Parrish had, but he wasn't some stupid kid either.

He was just about to say so when Agent Parrish continued, "That doesn't mean what you've done is useless, though. You've actually been extremely helpful. Castillo was probably counting on this being dismissed as a voluntary missing, just like the local police assumed it was. You're the one who didn't let that happen. Not to mention you got us both Castillo and his car. That's a solid lead and gives us something to go on. Don't knock that."

Lucas was more relieved than he probably should have been. Finally somebody was listening. Finally somebody was taking him seriously. "So now what?"

"Now you let me do my job," Parrish said. "We can take it from here. I'll get a team on this as soon as possible. I'd also appreciate it if you'd leave me your contact information, in case we have other questions as things come up."

"Of course," Lucas agreed. Gabriel took a business card out of his wallet and laid it on Agent Parrish's desk. Lucas picked up a pen from the pencil cup on the desk and scribbled his own name and number on the back of Gabriel's card.

Agent Parrish took the card from Lucas and clipped it to the printout of Castillo's picture. "Thank you, gentlemen. I really appreciate you bringing this to my attention. I assure you my team and I will work to get your friend back to safety as soon as possible, and I'll let you know as soon as we know anything."

Gabriel nodded. "I assume Moose is sending you a copy of the video. He couldn't get the tag number on the car, but he does have the make and model."

"It's on its way," Parrish confirmed.

"So what do we do in the meantime?" Lucas asked.

"You go home and let me handle it," Parrish said.

"That's great. Just great," Lucas said bitterly. "I've been running crazy on this for days. I've been telling anybody who would listen that something bad was going on. Nobody would believe me. Now we find out some big-shot gang guy is involved, and you want to pat me on the head and tell me to go home and wait like a good little boy. No, I don't think so."

Agent Parrish drew himself up. "Mr. Craig, with all due respect, you are a civilian, a friend. Yes, the information you've uncovered is extremely helpful and very much appreciated, but you have no place in this investigation. I'd ask that you not attempt to meddle. Frankly you'll only get in the way. You'll slow us down and waste valuable time that would be better used trying to find your friend."

"You can't just shut me out," Lucas insisted.

"Look, kid, you're in over your head here," Parrish told him.

"Now I'm in over my head," Lucas spat. "First I was making something over nothing, now I'm in over my head, yet I'm the only one who has realized what's going on the whole time."

"Do you want me to let you play or do you want me to find your friend?" Agent Parrish asked. "These are dangerous people. This is no time or place to be babysitting a kid who wants to stick his nose in. If you know what's good for you, you'll lie low and keep as quiet as possible. Castillo has probably left the area, but he most likely left scouts here. The best thing you can do is be as normal as possible and not do anything that might inadvertently let somebody know what's going on. If you tip them off, your friend's as good as dead. And he might not be the only one."

Lucas paled. All his righteous anger suddenly fled in the face of fear. Before he could gather his thoughts to respond, Gabriel stepped forward.

"You don't need to worry about that," he told Parrish. "I'm keeping an eye on him, and while I realize neither of us technically has jurisdiction here, we also both know I'm not exactly a civilian either. Lucas and I have started this, and it's hard to just let go in the middle. Could you do me a favor and keep us in the loop?"

Agent Parrish scrubbed a hand over his head and sighed like a deflated balloon, but he said, "Yeah. I can do that."

"Thank you," Gabriel replied. "We appreciate that. Now, unless you have any further questions for us, we'll let you get to it."

"I think I have everything for now." Agent Parrish tapped the business card with their information. "If I think of anything else, I know where to find you."

Gabriel nodded. "That you do. We'll wait to hear from you." He took Lucas gently by the shoulders and guided him out the door.

At the elevator Lucas shrugged him off. "I'm fine. You didn't have to play referee. I wasn't going to do anything."

"You can't be getting angry with people for just trying to do their jobs. I know this is frustrating, but you have to let him do his job. He's right. Us trying to get into the middle of it will only slow him down."

"I know, I know," Lucas said irritably. "It's just so frustrating. It's like we've done all the work, but now they just want us to turn it over and go away."

"Sometimes the best thing you can do is do your job and trust other people to do theirs," Gabriel replied. "Besides, I never said anything about going away quietly. Agent Parrish said he would keep us in the loop, and he will or he'll answer to me."

And that was the most comforting thing Lucas had heard all day.

BY THE end of the week, Gabriel had decided his worries about having to go back into the undercover world were unfounded. His biggest problem was preventing himself from killing Lucas. The kid was making him crazy. He was worse than some impatient rookie and could not seem to understand that investigative work took time. Castillo and his men were involved, but that didn't mean they could locate them instantly. And once they located them, it would take some time to put together a safe extraction plan. They couldn't just go busting in half-cocked.

Worse—the more irritated Gabriel became, the harder controlling his rage became. And then, to top it all off, his libido decided to get involved and conjured up all sorts of hot and creative ways he could shut Lucas up and occupy his time. It made his efforts to remain honorable damn near impossible. He'd taken more cold showers that week than he had since he was a hormonal teenager.

When the call finally came with an update in the case, Gabriel nearly sagged with relief. Finally some progress and a way to answer Lucas's insistent questions. Right on cue Lucas popped his head into Gabriel's home office and fidgeted in the doorway like an eager bird dog while Gabriel finished up the call. "Was that him?"

Lucas asked the same question every time Gabriel's phone rang since the day they met with Agent Parrish. "Yes, it was," Gabriel said. "And before you ask, no, they haven't found Eric yet. They do think they might have a lead on where Castillo may be keeping him, though. They want you to look at some photos to see if you can identify anyone. Parrish is sending someone to meet us at the police station this afternoon."

Visible relief washed over Lucas. "Finally."

"It might not be him," Gabriel cautioned. He of all people knew how often what looked like promising intel could turn out to be total crap. Lucas didn't need to celebrate just yet.

"At least it's something," Lucas insisted. "That's more than I've had before."

Gabriel nodded. That was undeniably true, and though he was cautious, he could understand Lucas's need to hold on to any scrap of hope, however scant it might be. Statistically the likelihood was that Eric could be dead. Kidnapping victims didn't usually live long, and prostitutes didn't have particularly long life spans either, but he kept the thought to himself. He wouldn't mention that possibility to Lucas. It would shatter him, and Gabriel couldn't bring himself to be the one who did that.

WHEN THEY arrived at the police station later that afternoon, the deputies were stunned. The one Lucas called Deputy Potbelly trailed behind the FBI agent who met them in the lobby. He looked like the shell-shocked victim of a natural disaster. The agent Parrish sent was very young and very green, but even he had more composure than the deputy. To Gabriel's surprise the FBI agent wasn't alone. Moose was with him.

"What are you doing here?" Gabriel asked as the agent led them into a small room, off the main area, that served as an interrogation room and conference room.

Moose shrugged. "You got me interested. I've been working with Parrish on the follow-up surveillance. If this tip turns out to be good, I'm going to handle the surveillance on the raid. Parrish's guys are good, but I'm better."

"You could have given me a heads-up," Gabriel told him.

"You know how these things go, Shadow. Hell, man, this time yesterday I was still sitting in my office in Dallas. I didn't exactly have time to plan out a social calendar."

Gabriel let that pass without comment. They took seats around the table, and the FBI agent opened a manila envelope, pulled out a packet of photographs, and handed them to Lucas. Gabriel examined them over his shoulder. They were all taken from the parking lot of a run-down motel and showed various people coming in and out. Castillo was clearly visible in several of them, holding conversations with an assortment of men on the walkway outside the rooms.

"Do you recognize any of them?" the agent asked Lucas.

Lucas shook his head, continuing to sort slowly through the photographs. "I recognize the guy from the video, of course, but no one else. I've never seen these men before." Then Lucas flipped over the next photograph and gasped. "That's Eric." It was a photograph of two men in a dark SUV. The photographer had gotten a shot through the window as the vehicle left the hotel parking lot, and a streetlight had given just enough illumination to see their faces, though they weren't particularly clear.

"Are you sure?" the agent asked.

"I'm sure." Lucas's voice was confident, though his hands had begun to shake. "I'd know him anywhere. He's alive. My God, he's really alive."

Lucas began to shake uncontrollably then, and the photograph slid to the table as Lucas curled into himself. Gabriel got up and gathered him into his arms. "It's okay," he murmured into Lucas's ear. "You found him. We'll get him now."

"Yes, we will," Moose vowed, catching the last of what Gabriel was saying. "You have my word on that." He quickly excused himself and stepped outside to make a call. When he came back in, he said, "Parrish is putting together a team now. We'll go in later today. Go home. I'll call you when it's done."

CHAPTER FOURTEEN

ERIC HAD barely closed his eyes when the door to their motel room burst open. He startled awake and struggled to shake away fatigue. He silently prayed it wasn't someone bringing in yet another client. He was sore and exhausted and would have been happy not to see another cock for the rest of his life.

"Get up," Julio said as he abruptly stripped the sheets off the bed.

Eric's stomach twisted. Shit! What had he done to deserve a session with Julio? He didn't remember doing anything wrong. Wincing, he pushed himself upright. He'd learned the hard way that delaying would only make it worse. The best thing to do was to get it over with as quickly as possible and pray Julio would go easy on him. But Julio liked to draw out his fun and toy with his victim like a cat with a mouse.

Rather than crawl in bed with him as Eric expected, Julio grabbed his jeans from the floor and threw them at him. "Get dressed."

Eric pulled on his jeans as best he could with his arm still chained to the bed, groaning with every movement. He found his discarded shirt on the end of the bed and shouldered it on. Monique was clearly doing the same as Julio moved to unchain first her and then him.

"What's going on?" she asked blurrily.

"None of your business, bitch," Julio replied. He took handkerchiefs from his pocket, blindfolded them both, and led them out of the room and across the parking lot.

Julio shoved him roughly into the back of a car alone. Eric called out to Monique as the door slammed behind him. His only reply was a sharp cuff to the head from someone in the front seat. Then there was the sharp prick of a needle stick, and everything slowly faded to blurry darkness. With his last snatches of consciousness, he realized the car was moving.

WHEN HE woke again, he was in another motel room. It was the same dingy, low-rent quality as the last one, but the cracks in the ceiling above his bed were unfamiliar. He turned on his side to speak to Monique and was shocked to discover that in the bed where Monique should've been, there was a thin white girl with corn-silk blonde hair that fell well below her waist.

"Who are you?" he blurted.

She jerked and skittered away to huddle in the corner of her bed, staring at him with wide, frightened blue eyes. "Don't hurt me," she pleaded.

"Why would I do that?" Eric asked. "I'm in the same boat you are. It's not me you have to worry about. Where's Monique?"

The girl blinked at him. "Who?"

"You know, Chyna. Black chick with braids. She shared this room with me," Eric explained.

"You're the only person I've seen," the girl whispered. "There's no one here but us, wherever here is."

Eric's heart sank into his stomach as he realized he not only had no idea where he was, but that the only friend he had left in the world was gone, and he would probably never see her alive again.

CHAPTER FIFTEEN

AFTER A day and a half of waiting, they got the call from Moose. Unfortunately it wasn't the news they hoped for. In the time it took them to set up the rescue operation, Castillo had fled. Whether he got wind of the planned operation or just decided to move on, no one was sure, but he was gone. The entire operation had seemingly disappeared into thin air.

Now Lucas wouldn't shut up. It was as though, after all the intense anticipation of waiting and the gut-wrenching disappointment of the near miss, the roller coaster of emotions had set his mouth on overdrive. Lucas's disappointment was cutting and palpable. He ranted and raved until he ran out of steam and then finally dropped into a heavy silence that went on for a long time. It should've been peaceful—a welcome quiet, and it was at first, but toward the end, it was surprisingly unnerving. Gabriel needn't have worried. Abruptly, Lucas sat up, almost tangibly shook off the silence, and started to talk. And talk. And talk.

He'd been at it for nearly two hours, practically nonstop. He dissected everything they knew of the investigation thus far. Then he reconstructed everything Moose had said about the day's attempted rescue, took it apart again, and questioned every move. When he exhausted his options for exploring what they had already done, he started to speculate about the next steps.

That was about the time Gabriel began to seriously lose patience. The men who had been out there were professionals—highly trained and talented people. The idea that a do-gooder social worker like Lucas thought he could do better than them when he had never seen and probably couldn't even imagine the horrible situations these men routinely walked in and out of was at once laughable and insulting.

Not that Lucas intended it to be. Deep down Gabriel knew that. His was the nervous chatter of a man about to go under the knife, a scared kid who had suddenly come face-to-face with the fact that his best friend was in more serious trouble than he had ever dreamed, and that despite all their efforts, there might not be a fairy-tale rescue. He was on the edge of falling apart, and he was clearly chattering to keep himself from giving in.

Gabriel knew all that, and if Lucas would just bloody shut up, he might actually be sympathetic. But the babble was driving him to the edge of murder.

It wouldn't be that hard to do, really. It was a lot easier to kill a man with your bare hands than people made it seem. All it would take was to slap a hand over Lucas's flapping mouth and nose and hold it there long enough to cut off the air supply. Getting an arm around his neck and over his windpipe would be even quicker. It wasn't as elegant or untraceable as the poisons Gabriel favored, but it would do in a pinch.

The impulse to kill that thrummed almost constantly beneath his skin grew stronger with every thought. By the time he became aware of what he was doing, Gabriel had spun around, pinned Lucas against the wall, and immobilized both of his arms above his head, where both wrists were captured in Gabriel's right hand. His left hand had frozen in midmotion as he reached toward Lucas's throat.

What the hell was he doing? Lucas wasn't a target. He didn't actually want to kill him. Christ, he needed to get to the range soon if it was getting that bad. He'd barely felt it at all since Lucas moved in with him, but clearly it wasn't nearly as dormant as he hoped. Dammit. He could've actually killed the kid.

It had accomplished one thing, though. Lucas had shut up. He was motionless and silent, wide-eyed as a frightened doe. Up close Gabriel could feel the heat coming off Lucas's body and see the pulse skittering in his throat—a tiny frantic drumbeat. By any standard of decency in the world, Gabriel knew he should back away and apologize. He was completely out of line and had likely scared Lucas senseless. There was only one problem with that. Once the haze of the killing urge had subsided, Gabriel was vividly aware of yet another urge—the one that flooded directly to his cock.

Unable to stop himself, he dropped his head and kissed Lucas hard. He was gratified beyond measure when Lucas, rather than trying to get away as he expected, returned the kiss in kind, groaned deep in his throat, and arched up to meet Gabriel's advances with demands of his own.

It was like drowning in sweet, hot lava. Gabriel's hips jerked forward involuntarily and thrust his cock into direct contact with the rough denim of Lucas's jeans. Even with multiple layers of clothing between them, the friction was delicious. Gabriel would have liked nothing better than to divest them both of all the restrictive garments between them and pound Lucas into the wall.

It was tempting—God, so tempting—but he knew he couldn't. It would be unfair to take advantage of him. It was undoubtedly one of the hardest things he had ever done, but Gabriel made himself break away and take several steps back.

Lucas blinked in confusion and wiped the back of his hand over red, swollen lips. "Where're you going?" he slurred, still punch-drunk and breathing hard.

"I'm sorry," Gabriel said. "I was out of line. I should have never done that."

"Why not?" Lucas asked. "I enjoyed that." He trailed his eyes slowly down Gabriel's body and zeroed in on the obvious erection straining at the front of Gabriel's pants. "And from the looks of things, so did you."

"I did," Gabriel conceded. In truth "enjoy" was far too pale a word for what he felt and was still feeling. He could barely contain himself. Sheer unadulterated need danced through his veins like a blazing fire. "But that's of little consequence right now. We can't do this."

"And just why the hell not?" Lucas demanded. "We're both willing, consenting adults. Who's going to stop us?" He pushed himself up off the wall and crossed the space between them with rapid, determined strides.

It was excruciating, but Gabriel made himself turn away before Lucas could land the kiss he could see coming. Lucas's expression turned confused and more than a little hurt.

Gabriel sighed. "If only it were that simple…."

"It is that simple," Lucas insisted, and he closed the gap between them once again. He reached out and touched Gabriel's face, and Gabriel very nearly crumpled. His legs trembled beneath him. He wouldn't have believed it possible, but his desire grew even stronger. The fierce need grew painful, almost blindingly so. In fact the need was so strong it had completely obliterated the throb of the killing desire that had been dominant only moments before.

That was an utter shock. It had never happened before—not for as long as he could remember. It wasn't just sex either. While he was always discreet, he had hardly been a monk. There were many men, from casual encounters to very hot love affairs. None of them ever made him feel like Lucas did. Who was this boy—this man—and what was he doing to him?

Lucas took advantage of his silence to trail kisses up his jaw. Gabriel's head dropped back of its own accord, and a groan escaped him. With a strength Gabriel would have never believed he possessed, Lucas guided them both in the direction of the nearest horizontal surface—which happened to be the sectional in the living room. Gabriel's logical mind rapidly retreated. He made one last feeble effort to protest, but then Lucas sank his teeth into his earlobe and all words fled. The backs of his legs hit the edge of the sofa, and he gratefully collapsed on the cushions. Lucas pressed him back, crawled on top of him, and thrust impatiently. Gabriel drew in a sharp breath and arched up to meet him.

"Too many clothes," Lucas growled. He backed away long enough to strip out of his own clothes, roughly and impatiently. Then he came back to attack Gabriel's. Gabriel had stripped off his shirt and was fumbling blindly with the fasteners on his pants. Lucas slapped his hand away and unbuttoned them himself. To Gabriel's surprise, Lucas didn't bother with pulling them down any farther. He just released his rock-hard cock and crawled back on top of him so their erections were pressed together.

The sudden sensations stole his breath—silk covering molten steel, at once soft and hot and hard. Then Lucas wrapped one strong, long-fingered hand around both of them and all sense of coherent thought fled. It disappeared in the shower of sparks that arched up his spine. There was nothing but sensation as Lucas stroked roughly up and down their joined members. Gabriel bucked upward, reduced to moans and incoherent murmurings that made no sense, even to his own ears. Holy hell….

Then, without warning, Lucas dipped down and laved his nipples like a cat bathing a kitten—rough and wet but with the same exquisite care and gentleness—and that was all it took. Gabriel exploded in a white-hot wave. He was vaguely aware Lucas was still moving his hand, milking him right through his orgasm. The harsh, fast movement edged on exquisite pain, but Gabriel had neither the voice nor the heart to stop him. He was still riding on the torturous edge of pleasure and pain when Lucas stopped, captured in the throes of his own release.

Lucas collapsed on top of him and they lay that way for quite some time, drifting between sleep and the haze of afterglow. For his part Gabriel was stunned. In most of his past encounters, he was the dominant one. There were very few people he had ever allowed to take control the way Lucas just had. One minute he was trying to explain why it was an extremely bad idea, and the next Lucas completely took over. He still wasn't entirely sure how that happened. He wouldn't have believed there was anyone who could control him that thoroughly, much less some skinny college kid. He should've been outraged, incensed that he could be dominated in such a manner, and he was sure, in the cold light of day, he probably would be. But he couldn't get past the fact that, despite his surprise, he enjoyed it thoroughly.

Lucas slowly pushed himself up and grimaced at the mess between them.

"You okay?" Gabriel asked. In the heat of the moment, he was sure Lucas enjoyed it every bit as much as he had. But he was struck by uncharacteristic insecurity. After all, he had just lain there like a boneless lump. He hadn't given a moment's thought to Lucas's pleasure. That knowledge sank like a boulder in his chest. Even in casual encounters, he was usually more considerate.

Before he could explain any of that, Lucas caught his eye with an absolutely blank expression. "No, I'm not okay."

Gabriel's heart rate shot up. How could he make it right?

Abruptly Lucas's blank expression dissolved into a grin. "I'm much better than okay. That was amazing."

Gabriel sat up and shoved Lucas off his lap. "Ass."

Lucas stumbled backward, laughing. "Come on, man. You had to know that was amazing."

"I knew I enjoyed it," Gabriel said. "But that doesn't necessarily mean you did. Especially since I left you doing all the work."

Lucas shrugged and shook back his messier-than-usual hair. "I'm not complaining. Besides, that just means it's your turn next time. I need a shower. Want to join me?"

"Tempting though the offer is, I'd better not," Gabriel said. "We'll just end up getting messy again."

"Yeah. But if we're in the shower, it's a lot easier to clean up," Lucas countered.

Gabriel laughed. "You're incorrigible. Get going, brat."

Lucas cast him an extremely cheeky grin and disappeared in the direction of the guest room. Gabriel retreated to his own bedroom and bathroom and gathered their soiled and discarded clothes to deposit in the laundry on his way. He barely noticed he was whistling the entire time.

CHAPTER SIXTEEN

UNFORTUNATELY MORNING inevitably came, and with it all the things he had successfully pushed out of his mind the night before. What the hell had he been thinking? No. Forget that. That much was obvious. He hadn't been thinking. Clearly any rational part of his mind fled the moment his cock took over. Gabriel flopped over onto his back, tangling his already mussed bed linens even more, and groaned. What was he supposed to do?

What he wanted was to do it again. Whatever the implications, the sex was fantastic, possibly the best he ever had. Who knew the kid would be such a demanding lover? More than that, who knew Gabriel would like that? In the majority of his sexual encounters, Gabriel was always the aggressor. It'd been an outlet for the dark energy that always pulsed beneath his skin—the urgent, driving need to kill. Though sex wasn't killing—at least he never used sex as a way to eliminate a target, though he knew others did—it was its own kind of violence and always had, in its own way, temporarily satiated the need. And the craving was gone. At least it was as close to gone as it ever got, reduced to little more than a tiny tickle far back in his consciousness. Not that it had been particularly strong lately... and come to think of it, that in itself was unusual. Gabriel realized he had barely felt the need at all in the time since Lucas began staying with him. And that made absolutely no sense at all. Why should having the kid around affect a need he had carried all his adult life?

Gabriel rolled out of bed, stood up, and pushed the thought away. That was a puzzle for another time. He had to figure out what to do about last night. He pulled out what he thought of as his at-home clothes—a polo and jeans—and headed for the shower. He stripped off and stepped into the shower. There was only one answer. No matter how much he might have enjoyed the sex, it couldn't happen again. It was far too dangerous. The kid had put him up on a pedestal as some kind of hero, but he knew how far from the truth that really was. Eventually Lucas would figure it out too, and that pedestal would come crashing down. When it did they were both likely to end up cut and bleeding from the rubble.

He'd developed a thick skin years earlier, forged by a lifetime of being forced to break relationships and leave people behind, often at a moment's notice. Lucas wasn't like that. He was the loyal type, the "settling down and sinking roots" type. Who else would move heaven and earth to look for a roommate he wasn't even having sex with? For family, probably. For a lover, sure. Gabriel had seen a few possessive types who might do that, but for a roommate? No way. They were just going to come and go anyway. Only an idealist would bother, and Lucas most certainly was one.

That's why they couldn't do that again. No matter how much Gabriel enjoyed it. He couldn't crush the kid's idealism like that.

With that fixed firmly in his mind, Gabriel finished up, dressed, and went in search of Lucas. He found him slumped drowsily at the table, rumpled as though he had just rolled out of bed, nursing a cup of coffee and poking a spoon desultorily around in a bowl of cereal.

"Morning," Gabriel said evenly and made himself a cup of coffee.

Lucas murmured something unintelligible in reply. It might have been "good morning," but it also might just as easily have been "go fuck yourself." Gabriel decided to assume it was the former. He gave up attempts at conversation, since Lucas clearly wasn't a morning person, and instead set about toasting himself a bagel. He watched Lucas covertly from the corner of his eye.

It was cute, really, and Gabriel didn't find much of anything cute. Even so, that was really the perfect word to describe a sleep-rumpled, not-yet-fully-awake Lucas. His oversized T-shirt had slipped off one shoulder and his hair was sticking up in all directions. He glared at his cereal bowl as though he couldn't decide whether to eat it or dump out the contents and turn it over to use as a pillow. He looked like nothing so much as a grumpy toddler, except he was also, bizarrely, sexy as hell. Gabriel had to stop thinking of Lucas as sexy. Still he couldn't help but wonder why he hadn't noticed how cute Lucas looked when he woke up.

But they rarely ran on the same schedule. While Gabriel taught every day, Lucas's varied from day to day, and though he had stopped his nighttime volunteering, Lucas still normally declined to get out of bed until he absolutely had to. Gabriel, on the other hand, habitually tried to make it in to campus early. Years of planning for unexpected contingencies had driven that habit deep.

"I take it you're not a morning person," he said lightly as he slid into the chair opposite Lucas and put his bagel and coffee on the table.

Lucas raised an eyebrow. "Ya think?"

Gabriel ignored the sarcasm. "I wasn't either at your age, but training drilled it into me quick enough. At this point I think I could sleep pretty much anywhere and anytime and still wake instantaneously." He said it casually, but he knew it was absolutely true. He could also go for several days without sleep, if necessary, but that wasn't a habit he wanted to encourage in Lucas. He ran on too little sleep as it was.

"We need to talk about last night," Gabriel continued, determined to get the unpleasantness over with so he could go on about his day without distraction.

Lucas shook his head. "Not now. Later. Too early."

Gabriel sighed. "We have to talk about this, kid. Putting it off isn't going to help things."

"Too early." Lucas scowled. "Talk later."

Gabriel could practically see him digging in his heels. Obviously any further attempts at conversation would be useless. He wouldn't put it past the kid to just sit there like a rock and refuse to answer. "Fine. We'll table this conversation until this evening. But we are going to talk about this."

"Yeah, yeah," Lucas said. He finally gave up poking at his cereal and took the bowl to the sink. He emptied the contents but left the bowl sitting there. Gabriel bit back the urge to remind him to rinse it and put it in the dishwasher, but the tiny irritation only added to the frustration he already felt.

Gabriel turned on his heel and strode abruptly into the living room, where he took out a jacket from the coat closet and shouldered into it.

"You're going out?" Lucas asked.

Gabriel's reply was a short, sharp nod.

Lucas frowned. "Where?"

"To the gun range." He had to do something with his frustration before he gave in to temptation and strangled Lucas, or worse yet, dragged him into the bedroom and fucked him into the mattress. "Lock the door as soon as I leave and leave it locked. Don't go out without letting me know. In fact I prefer you not go out at all. It's not safe for you to be out alone. But if you absolutely have to, let me know. Not sure how long I'll be, but if you need me for any reason—any reason at all—do not hesitate to call. Understood?"

Lucas nodded, wide-eyed and silent.

Instinct made Gabriel move without thought. He slipped two fingers under Lucas's chin and tipped his head up so they were eye to eye. "I need the words, kid. Do you understand?"

"Yeah," Lucas said quietly. "I understand." Satisfied, Gabriel turned and disappeared out the door before he could think to say anything more.

IT WAS time, Gabriel decided later that evening. The trip to the gun range had helped and let him release a lot of his frustration, but he had let it go on long enough. It was time to bite the bullet and talk to the kid—he broke off with an internal wince—no, not the kid, Lucas. His name was Lucas. That's how Gabriel had to think about him. Calling him the kid, even in his head, in the context of what they had done the night before, was just wrong. So very wrong.

He paused in the doorway and cleared his throat to get Lucas's attention. "We still need to talk about last night."

Lucas held up a hand. "Stop."

"No, not this time," Gabriel said. "I let you put it off this morning, but I told you then that we would talk about it tonight, and we are going to."

Lucas unfolded his legs and stood up from the couch. "Oh, I have no problem talking, but don't even bother giving me the whole 'that never should've happened' speech because I damn well wanted it to happen, and so did you. I don't regret it, and you're not going to convince me it was wrong, so don't bother trying. I know you think of me as a kid, but I'm not, and I haven't been in a long time. I'm not the blushing, innocent virgin you like to think of me as, and in case it escaped your notice, I was the one who initiated things last night. You didn't do anything to me. If anything, I did it to you. I came on to you."

"That doesn't matter," Gabriel insisted. "I'm older and should've known better. You may not chronologically be a child, but in terms of life experience, I'm the one with far more, and I shouldn't have let it go that far."

"Why not?" Lucas shot back. "I wanted it. You wanted it. We're both well above the age of consent. Why the hell shouldn't we have done what we wanted?"

"You don't know what you want," Gabriel said. "How could you possibly? You're right in the middle of what is probably the most traumatic situation of your life. Starting something with you now is nothing more than taking advantage of that. I shouldn't do that, and frankly, you shouldn't let me."

Suddenly Lucas closed the space between them and was in his face. He shoved Gabriel hard enough to make him take a step back. Though it probably wouldn't have budged him if Lucas hadn't caught him off guard, Gabriel was still shocked. But Lucas apparently was just getting started. "Don't you dare presume to tell me how to feel. Yes, I'm younger than you, but make no mistake. I know exactly what I'm doing. Get over yourself. I'm not some flighty little club bunny, and I don't appreciate being treated as though I were. I won't break, and I don't need protecting. So just get the hell over it."

"That's where you're wrong," Gabriel told him furiously, with his hands clenched at his sides. "You do need protecting, and the very fact that you think you don't tells me you're far more innocent than you think. This is a dangerous game we're playing. It could get either or both of us killed. It may have gotten Eric killed already. We can't afford to do anything—anything at all—that could be a distraction. We can't do this. Not now.

"I refuse to see you dead because we were too busy following our dicks to pay attention. And if you think it won't happen, you're wrong. It's taken down people with a hell of a lot more skill and training than an arrogant college kid." He expected Lucas to flee in the face of his anger, or at the very least to take a step back—not to stand his ground. Gabriel had seen trained agents back away from him in the middle of an outburst. It had certainly turned away more than one lover.

It didn't even budge Lucas.

"So let me get this straight. You think denying ourselves is somehow going to be better," Lucas countered. "Won't denying the attraction be even more of a distraction? And don't bother denying that there is an attraction, because we both know there is."

"Yes, there is an attraction," Gabriel admitted reluctantly. "But it doesn't mean anything. This happens in high-stress situations with people in tight quarters. It's just a symptom of the situation. That's all. A way for the body to release stress. Nothing more. So don't go getting stars in your eyes, kid." He needed to remember that himself. Maybe they could have occasional sex. Lucas was right about that. Trying not to do anything was likely to be just as much of a distraction. It certainly had been thus far. And he had severely underestimated how difficult it would be to have Lucas in the house. It would be a lot easier to be able to relieve the itch than to constantly try to deny it. But they both had to remember it was just sex, nothing more. No strings and no getting attached.

"I'm not the one making a big deal out of it," Lucas pointed out. "I'm not the one who's been insisting all day that we talk about it. You were the one insisting we had to talk. Christ, for a while there, I thought you were going to demand to know the status of our relationship and where this was going, like some clingy schoolboy."

Gabriel stared at him, utterly baffled. "I did no such thing. I was only trying to make sure you were okay. No matter what you say, you *are* very young, and it's not like you would be the first person to make an impulsive decision and end up regretting it."

"I don't regret it," Lucas informed him decisively. "In fact I really enjoyed it and would like to do it again. The sooner the better. Maybe we could even make it to the bed this time."

"Don't get me wrong. It's a very tempting thought," Gabriel said. "But I meant what I said about being careful. We need to take this slow and not get in over our heads."

In reply Lucas stepped even closer and rubbed down the length of Gabriel's body like a cat. "I can handle slow." He stretched upward and took Gabriel's lips in a gentle kiss. "I can keep it up for hours," he said softly, "kissing every inch of your body." He caught Gabriel's head and drew him down to plant a kiss on his temple. "Should I start at the top—" He slid a hand between them and cupped Gabriel with just enough force to be demanding. "—or at the bottom?"

It was like being slowly dipped in molten lava. Heat zipped over Gabriel's body like an electric current dancing over his nerves. Any noble intentions fled as he went instantly rock-hard. But two could play that game. He shifted his legs slightly and pivoted to bring Lucas around with him. Then he drew Lucas's arms above his head and pressed him into the wall, using his body weight to keep him there.

"Not this time. This time it's my turn." Before Lucas could draw breath to respond, Gabriel bent and devoured his mouth, and their tongues battled for dominance. When they broke apart, they both gasped for breath, hearts racing. "This time we're not making out on the couch like a couple of teenagers," Gabriel decreed. "Bed. Now."

Lucas snatched one more quick kiss and squirmed away, making sure he touched as much of Gabriel's body as possible while he did it. Gabriel got the hint and released him. "Tease," he growled.

Lucas grinned back over his shoulder. "Who, me? Never. My bed or yours?"

"Mine," Gabriel said and swatted Lucas's ass. "Move, brat."

Lucas didn't need to be told twice. He scampered across the room and into Gabriel's bedroom like a kid running for the playground. It was all Gabriel could do not to laugh. Gabriel followed him into the bedroom and found him standing at the end of the bed, looking hesitant. The change was so abrupt Gabriel blinked, not quite certain what to make of it. "What's the holdup?" he asked.

Lucas shrugged. "You're running the show this time. Remember?"

A smile spread slowly across Gabriel's face. That he was, and he knew exactly what he wanted to do. Stepping over to Lucas, he pulled his T-shirt from the waist of his pants and tugged it gently over his head. As he tossed the shirt away, Gabriel dipped his head and kissed Lucas again, hard. Then he worked his way slowly from Lucas's jaw down to his chest and paused in the space between Lucas's nipples to circle each of them with his tongue. Lucas groaned and thrust helplessly against Gabriel.

"Easy there," Gabriel said, and he chuckled.

Lucas huffed. "Come on, man, please."

"Please what?" Gabriel asked in a tone of perfect innocence. He left off teasing Lucas's nipples and resumed his path down to his navel.

"You know what, jackass," Lucas replied through gritted teeth.

"No, I don't believe I do," Gabriel said. He retraced his path and nipped and sucked his way back up Lucas's body.

"The... hell... you... don't," Lucas gasped. Abruptly it seemed to occur to him that his hands were no longer restrained. He ran them down Gabriel's back and then gripped his buttocks hard and slammed their bodies together.

"Oh, that," Gabriel said mildly. He stopped his ministrations long enough to slide a hand between their bodies and thumb open the fasteners on Lucas's pants. When he stepped back, he admired the rather impressive erection tenting the front of Lucas's jeans. Impatient, Lucas let go and hooked his thumbs in the waistband of his jeans, but before he could pull them down, Gabriel slapped his hands away and jerked them down himself. He skinned both jeans and underwear from waist to ankles in one swift tug.

Lucas let out an involuntary moan as the rough denim scraped over his ultrasensitive skin. Gabriel knelt, tapped Lucas's legs, and gestured for him to step out. He tossed the clothes to the side and continued the journey as he kissed and nipped his way down the rest of Lucas's body and paid special attention to the inside of his thighs and all the tender regions between them. Like a worshiping penitent, he pressed a kiss to the tip of Lucas's swollen cock and tasted the bitter, salty fluid leaking there. He ran a gentle hand up the length of it and back down again.

That was when he noticed Lucas's knees were trembling as though they might collapse underneath him at any moment. Gabriel rose to his feet and made short work of his own clothes.

"Pitch or catch?" he asked lightly. Given the choice, Gabriel generally preferred to top, but he didn't have a problem bottoming either if the situation called for it. He would gladly stand on his head if that was what Lucas preferred.

"Need you in me." Lucas's answer was soft and strained, as though even getting the words out took a supreme effort.

"Perfect." He leaned over and kissed Lucas again. Then he went to the table beside his bed to retrieve condoms and lube. "I want you on your back. I want to see your face."

By the time Gabriel was ready, Lucas had scrambled onto the bed and into position, eager and willing. Gabriel wasn't sure he'd ever seen anything more beautiful in his life. He climbed carefully onto the bed beside Lucas, coated both his hand and Lucas's hole liberally with lube, and eased a finger inside. Even that small intrusion made Lucas nearly arch off the bed. He whined and keened and wordlessly begged for more.

Gabriel fought the temptation to rush. As eager as they both were, the last thing he ever wanted to do was hurt Lucas. Finally, when Lucas had been reduced to babbling incoherently, Gabriel pulled Lucas's legs up over his shoulders and carefully pushed in.

Lucas thrust up off the bed. "Yes. Now more. Faster."

Gabriel followed his prompts and subtly adjusted until he found Lucas's sweet spot and hit it consistently. Then and only then did he give in to the driving need to pound into him, harder and faster, until there was nothing but their unintelligible noises and the sound of flesh on flesh.

"Gonna—" Lucas choked out, but the words were cut off as his orgasm exploded through him and tore the breath from his lungs in a silent scream.

Gabriel rode him through it until the spasms rolling through his body and milking Gabriel's cock spurred him to his own completion. "Lucian," he roared as his arms gave way and he collapsed on top of Lucas.

It was a long time before either of them spoke or moved again. Eventually Gabriel stirred enough to roll off Lucas, tie off the used condom, and toss it in the direction of the wastebasket. He had no idea whether it made it or not. He knew he should probably check, but he couldn't find the energy to care.

"What was that all about?" Lucas asked blurrily, his eyes still closed.

"I should think that was obvious," Gabriel deadpanned.

"Not that. You called me Lucian," Lucas told him.

Gabriel's eyes went wide. He rolled over and propped himself up on an elbow to look at Lucas. "No, I didn't. Maybe you just misunderstood me."

"It was kind of hard to misunderstand. You were screaming at the top of your lungs," Lucas said pointedly. "Besides, I know my own name, and it isn't Lucian."

"Actually it is, sort of," Gabriel replied. "Lucas is the modern equivalent of the same base name. If you had been born in the Middle Ages or before, your name could have actually been Lucian. I guess I must have been unconsciously channeling my inner 'knight of the realm' persona or something."

"Sure that's all you were channeling?" Lucas asked. "No ghosts of old lovers that I should know about?"

"Not at all. I promise," Gabriel assured him. He wasn't the kind to scream out old lovers' names. Most of them hadn't even been around long enough for him to remember their names. "It must've just been some kind of weird Freudian slip or something."

It had to have been. He'd never even known anyone named Lucian. It was just a random thing, caught up in the throes of passion. Who could be held responsible for what they said during sex? Half of it didn't make sense at all. So why did he feel like he was missing something far more important?

THERE WAS something very disconcerting about having the best sex of your life, only to have your partner call you by the wrong name, and try as Lucas might to brush it off, it still bugged him. It wasn't that he thought Gabriel was lying. Not exactly. His explanation did make some sort of sense. Kind of, anyway. Not that any of it really made sense.

Still, he had no business getting worked up about it. It wasn't as though they were in a relationship. Gabriel had made that very clear, and Lucas had agreed wholeheartedly. Just a little while earlier, he was the one who was harassing Gabriel about wanting to talk through things, and now he was freaking out because Gabriel called him Lucian instead of Lucas. At least the names were close, and it could plausibly be a mistake. It wasn't as though Gabriel had called him something totally wrong, like Eddie. That would've been harder to believe as a mistake. It could've been far worse. He shouldn't be worrying about a simple little slip.

That decided, he pushed himself up on his arms and turned to Gabriel. "I'm going to get cleaned up. Want to join me?"

"We'll just get messy again," Gabriel pointed out.

Lucas grinned. "I'm not going to let you use that excuse forever. Besides, we'll have a lot of fun doing it. Coming?"

He didn't wait for an answer. Instead he stood up, stretched slowly, and deliberately turned his back to Gabriel. He heard Gabriel give a quiet moan, and he smiled but didn't comment. He sauntered confidently into the connecting bathroom and turned on the water. Gabriel joined him before the water got hot. Fighting back a laugh, Lucas caught Gabriel's lips and kissed him. Then he ducked under the water.

Lucas felt as much as heard Gabriel step in behind him, but even knowing he was there, he still squeaked when Gabriel grabbed his hips and jerked him back so his ass fitted snugly against Gabriel's body. "Like that, is it?" Lucas teased. "And here I thought we just did that."

"So," Gabriel replied. "Sometimes once is just not enough. You know, it's like potato chips. You can't eat just one."

Lucas couldn't hold back the laugh. "Did you seriously just compare having sex and eating potato chips?"

"Okay. So maybe that wasn't the best analogy I could've made," Gabriel conceded. "But you're still equally irresistible."

"Nice save, professor," Lucas shot back and giggled.

"None of that," Gabriel admonished. "I'm naked in the shower with your ass against my cock. I don't want the professor anywhere around. Here I'm just Gabriel."

The corners of Lucas's lips quirked up. "Aw, man. There goes that sexy teacher/naughty student fantasy…."

"I'll show you fantasy," Gabriel growled and nipped the back of Lucas's neck.

"You will, will you?" The teasing fell flat when Lucas's voice suddenly went up sharply as Gabriel reached around him and took firm hold of his rapidly hardening erection.

"That answer your question?" Gabriel said mildly.

Not trusting his voice, Lucas nodded. Though he liked sex as much as the next guy, Lucas had never considered himself to have a particularly rampant sex drive. He'd always been able to go without for long periods of time and not experience the misery some guys did. He could make friends with his right hand on a regular basis and be perfectly happy. Okay, maybe not perfectly happy—the real thing was always better—but at least reasonably content.

It was different with Gabriel. With him Lucas felt a constant craving, one he couldn't get enough of. It was bad enough when Gabriel was just a fantasy, but once he really knew what it was like, it was even worse. Even having just had mind-blowing sex, he still craved it. For the first time, Lucas thought he might understand what an addict felt like. He was addicted to Gabriel, how he felt, how he tasted, and—all the heavens above—the things he did to him.

As if on cue, Gabriel spun him around so they were face-to-face. He moved Lucas as effortlessly as if he were a child. That in itself was its own sweet torture—knowing Gabriel could manhandle him as he pleased, without breaking a sweat. It didn't frighten Lucas as it might have some.

He had absolutely no fear that Gabriel might hurt him. For all Gabriel's gruffness and all his shadowy, dark, and mysterious past, he was incredibly gentle. As though to prove the point, Gabriel slowly ran his hands over Lucas's shoulders and dropped a gentle kiss on his lips. Lucas smiled. The combination of manhandling and gentleness was delicious. He couldn't stop his soft moan in response. Gabriel thrust up against him, matching their groins together. Then he wrapped one large hand around them and stroked excruciatingly slowly.

At first the tender movement was ecstasy, but it didn't take long before ecstasy became a kind of torture, exquisite torture, but torture nonetheless. "Faster," he whined as he squirmed.

Gabriel took a step closer, splayed his hand against the tile, and effectively penned Lucas in. "Settle down. You're just going to have to be patient."

"Patience is overrated," he said through gritted teeth.

Gabriel laughed. "You'll live." Throughout it all he never stopped moving his hand, but he hadn't sped up any either.

Lucas dropped his head back against the tile and whined helplessly. Gabriel laughed again but continued to ignore him. Finally Lucas couldn't help but squirm, and his hips thrust uncontrollably. He had to do something, anything, to get some relief, so he gripped Gabriel's broad, solid shoulders and clambered for purchase.

All at once his fingers brushed over a slightly raised patch of skin on the back of Gabriel's left shoulder. Instinctively he traced the shape of it. It was two lines—one horizontal, the other vertical—but the end of the vertical line was rough, ragged. It wasn't like the smooth planned lines of a tattoo. It was more like a scar with its puckered lines long healed, except for that distinctive shape. What was it? A cross. The shape matched, but he doubted it. He'd had no indication Gabriel was a particularly religious man. It wouldn't be a military tattoo. He had never heard Gabriel mention any type of military training, though he was sure the CIA had given him some sort of equivalent. And he couldn't imagine the CIA encouraging any kind of identifying marks.

Before Lucas could ask, Gabriel finally sped up his steady strokes. His breath caught, and his movements became jerky and less controlled. Lucas put his hand over Gabriel's and encouraged him along, pushing them both faster and faster toward the finish. When that finish came, it was a joint explosion of pleasure, splattering walls, floors, and bodies. By the time they got around to actually cleaning up, the water had long since gone cold.

When Lucas thought of it again, they were out of the shower and drying off. "What's that place in your shoulder?" he blurted.

Gabriel, who was standing at the sink, caught his eye in the mirror with a puzzled look. "What place? Have you been leaving marks on me, you little hellcat?"

Lucas smirked. "It wasn't me, but I'll be glad to do that next time. If you're going to accuse me of it, there might as well be a reason for it." He watched Gabriel's eyes darken in the mirror as he stepped up to touch the skin on the back of Gabriel's shoulder. Hmm… it seemed like Gabriel liked that idea. He would have to remember that.

Though he was pleasantly sated, Lucas's fingers still tingled at the feel of Gabriel's skin. Did the wanting ever stop? He could see the mark clearly—a small, dark area, puckered like a scar, but it wasn't a scar. Neither was it a tattoo. It wasn't a cross either. Instead, it looked oddly like a sword.

"Oh that," Gabriel said. "That's a birthmark. I've always had it. I forget it's there most of the time." He twitched his shoulders lightly, not as though he were trying to shake Lucas off, but reflexively, like a habitual movement he wasn't quite aware of.

Lucas planted a soft kiss between Gabriel's shoulders. "Is it just me, or is it shaped like a sword?"

"You're not the first to make that observation," Gabriel told him. "But I've never been quite sure about exactly what it looks like. I can see what you mean about it resembling a sword, but it's not pointed. A sword without a point is rather useless, isn't it?"

"Maybe it's broken?" Lucas suggested.

"What's the difference? Either way it's not much use."

Lucas shook his head. "It's not useless at all. If anything, it's been worn down from constant use and broken from the strain. That's not being useless. That's rather selfless, I think. Trying so hard to keep going that it ended up broken in the process. Reminds me a lot of some of the kids I work with, actually."

Gabriel laughed, but it was soft and more wistful than humorous.

"What's so funny?"

"You," he said. He gave Lucas a wry look in the mirror as he finished his shave, rinsed his razor, and put it away. "It's a birthmark, a trick of birth or genetics, not an abstract painting. It doesn't have a meaning. It's just there."

Lucas huffed and smacked Gabriel's shoulder. "You just have no imagination."

"You have no idea, kid. My imagination has gotten more of a workout since I met you than it has in years."

"Bet that hasn't been the only thing getting a workout." Lucas smirked. He trailed his eyes down Gabriel's body and paused to look pointedly at his hands and his cock.

Gabriel shot him an unrepentant grin. "Bet I'm not the only one."

"You'd be right about that," Lucas admitted.

"Care to share?"

"I'd love to," Lucas told him. "But it would probably just end up with us needing another shower, and I'm starving. I need food before we attempt round three."

"If you insist," Gabriel teased. "I suppose you better go get dressed, then."

"You know, clothes aren't necessarily mandatory for eating," Lucas said. "I could probably even manage cooking without getting dressed, as long as I had an apron to cover the important bits."

"As much as I might love to see that someday, I was thinking more about going out," Gabriel replied. "You've been stuck inside all day while I was at the range. I thought you might enjoy getting out for a bit."

Lucas's expression brightened. "What happened to needing to stay inside for my own safety and not leaving the house unless I had to for work or school?"

"I still don't want you going out alone," Gabriel said. "But you're with me. I can handle keeping us both safe. We're still going to have to be very careful, but I think we can handle a couple hours for dinner. That is if you're willing to concede to get dressed."

"If I'm willing…," Lucas sputtered.

What kind of a dumb question was that? He hadn't been anywhere but work and school and the house in days. Ever since Gabriel found out about the gang connection, he watched him like a hawk. Lucas couldn't even hang out in the co-op between classes anymore. Gabriel insisted he come to his office between classes. Lucas didn't really mind since it meant they generally had lunch together, which was far more enjoyable, anyway. But he wasn't about to turn down an opportunity to actually go out. Hell, he couldn't remember the last time he'd gone out even before the whole mess started, not to mention the last time he'd actually gone out with someone he wanted to be with and whose company he enjoyed.

"Give me ten minutes," he told Gabriel as he strode out the door.

He heard Gabriel chuckle behind him.

GABRIEL BREATHED a sigh of relief when the bedroom door closed behind Lucas. Though he knew Lucas had no way of knowing it, their conversation, easy as it seemed, had touched on some pretty sensitive things—things he never talked about, and he meant never. He had never even mentioned his birthmark to another lover. It wasn't as though they had ever had cause to question it in their discreet and often hurried encounters.

He hadn't even told the CIA doctors the whole truth about his birthmark. They knew he had it, of course. It had been documented along with his other scars and anything else that might be considered an identifying mark, but he simply said it was a birthmark, and it wasn't questioned. Certainly no one had ever touched it beyond the briefest cursory clinical examination with gloved hands.

Until Lucas. From that first moment when their hands brushed as he handed over Lucas's coffee, Gabriel never failed to be intensely aware of Lucas's touch. But when Lucas's bare fingertips brushed oh so gently over the skin of his birthmark, his heart made a valiant effort to climb out of his throat. Could Lucas feel it too? Gabriel hoped with everything in his being that he couldn't.

He hadn't been truthful with Lucas about the birthmark. The fact was he was almost never unaware of it. It pulsed nearly constantly. In fact Gabriel was relatively sure the birthmark was the source of the need for violence and killing that hummed continually in his blood. He had noticed some time earlier that the stronger the need became, the more his birthmark pulsed, and vice versa. Though he had no idea how or why, the two were mysteriously connected. Not that he had ever done much research on the subject. In his experience, admitting you had homicidal tendencies ended only one way—with you locked up. Whether it was in a prison or psych facility didn't make all that much difference. At the end of the day, it still ended with him in a cage, and that wasn't something he was about to let happen. He'd swallow one of his own poisons first.

Since Lucas hadn't said anything, Gabriel supposed it was safe to assume he wasn't adversely affected. Thank fuck. Hell only knew what he would have done if his do-gooder social worker suddenly started exhibiting violent tendencies. He was a spook. Everybody knew they were crazy in the first place. Lucas would have been another story entirely.

A glimpse at the clock beside the bed broke that train of thought and sent him rushing to his closet. If he didn't get moving, Lucas would be dressed and waiting for him, and that wouldn't do. Gabriel prided himself on never being late, at least not unless it was an intentional part of an undercover plan.

He hadn't planned on going anywhere that required dressing up, but he didn't want to look like most of those ridiculous college kids either. He didn't know how some of them were ever going to make it when a professional dress code was called for. A lot of them looked like they just rolled out of bed. Then again he used to think the same of Lucas when he only ever saw him on campus. Since he had been living with him, Gabriel had learned that impression wasn't entirely accurate.

Lucas knew perfectly well how to dress professionally on the days when he was going to work. It was only on his campus days that he looked like a bum, and having seen the rest of the campus population, Gabriel had begun to wonder if it wasn't intentional. Even as young as he was, Lucas was some years older than most of the students. It was entirely possible Lucas was trying to camouflage that by dressing the way he did, to blend and make himself less conspicuous. Gabriel couldn't complain about it. He not only completely approved, he appreciated the skill it took to do that, having spent a good chunk of his life doing it himself.

He settled on a deep red button-down and dark-wash jeans. He was so intent on not making Lucas wait for him that it was only after he had quickly dressed, finished his grooming, and was headed down the hall to check on Lucas that the reality of what he had been thinking earlier suddenly dawned on him—"*his* do-gooder social worker."

Since when had Lucas become his anything?

CHAPTER SEVENTEEN

LUCAS DECLARED he didn't care where they went for dinner, so Gabriel took him to one of his favorites, a small, local, hole-in-the-wall Italian place run by a family who had been in the business for generations. As far as Gabriel could work out, the third generation currently ran the place and the fourth generation worked as servers and busboys. It was one of the few restaurants in town that was, by some miracle, not generally overrun with college students. That was his primary reason for choosing it.

With Lucas he no longer wanted to be Professor Ingram. His professional persona might be necessary to his career, but it wasn't who he wanted to be with the man who shared his bed, even if said man was a student. He also didn't particularly want to set tongues wagging on campus. Lucas might claim to be perfectly okay with their age difference, but it was likely to be a horse of a different color if that age difference turned into a campus scandal. The politics of academia might be nothing compared to the games he played in international politics, but he'd seen them get ugly before, and Lucas didn't have his experience to know how to handle them. What's more, he didn't want Lucas to gain that experience. He wanted to shield Lucas from that and from the cynicism it would likely engender.

Not that they were doing anything wrong or even against policy. Lucas was right about that. He was well above the age of consent, and he wasn't Gabriel's student. Even if he had been Gabriel's student, there were ways to work around that by having someone else grade his assignments. Gabriel knew more than one couple who did just that. But he also knew it didn't necessarily have to be wrong to be a scandal. Gossip spread like wildfire, and perception was sometimes more important than reality.

All of the staff greeted him with smiles when he came in the door of the restaurant. "Gabriel," the owner, Giovanni, a man in his forties, called out. "Long time no see."

Gabriel waved as he guided Lucas through the maze of tables covered in checkered cloths to his preferred seat in the back corner. By habit he took the chair facing the door that gave him a clear view of the entrance over Lucas's shoulder.

"They seem to know you well here," Lucas commented as he took his seat.

"I've been coming here for years. Giovanni knows all the regulars. This place is his baby."

"I never even knew it was here," Lucas told him.

"And that's why I'm a regular," Gabriel replied. "It's one of the few places in town that's not overrun by college students. I don't have to be Professor Ingram."

"But you are Professor Ingram," Lucas said, giving him a quizzical look.

"Not all the time, or at least I hope not. God knows Professor Ingram had no business doing what I've been doing with you."

"What?" Lucas asked. "You think just because you're a professor you're not allowed to have a sex life? Because I hate to tell you that there are any number of your colleagues who don't share that opinion."

Gabriel raised an eyebrow. "Are you speaking from experience?"

Lucas went red from his chin to the roots of his hair. "No. But it's not exactly privileged information on campus either."

"Is that so?"

Lucas was saved from responding when Giovanni's oldest son, Tony, appeared at their table. He filled their water glasses and handed Lucas a menu. Then he held out the second menu to Gabriel with a quizzical look. "You want it or you want your usual?"

"The usual will do," Gabriel told him. "Why don't you get us an order of mozzarella sticks while my—" How did he describe Lucas? Friend? They were certainly that, but that no longer seemed accurate, given what they had spent much of the past two days doing. Lover? That was accurate enough, but that made Lucas seem like a convenient side piece, and he was far more than that. Companion was even worse. Boyfriend? What were they? Fourteen? "—friend," he went on, deciding that was the most neutral of the lot, "decides what he wants."

"You got it," Tony said and trotted off in the direction of the kitchen.

"Friend?" Lucas questioned. "I wasn't aware that you made a practice of doing what we've been doing with your friends."

"Of course I don't," Gabriel said. "Frankly I don't usually make it a practice of doing what we've been doing at all. I can't remember the last time someone was actually still there when I woke up in the morning, much less the last time I took anyone to dinner who wasn't a colleague or an operative. Maybe it wasn't the best choice of words, but if Tony gets the idea we're seeing each other, the next thing you know, Giovanni will have us married and giving him honorary grandbabies."

"Would that be a bad thing?" Lucas asked.

Gabriel didn't have the foggiest idea how to answer. Having a partner, much less a family, was an option he never allowed himself to contemplate. With the rage that lived inside him, it was never safe. Growing up in foster care gave him an up close and personal view of what men who couldn't control their tempers did to their families. And what he had was something else again. He swore at an early age he would never be that kind of person. An enemy was one thing, but an innocent was yet another.

At least he never thought he could before he met Lucas. For some inexplicable reason, the rage calmed around Lucas, and if it could stay that way, then a lot of things might be possible. He shut that thought down before it went any further. Indulging in fantasy was dangerous. They were in a high-stress situation, and emotions ran high. Who knew what they would feel after it was all over? The best thing he could do was enjoy the evening and leave it at that.

"Well, would it?" Lucas pressed.

"We've got enough to worry about right now without complicating it with things that may or may not happen. When we find Eric and get him home safe, then maybe we can think about the future."

He didn't mean it as a condemnation, but Lucas took on a look like a scolded child. "Of course. That's the most important thing right now." Lucas opened his menu and bent his head to study it, putting up a wall between them as surely as if he had built it with stone.

Gabriel felt like he was getting whiplash. Why was Lucas suddenly so worried? It wasn't as though he had ever promised him anything. For that matter, it wasn't as though they had actually talked about their relationship at all, if it was a relationship. It just happened suddenly and without warning.

Did he regret it? Not really. How could you regret someone like Lucas? Did he want it? Absolutely. Without question. Did he understand it? Not in the slightest. It felt like he'd been thrown on a roller coaster without warning. Was it such a bad thing that he needed a little while to get his feet under him? Why did everybody seem to want to jump directly from the first date to the white picket fence? He couldn't promise forever. He didn't even know what would happen tomorrow.

"Any idea what you want to eat?" Gabriel asked, mostly as a way to dispel the uncomfortable tension rising between them.

"Not really," Lucas replied. "I'm not a picky eater, and everything looks good." He laid the menu on the table and looked up at Gabriel curiously. "You told the waiter you'd have your usual. What's that?"

"Vegetable primavera." Gabriel flicked open the menu and pointed it out. "If you like mushrooms, the chicken-and-mushroom manicotti is good too."

Lucas wrinkled his nose. "Not a huge fan of mushrooms. Will you laugh at me if I just go with plain old spaghetti and meatballs?"

"Of course not," Gabriel assured him. "It's a classic for a reason. You can't go wrong with classic comfort."

"My mom used to make it by the vat," Lucas said as a nostalgic smile played on his lips. "My parents were foster parents, so we never knew exactly how many kids were going to be in the house on a particular day. Spaghetti was cheap, easy to make in large quantities, and most kids like it, so it became something of a staple around our house."

So the kid's parents had been foster parents. The do-gooder kind, he'd wager, rather than the "pack as many kids into the house as possible" kind who used kids as their primary source of income. It explained a lot about Lucas's nature—in particular his drive to help people and make things right. Not that you could always make things right. None of Gabriel's foster parents had ever been able to fix him, though there were a few who tried.

His inborn aggression was stronger than any therapeutic intervention could outlast. It wasn't until he made up his mind to leash the monster himself that he found even some small measure of peace. True peace still eluded him, though he had to admit the constant rage was a lot less palpable with Lucas around. The kid seemed to be his own, personal calming balm, better than any concoction of lavender or valerian root he had ever tried, including the ones he bottled himself. Nothing had ever worked, until Lucas.

He realized suddenly that Lucas was staring him. It was clear from his expression that he had asked a question Gabriel hadn't heard. He was saved from admitting that when Tony came back to deliver their appetizer and take Lucas's order.

Tony cast a sly glance at Gabriel. "How was it you two met?"

"At work," Gabriel said.

At the same time, Lucas said, "School."

Tony smiled knowingly and winked at Lucas. "Ah, so you were hot for the teacher, huh?"

"He's not my teacher," Lucas blurted, going red from the neck up.

"No worries, man," Tony said as he patted Lucas on the shoulder. "You'll get no judgment from me. I've had a crush on a teacher or two myself. Just never had the guts to act on it. Good for you."

"How do you know this isn't work related?" Gabriel asked. "We could be having a working dinner."

Tony scoffed. "I've got eyes in my head, don't I? It's written all over the both of you. You're so sweet we could sell you for dessert."

"We're never going to get dessert if you don't get that order in," Gabriel said pointedly.

"Right," Tony agreed as he turned back in the direction of the kitchen. "I'm on it."

"Pay him no mind," Gabriel advised Lucas. "He's incorrigible. What were you saying before we were so rudely interrupted?"

"It wasn't anything important," Lucas replied. "I think I asked what kind of movies you like."

"Good question. I can't remember the last time I've actually gone to see a movie."

"Don't you like them?"

"I do," Gabriel assured him. "I just rarely get the chance to take one in these days."

"We'll have to remedy that," Lucas said. "Is there anything out that you've been wanting to see?"

Gabriel thought back through the occasional preview he had run across and named the one that seemed the most interesting. After that, conversation became surprisingly easy. They talked movies and music and hobbies—all the inane small talk that normally would have driven Gabriel crazy. It was different with Lucas. He was curious about all the mundane details.

Much to Gabriel's surprise, it took almost no work at all to keep the conversation going between them. It was effortless, and he enjoyed it. A comfortable intimacy developed between them, and they continued to talk easily and paused only briefly when their food came. Gabriel couldn't remember ever talking to anyone like that. Not without some objective or ulterior motive. Lucas was guileless, a wonderful rarity, and Gabriel was determined to appreciate him.

As if in defiance of that determination, an unfamiliar ringtone shattered the conversation. Scowling, Gabriel slid the phone out of his pocket. The irritation melted away when he recognized Moose's number on the screen. He answered immediately.

"What's going on, Moose?" he asked by way of greeting.

"We've located Castillo again," Moose replied, not missing a beat. "He's holed up in a motel near Richmond. Parrish is planning an undercover operation. He wants to send an agent in undercover as a potential victim."

Gabriel frowned. While it was true they needed to prove what Castillo was doing, the plan sounded like a really good way to get an FBI agent taken hostage. Not to mention there was no guarantee that Castillo would actually take the bait.

"He's a kid, Shadow, barely out of the Academy," Moose went on.

Gabriel rubbed a hand across his forehead. It sounded like another clusterfuck in the making. "And just when is this supposed to be taking place?"

"That has yet to be determined," Moose said. "Parrish has called a war counsel of the involved parties at the Richmond FBI office in the morning."

"Funny how he didn't see fit to inform Lucas or me of this plan. I'd be willing to bet he doesn't know you are either, does he?"

Moose snorted. "What can I say? You know I'm not so good with following the chain of command."

"Neither am I," Gabriel countered. "I just love the element of surprise, though. Not to mention that crashing Parrish's party sounds like far too much fun to miss."

"That's what I thought you'd say," Moose said. "See you in the morning." He hung up.

"Looks like we're going to have to cut our night short, kid," Gabriel said to shut off the rash of questions before Lucas could start. "That was Moose. Castillo's in Virginia, and we need to move now."

At one point in Gabriel's life, making last-minute trips to anywhere in the world was commonplace. For the past ten years, such an occurrence had been nonexistent, but he was pleasantly surprised to find that habit had never really left him. A confident and seasoned traveler, he had them booked into a hotel in Richmond before they made it back to his house to gather Lucas's clothes. He had no need to pack. Despite his years out of the agency, he still kept a packed go bag in the front closet by the door.

He picked it up and added his tools while Lucas gathered his clothes. He couldn't help but feel a bit of nostalgia at picking them up again. He never expected to have to, but he could never bring himself to give them up completely either. A knife and gun went into the bag automatically, but he hesitated over his truly specialized tools—herbs, powders, tinctures. To the naked eye, they seemed innocent enough— mesh bags, small glass bottles, wrapped packages. The kind of thing any naturalist or health-conscious person might keep in their home.

Only he knew they were deadly poisons. The right combination of any of them would be deadly. Some would kill in minutes. Others might take days. He was an expert. One of the few in the world.

After a moment's hesitation, he selected a couple of the quick-acting, fast-absorbing poisons. With any luck he wouldn't need them. He honestly hoped Parrish and his FBI boys would be able to handle it without him. He was content to live as a civilian and hoped to be able to remain so. But walking into a potentially dangerous situation without some protection felt too much like walking in naked. He might be out of the field, but he wasn't stupid.

Gabriel zipped the bag and shouldered it. Then he crossed the house to check on Lucas. "You ready?" he asked, stepping through the partially open door into Lucas's room.

"I think so," Lucas replied hesitantly as he came out of the attached bathroom with his toiletries. "We only need enough for a few days, right?"

"I think that will be sufficient," Gabriel replied. "This thing is going to have to move fast if it's going to work. The longer it drags on, the more likely Castillo will get wind of it and move again. Let's go if you're ready."

As they passed through town, they stopped first at X-press Rent-A-Car, where Gabriel rented a nondescript, older-model sedan in the name of the one alias he had kept intact. Lucas raised an eyebrow at the change but swapped vehicles without complaint.

"My car is identifiable," Gabriel explained when they were back on the road. "An average, unremarkable car is better for something like this. People are less likely to remember it or be able to describe it."

"That sounds like you expect to be actively involved in whatever happens," Lucas commented.

"If Moose called me, he's got doubts about whatever the current plan is," Gabriel admitted. That was the elephant that had been in the room since the moment his phone rang. "If Moose thought whatever Parrish had planned was the best solution, he wouldn't have bothered involving us until it was all over."

"So he wasn't just giving us a heads-up because he thought we'd want to know? He thinks something's going to go wrong." The worry lines that had settled between Lucas's brows when they left the restaurant had deepened into crevices that were noticeable even in the thin glow of the streetlights.

"Not wrong, necessarily," Gabriel corrected. "Just not as well as it could either. Moose is a professional who's done this a long time. He doesn't have much tolerance for sloppy ops. After the first time, he's probably been watching Parrish pretty carefully. My hunch is he let Parrish do it his way the first time, out of professional courtesy and so that Moose could get a handle on Parrish. That phone call means Moose has decided that he's in over his head, and Moose wants me to get involved before things get any worse."

"Why didn't Agent Parrish just tell us what was going on himself?" Lucas asked.

Gabriel snorted. "That was likely part of an agency pissing contest with Moose. The intelligence and law enforcement community, especially at the high levels, is very territorial. Parrish just didn't want a retired spook like me or Moose sniffing around on his territory, and a civilian like you is even worse."

"Why does that even matter?" Lucas demanded, and frustration oozed off every word. "Shouldn't finding these people and getting them out of there before they get hurt worse be what's most important?"

Gabriel laughed. "You really are an innocent, kid."

Lucas shot him a glare that was mostly lost in the dark, but he felt it, nonetheless. Then, in the space of a passing light, the glare faded and melted into a wicked grin. "I should think you would know better than that. Even if I'd been innocent before I met you—and I wasn't—I'm certainly not now."

"So you're saying it's all my fault," Gabriel teased. "I've corrupted you?" The tone was lighthearted and teasing, but Gabriel was afraid it was true. He had corrupted the kid, and God help them, things would get even worse, especially the way it looked to be shaping up. No matter how hard he tried, Gabriel couldn't see a way to avoid getting right in the middle of the action, and that would do more than corrupt Lucas. It would destroy everything.

"Oh no." Lucas matched Gabriel's teasing tone with one of his own. "You didn't corrupt me. As I recall I was a very active and willing participant." He trailed a hand down Gabriel's thigh—part teasing and part offering.

Gabriel removed his hand from the steering wheel, laid it on top of Lucas's, and twined their fingers together. "As much as I would enjoy taking you up on that, I'm going to have to take a rain check, at least until we get to the hotel. I don't know this route that well. I need to concentrate on the road."

"Sorry," Lucas said sheepishly and pulled back.

Gabriel didn't let go of his hand. "Don't apologize. Another time I'd be more than willing to take you up on it. Just let me take a rain check until we get to the hotel. Okay?"

Lucas nodded. "You got it, but I'm taking you up on that later." His wicked grin was back, curling the corners of his mouth upward.

"It'll give me something to look forward to," Gabriel told him. "Why don't you try to get some rest? It's going to be a long night. We've got about a four-hour drive ahead of us, and you're going to need your energy up if you're going to make good on that rain check."

"There is that," Lucas agreed. He shrugged out of his jacket and balled it up to make a pillow. When Gabriel glanced over again, a few minutes later, he was sound asleep.

He looked even younger when he slept. It almost made Gabriel feel guilty, but Lucas was right. He was no innocent, at least not when it came to sex. He knew what he wanted and didn't hesitate to go after it.

Gabriel's heart swelled at the memory and with something else too—an emotion he couldn't quite name. There was fondness there and deep affection, perhaps deeper than he'd ever felt in his life. There was attraction too. Heavens above, was there attraction. Lucas was fast becoming an addiction he couldn't live without, and that was dangerous.

Lucas might have no idea what they were potentially about to get into, but Gabriel did. As much as he wanted to stay uninvolved, as he had told Lucas, Moose wouldn't have called them in without a good reason. If Moose was calling, the most likely explanation was that he needed Gabriel's help.

The very thought made him go cold. That's what he'd been afraid of since the moment Lucas appeared in his office. That's why he hadn't wanted to get involved. Yet, slowly but surely, he had become far more entangled than he intended.

Lucas had wormed his way into his heart and soul far deeper than anyone ever had before. He gave him the peace he'd been searching for most of his adult life. Lucas alone soothed the murderous rage that always plagued him. For that alone Gabriel would to do anything Lucas asked, even go back into the life he swore to walk away from. And there was so much more to Lucas than just that. So whatever came in the morning, Gabriel would face it, even if it meant walking back into the darkness. He always knew the end would come someday, anyway, and he couldn't think of a more noble cause than saving innocents. If he had to give in to the rage, at least his sacrifice would mean something. It would be more than slaughter and bloodshed and following orders.

He rubbed a thumb over Lucas's knuckles. He had fallen asleep with their hands still intertwined. It might be a fantasy, but just for one night, he could still enjoy it, and he would.

When they reached their hotel—a suitably anonymous chain like a thousand others all over the country—Gabriel checked them in and guided a half-asleep Lucas to their room. He should probably let Lucas sleep, but he couldn't help himself. Instead Gabriel carefully undressed and pushed Lucas gently down onto the mattress, crawled up beside him, and covered his face with kisses. It didn't take long for Lucas to respond with equal enthusiasm.

"I'm taking you up on that rain check," Gabriel said as he worked his way down Lucas's neck and chest with nips and kisses.

"I thought that was supposed to be *me* taking *you* up on it," Lucas murmured. "Not that I'm complaining."

"Changed my mind," Gabriel replied. "Decided I wanted to do this my way."

"By all means, carry on," Lucas said. "Far be it from me to stop you."

Gabriel chuckled. "As you wish, good sir."

Before that moment Gabriel had never truly made love. Had sex? Sure. Any number of times on any number of continents with any number of men. But that was about satisfying needs. He would never have called it making love. This was different.

He made gentle, passionate love to Lucas, took his time, and savored it. He had no idea what the future held, but he was damn sure going to remember this night.

CHAPTER EIGHTEEN

THEIR ARRIVAL sent shock waves through Parrish's team the following morning. All the air seemed to go out of the room when Gabriel opened the door of the conference room where they were meeting. Only Moose remained unaffected.

Anger and shock warred in Parrish's expression in equal measure. Gabriel felt a grim sense of satisfaction. It served the bastard right for trying to shut them out after they practically dropped the case in his lap. Parrish hadn't even managed to coordinate a simple snatch and grab without tipping Castillo off, and if Moose's call was any indication, the agent was poised to do it again.

"What are you doing here?" Parrish sputtered.

Gabriel raised an eyebrow, crossed his arms, and leaned casually against the wall directly in Parrish's eye line. "You didn't think we were going to let you carry out the mission without us, did you?"

"Yes, actually, I did," Parrish replied coolly. He met Gabriel's eyes steadily, but to Gabriel's experienced eye, the effort was obvious. "This is an FBI matter. It doesn't concern you."

"Bullshit." Gabriel didn't raise his voice in the slightest, but the word rang around the small room like a bullet. There were a few younger agents gathered at the table, and every one of them startled like scared rabbits. Gabriel didn't dare look around to Lucas, standing at his shoulder, but he could feel the mix of awe and amusement shimmering off the kid in waves. It was all he could do to swallow his own grin in response.

"You wouldn't have a case if it weren't for Lucas. It might've been months or even years before you located Castillo again. Hell. He was kidnapping victims practically in the backyard of the damn FBI, and no one had a clue. How many agents are there in Maryland and Virginia, not to mention DC, and who locates one of the most-wanted human traffickers in the country? A social worker not even out of grad school in backwater Maryland."

"Yes, and of course we're all grateful for Mr. Craig's assistance. But when the two of you brought your information to me, this became an FBI matter. I assure you we are quite capable of seeing the matter through."

"Of course you are," Gabriel continued dryly. "Because you did such an exemplary job of that the last time you tried to take care of this matter. Right now, in your position, I would think it would be in your best interest to take any help you can get and hope like hell none of the victims are further injured or, God forbid, killed because of your incompetence."

"And just how do you think you can help?" Parrish asked, clearly skeptical.

Gabriel pushed up, leaned over the table, and scanned the papers scattered across its surface. "I'd say that depends on just what sort of operation you have planned here."

Parrish drew himself up, plainly planning to unleash yet another protest, but Moose cut in. "The current plan is to send him"—he nodded in the direction of a junior agent who looked barely old enough to be out of high school—"in undercover in a club Castillo's gang has been seen frequenting."

Gabriel considered this and eyed the younger agent critically. The man had the right look—slim and wiry. Gabriel would bet he had a deceptively strong build. And from the pictures he'd seen, he could've been Eric's cousin. "A gay bar?"

Moose nodded. "Local spot. Popular with the college crowd."

Gabriel met the agent's eyes. "Stand up."

He got instantly to his feet and practically stood at attention.

Gabriel circled him like a predator assessing his prey. "It'll never work."

"It will work," Parrish insisted. "Agent Harris is fully qualified. He's done undercover work before."

"When?" Gabriel muttered. "In preschool? He's so green he glows. They'll make him in less than ten minutes."

"I know he's young, but that's the point," Parrish countered. "He's exactly the type that Castillo's crew seems to be looking for."

"In what way?" Gabriel demanded. "He practically screams cop, and it's perfectly obvious he's straight as an arrow. He's never going to fit in at a gay club. Hell, his eyes will probably pop out of his head just walking in the door."

"I'm not quite that naïve," Harris protested.

Gabriel reached around and cupped his ass. Harris squeaked like a schoolgirl and involuntarily turned a fiery red.

Gabriel simply lifted an eyebrow.

"I wasn't expecting that," Harris protested weakly. "It'll be different once I'm in character." No one bothered to respond. Everyone, Harris included, knew it was a token protest.

"And I suppose you have a better idea, Einstein?" Parrish shot back.

Gabriel didn't reply. The truth was he didn't have a better idea. Not at all. The idea he had was worse, much worse, but that didn't make it any less inevitable. He caught Moose's eye across the table and held it. He could see the exact moment when the inevitable conclusion that had already dawned on him also dawned on Moose.

"Send Shadow in," Moose blurted.

Parrish gaped at him. "You don't think Harris can pull it off, but you want me to send him in? Just how in the hell is that supposed to be a better idea? There's no way he can pass for a club kid."

Moose shook his head. "Not as a club kid, as a client."

"He might pull it off," Parrish conceded.

Gabriel held back his derisive snort. Who the hell did Parrish think he was? He survived ten years in the goddamned CIA. He could hold the cover so damn tight that Parrish himself wouldn't even know him, even if he were in on the mission.

"But he's a civilian," Parrish went on. "You cannot expect me to send a civilian in on a mission like this. The brass would have my head for even asking. There's no way they'll sign off on this."

That time Gabriel did roll his eyes. That stupidity didn't even bear commenting on.

"He's not a civilian," Moose replied. "He's a former CIA agent who now works in the private sector, and for the purposes of this mission, he's also a contractor with my company."

It was only Gabriel's years of training that kept him from smirking. He did not do, nor had he ever done, any work for Moose's company, but if it meant they could get those kids out of there, he'd sign the paperwork without a second thought. He was already damning his own soul. What difference would a little backdated paperwork make?

Parrish raised a skeptical eyebrow. "And you're just seeing fit to tell me this now?"

Moose shrugged. "You're the one who assumed I would bring a civilian into this investigation. The kid is here by necessity. He's a witness. But Shadow hasn't been a civilian in a long time."

"And I'm just supposed to believe you?" Parrish replied.

Moose fixed him with a look that reminded Gabriel suddenly that, for all his laid-back personality, Moose had been trained by the CIA too. He was far from your typical middle-aged gamer living in his parents' basement. "Yes, you are. How am I supposed to trust you to supervise an op I'm involved in if you can't trust me about my own people?" Deliberately Moose picked up his phone and clipped it back into the holder at his belt. "Frankly none of us would know anything about Castillo or any of this if it weren't for Shadow and the kid. If you're not prepared to trust them, maybe we should all just leave you and your agents to deal with this mess on your own. After all, that worked so spectacularly well the first time. Speaking of the first time, I'm sure the media would love to know about how your incompetent agents allowed human traffickers to escape with their victims right under your noses."

Parrish glared at him. "Are you threatening me?"

"Not at all," Moose said coolly. "It's not a threat. I'm simply making you aware of the potential consequences of your actions." He held Parrish's gaze for a long, tense moment.

Parrish swore vehemently under his breath. "Okay, okay. He's yours. That still doesn't tell me why you think your man will be so much better than mine."

That was so ridiculous that Gabriel nearly laughed. Moose did laugh. "No offense to your boy or the FBI Academy," Moose told Parrish, "but Gabriel was trained by the CIA. His life depended on maintaining his alias. He could do deeper undercover in his sleep than your boy has ever seen, and that's assuming he were just an ordinary field operative. Shadow isn't. He's a legend. They teach his ops to new agents these days."

Both Lucas and the younger agent—what was his name again? Harris?—went wide-eyed. Gabriel stifled a wince. No doubt he'd have to explain that one to Lucas later. So much for his cover as just a translator. Lucas would just have to understand the falsehood was necessary. You did what you had to do to maintain the cover, even with people you cared about.

Who was he kidding? It didn't matter anymore anyway. There was no way Lucas would be with him once he saw the monster he really was. Bit by bit his carefully constructed fantasy world was slipping.

In a way it was a relief. It couldn't last. He could only hide who he really was for so long. Now at least he could stop waiting for the other shoe to drop.

"He's that good, and they let him go?" Parrish asked incredulously.

"I didn't give them much choice," Gabriel replied. "They tried everything they could think of to keep me in, but I knew I had to get out."

"Yet you're willing to go back in now?" Parrish pressed.

Gabriel shrugged. "This time I don't see how I have much choice. If you send your boy in, he's going to end up hurt or killed. No ifs, ands, or buts about it. If we wait on you to pull somebody else and read them in, then we stand a chance of Castillo rabbiting again and losing sight of the kids again, and that's if he doesn't decide to just kill them all and start over again somewhere else. We need to move, and we need to move now. And I'm what we've got."

Parrish sighed but nodded. He dismissed Harris and settled down to make battle plans.

Gabriel knew he would. It sounded simple and straightforward. So why did he feel like he was losing everything?

CHAPTER NINETEEN

WHEN HE came out of the shower later that evening, Lucas found Gabriel sitting on the small sofa on the opposite side of their motel room, fiddling with a number of vials and mesh packets spread out on the low, rickety table in front of him. Gabriel didn't acknowledge his presence, and Lucas wasn't particularly surprised. Gabriel had been getting steadily more tense throughout the long, complicated meeting with Moose and Agent Parrish.

In the beginning Gabriel coached Lucas on the finer points of going undercover, even though Lucas would only observe from the surveillance van with Moose, and that was a hard-won victory. He expected that meticulously going over the details would make Gabriel more comfortable with the coming mission, more confident and relaxed as he got familiar with the details, but it hadn't. Gabriel had grown steadily more distant on the trip home, and he was projecting back-off vibes so loud they could probably feel them in the next room. Every instinct Lucas had told him he should go far away and stay there.

But he had his own questions as a result of the afternoon's meeting, and he needed answers. He crossed the room and leaned against the wall next to where Gabriel sat. He didn't say anything, just waited until Gabriel finally glanced in his direction. His eyes moved just as quickly away, but Lucas had dealt with enough skittish and defensive teenagers to know Gabriel was paying attention whether he wanted to be or not.

Lucas pushed off the wall and stepped in Gabriel's direction. Gabriel didn't speak or make any other indication that he was aware of the movement, but Lucas saw the pulse in his neck kick up and the muscles in his shoulders tense. Gabriel knew he was there all right.

"What was that Moose was going on about?" he asked bluntly. "From what he was saying, it certainly didn't sound like you were just a translator like you led me to believe."

Gabriel shrugged. "I was a translator at first. That was the truth, and that's all my official CV says, but eventually my supervisors realized I was capable of more than just translation and moved me over to the specialized skills program."

"Specialized skills?" Lucas asked. "What does that mean?"

"I had specialized skills that the government was interested in exploiting," Gabriel said dryly. The bitterness in his voice was almost palpable. "Technically SSO is only open to people with military special-ops experience—paramilitary, counterintelligence, and the like—but I was an exception, an anomaly with a natural talent for disappearing into a crowd and becoming a ghost. Our benevolent government wasn't about to pass up the chance to take advantage of that."

"So you worked undercover. So what? Why not just tell me the truth?" Lucas demanded.

"Because I couldn't," Gabriel snapped. "Hell, the majority of the missions I went on don't even exist on paper. I wasn't some Fibbie paper pusher like Parrish, kid. I did things you don't want to know about."

"Don't presume to tell me what I don't want," Lucas shot back. "Contrary to what you seem to believe, I'm not some innocent kid you need to protect. You may not be able to be honest with the rest of the world, but I need to know."

"Like hell you do," Gabriel flared. "Trust me, kid, sometimes the truth is overrated. Some demons need to stay buried."

"Burying them only allows them to haunt you," Lucas countered. "There's nothing you could have possibly done that I would judge you for. Everything you did, no matter what, was in the service of our country. That's honorable and nothing to be ashamed of."

Gabriel snorted. "And you say you're not an innocent. Only an innocent could possibly believe that claptrap."

The derision cut deep. Lucas swallowed hard. "You say that, but you don't believe it."

"I don't just believe it, kid. I know it. You have no idea."

"So tell me."

Gabriel put down the mixture he was wiping over the blade of a knife and drew himself up to full height. He turned to face Lucas for the first time. "Fine. You'll know the truth tomorrow anyway. You want to know what I did? That oh-so-honorable mission I fulfilled in the service of our country."

Lucas met his eyes squarely and forced himself not to flinch in the face of the black ire that flashed there. "I do."

"I was an assassin—a hired killer—and I was damn good at it. You think I was honorably serving my country? Hardly. I have more blood on my hands than I can measure. I've killed so many people I don't even remember them all. I'm a living, breathing weapon, pure and simple. I destroy everything in my path, and it's best you get out of the way before I end up destroying you too." Gabriel spun on his heel and picked up the knife again. And Lucas, too stunned to do anything else, fled.

GABRIEL WAS up the next morning at the crack of dawn. He'd spent a restless night tossing and turning, staring morosely at the blanket-covered hump that was Lucas on the pullout bed. For the first time since that glorious night when Lucas finally overcame his hesitance, Lucas refused to share his bed. Not that Gabriel blamed him. He felt like the worst kind of bastard for hurting Lucas the way he had. Hell, he'd hurt them both. Before that he always thought the pain of heartbreak was merely an emotional wound, but his chest ached with a raw, physical pain. His heart felt like it was slowly coming apart at the seams with every breath he took.

Despite the hurt, Gabriel knew it was for the best. Once he walked into that hotel room today, his life as he knew it would be over. Even if everything went perfectly, his ten-year illusion of a normal civilian life would be over. He'd managed, barely, to leash the monster once, but when he uncaged it, there would be no more containing it. The urge to kill would take over. Nobody got that lucky twice. Particularly not him. If it weren't for bad luck, he'd have none at all. He was right back where he had started, and he had managed to hurt Lucas in the process.

That was his biggest regret. He could deal with his own shattered dreams and disappointments, but Lucas didn't deserve to be hurt. Maybe it had been better when he was with the agency. Back then missions and roles and objectives had changed so quickly that he never got the chance to get attached. He'd have to resign his position at the college when it was all over, anyway. A little time at the gun range wouldn't come close to satisfying the need to kill. He wouldn't be safe around civilians. War zones and combat were the only places he would be safe, where he would have enough of an outlet that he wouldn't hurt someone who didn't deserve it. When Lucas and Eric and the others were safe, he'd go back.

His superiors would be thrilled. They never really wanted him to leave in the first place. With all the lunatics and terrorists running around, he wouldn't be short of missions. Maybe it wasn't the life he preferred, but it was a useful one. Fate was the one enemy he couldn't fight. He'd just have to make the best of it, and he could do that.

But first he had a mission to complete. He had to get Eric out of the clutches of that bastard Castillo and back safe with Lucas. It was the one thing he could do for Lucas to make up for the hurt he'd caused, and he was damn well going to do it or die trying.

He wrote a quick note for Lucas and then donned his running clothes and set out. They weren't meeting with the others for several hours yet. A long, hard run was just what he needed to get his mind on the task ahead. An hour at the gun range wouldn't have gone amiss either, but he wasn't familiar enough with the local area for that to be an option. A run would have to do.

He made a detour on the way back to grab food for both of them, assuming Lucas would be up when he returned. He was right. Lucas was dressed and had folded up the pullout mattress, so the sofa was intact again. He sat cross-legged, with his back against the low arm of the sofa and the textbook spread over his lap. But if Gabriel had to guess, he doubted Lucas was actually focusing on anything.

Lucas took the food he offered and dug in, but he didn't seem inclined to talk. Gabriel was grateful. He wasn't sure he could've managed small talk, in any case. He was already becoming hyperfocused on the mission. It was hard to concentrate on anything else. He could manage social graces when the role called for it, but the warrior had little time for that, and today he was definitely the warrior.

After the meal he left Lucas on his own while he gathered what he would need. The attire they had agreed upon was hanging in his closet—dark jeans, a deep red button-down shirt, and boots. It was the kind of ordinary clothes any man might wear on a casual outing. But the shirt had long, close-fitting sleeves that would allow him to conceal a knife without worry that it would fall out, and it fit loosely enough to conceal the wire Moose would fit him with. The boots were steel toed and would protect his feet from injury and double as a weapon. Nothing could be left to chance, not even clothing.

As he showered and dressed later that afternoon, he felt the focus taking him over. Their makeshift staging area was a grocery-store parking lot down the road from the motel where Castillo's gang was holding court. By the time they met Moose and Parrish there, he was fully back in the mindset of an operative.

He catalogued everything, from the old man in a V-necked undershirt and blue shorts on a black scooter to the heavyset woman with the gaggle of kids crossing the main street. The smallest child, a girl, had a ring of blue around her mouth from some sort of candy and a Band-Aid on her knee. He reeled away the information in seconds and then dismissed it. None of it mattered if it wasn't mission critical.

The one hitch in his focus was that he had underestimated the effect of having Lucas there. It was simultaneously nearly impossible to remember things like basic courtesy and equally impossible not to be aware of his presence. Gabriel clocked his every movement, from the rise and fall of his chest to the rapid tattoo of his fingers against his jeans. It was almost a relief when Lucas stepped into the back of the surveillance van with Moose.

Except for one thing.

"Hey, kid," Gabriel called in the last second. "I'll bring him back to you. I promise."

He saw Lucas nod, just once, and the door slammed shut. Then he took one last deep breath and got in his car to head to the hotel. He meant that promise with every fiber of his being. It was time to make good on it.

CHAPTER TWENTY

ERIC HEARD the murmur of voices outside the door. He caught Damien's voice among them and swore internally. Damien was negotiating with a client already. Damn. He hated the days when they started so early. Didn't the bastards have the decency to wait until nightfall and let them recuperate from the night before? He almost hoped the client wanted Dawn and not him, but he couldn't do that to her. The poor girl was still terrified, despite the fact that she was going into her second week with them. She still jumped at her own shadow and cried every time a client chose her. She was sweet, but he found himself missing Monique's spunk. God, he hoped she was okay. *Please let her be okay.*

The door opened, but to Eric's shock, it wasn't any of Damien's crew who came in. It was a dark-haired man with ice-blue eyes. "Look, man, if you're a client, you need to get out of here," Eric told him. "Damien doesn't allow clients in our rooms. We're all gonna be in deep shit if he finds you here."

"I'm not a client, Eric," the man said in a hushed, tight voice. "I'm here to get you out of here."

Eric stared at him, dumbfounded. "Who are you and what are you doing here? How do you know my real name?"

"I'm a friend of Lucas's," the man replied. "He's been looking for you all over. Now come on. I've got to get you out of here before those bastards show back up. It won't take Damien that long to process my credit card."

"He takes credit cards?" Eric said blankly.

"Don't worry about that," the man snapped. "Just move."

"I'd love to," Eric said, and he held up his chained arm. "But I can't. Damien has the only key."

The man swore vehemently in what, to Eric's ear, sounded like several languages. He moved toward the beds, and Dawn started to scream. At that Julio burst in, and all hell broke loose.

CHAPTER TWENTY-ONE

GABRIEL KNEW the gig was up the moment the girl started to scream. The piercing screech might as well have been a tornado alarm, guaranteed to bring anyone in the vicinity. Castillo's muscle-bound lackey exploded through the door, cursing in Spanish.

Gabriel spun around to meet the man who crashed in the door, but he wasn't quick enough to prevent the man from landing a quick and nasty punch to his gut. Pain glanced up through him like a sharp knife releasing an icy rage.

Castillo's thug watched him with a maniacal glint in his eye. Gabriel recognized it immediately. The bastard enjoyed inflicting pain.

"I'm going to enjoy killing you, *cabrón*," he told Gabriel. "Maybe *Jefe* will even give me the girl as a reward."

Behind him Gabriel dimly registered the girl starting to cry. He wasn't sure which of them swung first. For the first time in more than a decade, reality swam in a haze of black and red as he let the rage slip its leash. He ceased to be aware of individual blows as the killing fury pulsed through him. He heard bones crunch and the thud of flesh against flesh, but it ceased to be more than background noise against the driving need to kill. At some point blood spilled and ran, but he could no longer tell if it was his or somebody else's.

He was dimly aware of Castillo's other henchmen and then finally Castillo himself as he rushed into the room and joined the fight. It was of little consequence. They simply gave the rage more targets, swept it up higher, spiking it into a frenzy that was akin to a twisted form of glee. It intoxicated him. It drove him. It overwhelmed him. They were no longer people, only targets, and he wouldn't stop until they were dead.

CHAPTER TWENTY-TWO

INSIDE THE surveillance van, Lucas huddled silently in a chair, his feet up in the seat and his arms wrapped around his knees as he watched Gabriel approach the hotel room on one of the half-dozen screens mounted on the adjacent wall. Although there were only inches between him and the screens, he felt like he was watching from a great distance. It had been like that since Gabriel admitted he'd been an assassin.

It hurt to even form the thought. He wasn't a fool. He knew Gabriel had probably done or been party to some less-than-scrupulous things in his time at the CIA, even if he had only been a translator. But he never imagined Gabriel had been a professional killer. He still couldn't wrap his mind around it. Sure, Gabriel had some hard edges, and he had a reputation for being aloof and moody. But a killer? Never.

And a liar as well, apparently. Lucas should've been suspicious of the whole only-a-translator thing, right from the start. Gabriel clearly knew his way around law enforcement, but Lucas had just thought that Gabriel had probably assisted various agencies as a translator. It made sense at the time.

But if Gabriel had been lying to him the entire time, was everything else a lie too? Lucas thought they were building something between them—more than just hot sex born out of desperation. He felt things for Gabriel that he had never felt for anyone else. It was nothing like the giddy, youthful affection he'd felt for his few past boyfriends. It was a far deeper connection.

Moose swore furiously and shattered his reverie. His eyes went immediately to the screen he had been watching, but there was nothing to see. Gabriel was inside the hotel room. They had lost visual contact. Gabriel had chosen to go without a body camera on the grounds that it was too conspicuous, and the tiny cameras mounted on the front of the van could no longer track him. They only had the audio feed from the wire Gabriel wore. Moose monitored it through his headphones, and whatever he was hearing, it wasn't good. Lucas wasn't even sure his rant was entirely in English, but the tone was clear enough. The already-charged atmosphere in the van shot up several more levels.

"What is it?" Parrish demanded. "What's happening?"

"Shadow's gone berserk," Moose said, spinning around in his chair. "Dammit. I should have known better than to send him in there alone."

"What the hell are you talking about?" Parrish said. "You're the one who vouched for him. You told me he'd be fine. You said he was the best there is."

"He is," Moose insisted. "I just hadn't counted on him slipping the leash. He hasn't done this in years."

"Hasn't done what?" Parrish's face rapidly darkened and a vein in his forehead stood out alarmingly.

What the hell was wrong with Gabriel? It had to be serious to upset Moose. From what Gabriel said, Moose was a veteran of undercover operations. Someone like that wouldn't shake easily.

"He goes into these berserker rages. Just loses it. I've never seen it in the flesh, but I've seen tapes. It's like he loses all touch with reality, and he won't stop. I've seen him throw off three guys. Guys in his class used to talk about the instructors trying to douse him in ice water to stop him."

"Did it work?" Parrish asked.

"Not usually," Moose said grimly.

"So what does?"

"He'll stop when they're dead."

"Goddammit, Moose. That's not funny. There are victims in there."

"I know that," Moose flared. "That's what I'm trying to fucking tell you. If we don't get him out of there, he won't stop until everyone else is dead."

Parrish let out his own string of colorful profanity, every bit as vehement as Moose's. "We're going to have to abort the plan. We have to get in there now."

The look Moose gave Parrish made it clear he thought he had lost his mind. "You want him to kill you too? Even when he's in his right mind, breaking Shadow's cover before he gives the signal will get your ass kicked. If you value your life, I'd wait until he gives the signal."

"And we just take our chances with the victims?" Parrish demanded. "You said yourself he won't stop."

"I know," Moose said. He spun away from Parrish and glared at the blank screen on the wall, as though his sheer will would make Gabriel stop.

"Just how the hell are we supposed to do that if we can't go in?"

"I can do it," Lucas piped up.

Both men turned and gaped at him.

"You're out of your mind, kid," Moose said. He kept a straight face, but it did nothing to conceal the condescension in his voice. "Shadow will snap you like a twig. You wouldn't last a minute."

"He'll recognize me," Lucas insisted. He would. Lucas was sure. He couldn't explain, but he knew it as well as he knew his own name. It was like that night when Gabriel pushed him against the wall. For a split second, Gabriel went blank, and Lucas had been terrified. But just as quickly as the moment came, Gabriel recognized him and pulled back. He'd seen it happen in Gabriel's eyes. Gabriel would know him.

Tired of arguing, Lucas stood up and pushed the door open in the same movement. By the time Parrish and Moose even realized he was moving, his feet were on the asphalt. He hit the ground running.

He could hear Parrish yell, "What the hell, kid? Get your ass back here. You're going to get yourself killed."

Lucas kicked it into high gear, expecting to hear the other man hot on his tail at any moment. Miraculously that never happened. He stopped halfway across the parking lot to catch his breath. He'd never been much of an athlete, and it had been a long time since he had run that hard. When no one came to drag him back, he assumed they had decided to let him get on with it. He started to take off running again, but at the last moment changed his mind, thinking of what Gabriel had said to him last night—God, had it really only been last night?— about going undercover. "The key is to blend in, look natural, like you belong there, and no one will think twice."

Lucas stuck his hands in his pockets and slowed to a more natural walk. He needed to look as though he were just another motel guest, ambling back to his room. If he burst in there running flat out, he was certain to attract attention, and the last thing they needed was other people getting involved. The room where Gabriel—and presumably Eric—were located was at the middle in a row of rooms that ran along an interior breezeway. Though they, like all the rooms, were entered from the outside, that particular set opened into the breezeway rather than directly into the parking lot. There were no windows and no way to tell what was going on inside.

He should have had Moose fit him with an earpiece. Then he would at least be able to hear what it sounded like in there. But Lucas wasn't sure he wanted to know. If Gabriel was as bad off as Moose claimed, even hearing it would be pretty bad.

He stepped onto the sidewalk and turned into the breezeway as though he were simply going for the snack machines that were located in an alcove at the far end, opposite the rooms that were his actual target. Even if he hadn't already known the number of the room Gabriel had entered, it would've been easy enough to pick it out. The door had been kicked in and was barely hanging on its hinges. And there were clear sounds of violence coming from within—punches, groans, cursing, and then the distinct sound of a body being thrown against a wall with great force. Lucas took a deep breath and stepped inside.

He didn't get even a brief glance at the interior of the room before someone large and clearly angry grabbed him. He felt the hands closing around his neck, thumbs pressing on his windpipe. Panic washed over him. Every cell of his body urged him to fight, to run, to get away before he was killed. Dying seemed an inevitability that might be only seconds away. It took every ounce of will he had, but Lucas forced himself to stand still and hold his ground. He dragged his eyes up to meet his captor's and found himself looking into Gabriel's distinctive, but blank, blue eyes. If it weren't for them, Lucas might not have recognized him. He looked nothing like his normal self. His face was etched with fury, and anger boiled off him in waves.

"Stop." Lucas forced the word up through his rapidly closing throat. It felt like trying to cough up glass, but getting through to

Gabriel was his only chance. "It's me—Lucas. I'm not a threat. Look at me. You know me." The blank expression never faltered. "Gabriel, I know you're in there. Come on. Look at me. Look. At. Me."

It was barely a flicker of movement. Gabriel's eyes flitted up to his face like the briefest touch of butterfly wings, and the pressure on his throat subtly eased. Lucas swallowed. "That's right. That's good. You know me. Remember? I'm an ally. I'm not a target or combatant. I'm your friend." He was a good deal more than that, but he didn't dare admit it with Parrish listening in.

Gabriel blinked hard and then stepped back abruptly, dropping his hands from Lucas's neck. "Lucas, what the hell are you doing here?"

"Things got a little out of hand," Lucas said. "You went a bit off the script."

Gabriel furrowed his brow. He started to speak, but whatever he was about to say was cut off when another voice broke in. "Lucas? You're here?"

Lucas pushed around Gabriel to step fully into the room. There, huddled on one of the two beds, a metal chain connecting his wrist to the headboard, was Eric. He was thinner than Lucas remembered. His normally spiky hair was plastered to his head, greasy and unkempt. Lucas could see fading bruises in several places, but he was there and gloriously alive. That was his greatest fear throughout the whole ordeal, though Lucas never let himself say it and had tried not to even think it, but it was always there, lurking in the back of his mind, the ever-present fear that, when they finally found Eric, it would be too late. The crushing relief nearly had him bursting into tears on the spot, but he swallowed them back.

He couldn't stop himself from diving on the bed with Eric and gathering him in a hug, though. "I'm so glad to see you!"

Instead of returning the hug as Lucas expected, Eric flinched and his body went stiff. "I'm glad to see you too," he said.

Lucas pulled back, confused. Eric might be saying he was glad to see them, but he didn't sound like it. In fact, he didn't sound like himself at all. There was no expression in his voice and the words sounded almost mechanical. Frankly, he both looked and sounded like some of the abused children Lucas had interviewed. It was an image that crunched badly against what he knew about his friend. Then suddenly the professional part of his brain kicked in and he realized what he had just done. Sudden and abrupt touch, particularly touch that could be interpreted as restraint, was a very bad idea with someone who had been through severe trauma. Lucas wasn't used to including Eric in that category, but rationally Eric most definitely qualified.

Cursing himself as the worst kind of idiot, Lucas slowly pulled away. He moved cautiously off the bed, knelt on the floor, and meticulously examined the chain that connected Eric to the bed, trying not to touch it or move it too much. It didn't take long to determine it would be impossible for him to do anything with it on his own.

He looked up and searched for Gabriel. It was only then he noticed the other occupants in the room. On the other bed, there was a thin, willowy girl with long blonde hair that fell nearly down to her butt. She huddled as far away from him as she could manage and gaped in open terror.

There were also several men scattered throughout the room. The one against the far wall, a heavyset Hispanic man, was clearly dead. His neck and head jutted at a grossly unnatural angle. It was hard to tell with the other two. Both were at least unconscious. A black man was sprawled in the middle of the floor. The other Hispanic man—Lucas thought he was the one from the video, but his face was so bloodied and bruised it was hard to tell—was slumped against the air conditioner.

Gabriel stood in the shadow of the doorway. Though the murderous look had left his face, he was still on high alert. He scanned the room, hypervigilant for any movement, a feral wolf watching for potential challengers or interlopers.

"Gabriel," Lucas said quietly. Gabriel swiveled his head in his direction. "We need to get them out of here, but I can't do anything with this chain. Can you take a look at it?" When Gabriel began to move toward him, the girl on the other bed began to tremble and sob.

"Hey, hey. It's okay," Lucas said and instinctively reached in her direction. He couldn't even come close to her from his position. She was curled in the corner of the bed on the far side of the room.

While Gabriel examined Eric's chain, Lucas slowly moved closer to the girl. He was careful not to crowd her like he had Eric, but it did little good. She scrambled off the bed and wedged herself into the corner against the wall, as far away as her restraints would let her move.

"I'm here to help," Lucas told her. "I'm Eric's friend."

"Leo," Eric corrected. "They call me Leo." To the girl, he added, "It's okay, Dawn, really. Lucas is my friend. He won't hurt you. Besides he's gay like me. He's no threat to you."

The girl—Dawn—didn't look particularly convinced, but she let him move a bit closer without protest. When he tried to move farther, she whimpered again and started to cry, so he stopped.

"Okay. I get it. I won't come any farther." He backed to the position at the end of the bed where she had been comfortable with him. Eric shouted his name. He turned to see what it was Eric wanted, but before he could ask, an arm came around his chest and the cold steel of a gun pressed against his temple.

Lucas had always heard people talk about time standing still, but he had never experienced it until that moment. Everything froze. He hardly dared breathe.

Guess at least one of them wasn't dead.

A glance downward at the arm that held him identified his captor as the Hispanic man who had been slumped against the heating and air unit. The heating and air unit that was mere inches from where he had been standing at the end of the bed. Dammit, he had practically walked right into the bastard's arms.

CHAPTER TWENTY-THREE

THE CHAIN dropped from Gabriel's fingers. Dammit. Why hadn't he seen the motherfucker move? He thought they were safe. He was sure he neutralized all the targets. Two of them were still breathing, but he hadn't expected them to regain consciousness anytime soon. Trust Castillo to defy the odds. Gabriel was on his feet and moving before he even finished the thought.

"Get your hands off him."

The bastard had the nerve to laugh. "Why don't you come make me, *pendejo*. Oh yeah. That's right. You can't. Take one step closer, and I'll put a bullet through the little *maricón*'s brain. Wouldn't that be a pretty sight? Your little boy toy's brains splattered all over these white walls."

Gabriel froze. It wasn't an empty threat. A man got a certain look when he was prepared to kill, and Damien had it. What's worse, he was damned twitchy. That was the most dangerous type of all. They would kill before they meant to because they got jumpy on the trigger. He couldn't rage, no matter how much he would like to snap the son of a bitch's neck like a twig. He had to think.

He slid a hand into his pocket and closed his fingers around the switchblade hidden there. Carefully he tucked it up into his sleeve.

"There's no use going for a gun," Damien taunted. "He'll be dead before you can even pull the trigger."

"It's not a gun," Gabriel said. "Don't you think if I had a weapon, I would've pulled it by now." Knife safely hidden, he got hold of his cell phone and pulled it from his pocket. "It's just my phone." He thumbed open the app that surreptitiously alerted Moose for help and then raised his hands and turned the phone so Damien could see it. The secret app had no visual display, so it looked like nothing more than the normal home screen.

"And just what did you think you were going to do with that, *cabrón*? Call the police. Go ahead. Call them. By the time they get here, they can collect your body and boy toy's too. Then again, maybe I won't kill him. Maybe I'll make it a recoverable wound. Then I could keep him. He's got a pretty face. He could make me a lot of money."

Gabriel had the knife out and open in one fluid movement.

Damien shot him an amused look. "*Pinche idiota*, didn't anyone ever tell you not to bring a knife to a gunfight?" The words ended in a choked gasp as he stared disbelievingly at the knife suddenly protruding from his thigh. The wound bled profusely. He closed his fingers on the trigger and fired wildly, getting off multiple shots with little regard for where they landed. Lucas had already begun to twist away. The bullet intended for his head instead caught him in the back as Damien suddenly crumpled.

Gabriel lunged forward and caught Lucas before he hit the floor. He wasn't worried about Damien. If bleeding out didn't kill him, the poison would. The blade was coated in fluoroacetate. With that in the wound, he wouldn't live more than a few hours at most. In the background Gabriel was faintly aware of Moose and Parrish storming into the room, along with what sounded like at least a dozen junior agents. The girl started to scream again, but Gabriel ignored them all.

All his focus was on Lucas. With extreme care he gathered Lucas into his arms, mindful of his neck and spine. He was pale and moaning, barely responsive. "I've got you, kid. You're going to be fine." He would. He damn well had to be. Lucas was the only person on the planet who had ever been able to make him feel real, like a normal person, and he was the only one who could ever reach him when he fell that deep into the darkness. There was no way in hell Gabriel was going to lose him. "Come on. Open your eyes. Look at me."

Lucas's eyes fluttered open. "Did you get him?"

"Of course I got him," Gabriel replied, affronted. "The day I can't take out a small-time thug is the day I need to retire."

"Already retired," Lucas pointed out weakly. Gabriel grinned. If he was able to be a smartass already, he'd be fine.

Lucas's eyes drifted downward, and for a moment, Gabriel thought he was going to lose consciousness again. Instead Lucas's eyes fixed on Gabriel's chest. "You're bleeding."

"What? No, I'm not. He didn't hit me. I'm fine."

"Look," Lucas insisted. Gabriel looked down at his own chest. To his shock, deep red blood was rapidly spreading across his chest. *How the hell did that happen? Bastard must've gotten in a lucky shot.* That was his last coherent thought before the world went black.

CHAPTER TWENTY-FOUR

GABRIEL FELL through the darkness for what seemed like an eternity. Then the pictures came. Grainy images floated before his eyes like an old silent film—only it wasn't silent. He could see and hear everything in them as if they were his own memories. The first ones flew past in a blur. Gabriel caught only the faintest glimpses of them. They were flickering streams of light.

Then he slowed, and the interminable fall seemed to finally come to an end. He found himself surrounded by one of those memory images, as though he had somehow stepped into it. He was following a boy, no more than sixteen or seventeen, clad in a rough, homespun, knee-length tunic, who was hurrying down a dirt road into what appeared to be a medieval village. The closer they got to it, the more obvious the sound of the bustling villagers became.

Suddenly the sound of the crowd became restive. The boy came to an abrupt stop, looked around warily, and gave Gabriel a sudden clear view of his face.

What he saw shook him to the core. The face was his own, right down to his distinctive ice-blue eyes. It couldn't possibly be. It was centuries before he was born, but it was him. The face was younger and far more innocent, but it was unmistakably his. As he watched, the younger version of himself seemed to come to a decision, draw himself up, and plunge into the crowd.

Drawn by an irresistible curiosity, Gabriel followed. The boy pushed his way through the crowd. Gabriel winced as his younger self was jostled and stepped on by countless thoughtless adults who didn't even seem to notice his presence. Then the crowd broke open, and the boy skidded to a halt. Like much of the crowd around them, he was mesmerized by a wizened man who was holding court from the back of a wagon, surrounded by an ever-growing crowd of people. When Gabriel looked up, the man caught his eye, and with a sudden jolt, Gabriel recognized him.

Moriel.

Was that why he was brought there? To be tortured by the memory of the moment he sold his soul to the devil? Even as the thought formed, young Gabriel stepped up to the parchment Moriel had unrolled and began to read it over. The boy reached for the quill Moriel offered, took out a penknife, made a small cut on his shoulder, and dipped the quill in the blood that welled. As soon as young Gabriel signed his name, the wound healed, leaving the sword-shaped birthmark in its place. Adult Gabriel touched his shoulder with a mix of curiosity and growing horror. So that's how he got it. It was a mark of the curse.

Before his eyes the younger Gabriel changed. His shoulders straightened. He drew himself up to his full height. A new confidence and strength imbued his frame, but it was his face that was the most telling. All trace of innocence had drained from it. The lines became hard and his eyes filled with an icy rage.

It was a rage the adult Gabriel knew all too well. It had flowed in his veins for so long that he didn't remember a time without it, save those last few precious weeks when he was with Lucas.

Everyone, including Gabriel himself, always assumed his unending pit of anger was the result of his hard childhood. Maybe some of it was, but he knew it was more than that. The rage was born of the curse—born of that one stupid decision when a lonely boy who wanted nothing more than to belong and to have power in a society that made him powerless fell victim to the manipulations of a silver-tongued wizard.

He should have stopped the boy before he signed that damn contract. No other man deserved to live his life fighting that ridiculous rage in what would ultimately be an even lonelier and isolating existence. God knew the boy deserved more than that. He was just a boy, not yet a killer.

Then the double-sided words of the oath came back to him, and Gabriel knew exactly what he needed to do.

The boy made to jump out of the wagon, but Moriel stopped him. They traveled deep into the woods, and Gabriel followed them. Several days went by before his eyes as Moriel led the boy through the forest and taught him of plants and poisons.

That explained where Gabriel's affinity for the subject had come from. When the boy took off one night, Gabriel followed him as he slipped into the castle. When the boy went to kill the man who had been his master, Gabriel opened his mouth to speak, to stop him, but the boy had learned his craft too well, and the sleight of hand was over before Gabriel could even draw breath to say anything.

When the boy left the room and encountered the young man in the hallway, Gabriel realized why. It wasn't the old man's death that mattered, for his cruelty had reaped exactly what he had sown. It was the young man's.

The younger man was so like Lucas it was almost painful to watch. Gabriel understood now what that damnable oath meant. This was the One. The boy and young man were still talking, but something in the boy's face had changed. His eyes had gone lighter—icy and cold. The young man who looked like Lucas didn't know it yet, but he was living on borrowed time. The boy hesitated. He was still young and not yet hardened to the effects of killing, but Gabriel knew that expression all too well.

If the boy took that step and murdered the young man, he would be bound by the oath forever. His life would be driven by the ever-deepening urge to kill, and he would be forever doomed to be alone. Gabriel couldn't let that happen, but how could he stop it?

If he stepped out, would the boy see him? Would the boy hear him if he spoke? Gabriel had no idea how he had come to that place or even where he was, so it was impossible to speculate what, if anything, might work. All that was left to do was try.

"Gabriel," he called, and he tried to ignore the oddity of calling someone else by his own name.

The boy startled and looked around, but the other man didn't seem to be affected at all. Satisfied with the result, Gabriel tried again. That time the boy looked straight in his direction. Gabriel shifted and tried to move more directly into the light. He knew the exact moment when the boy saw him. His face went white, and his eyes went impossibly round. Gabriel pressed a finger to his lips in the universal sign for silence. Thankfully the boy got his message, coaxed the other man back into his bedchamber, and came to speak with Gabriel.

"You called, sir?"

Gabriel nodded. "I did." He bent down so he could look the boy in the eye. He had grown taller since taking the mark, but he was still quite young and had some growing to do. "I know what you're thinking about—what you've just done and what you are considering doing now," he told the boy.

Looking into the face of the boy who was at once him and not him was surreal. The face was so like his own, but there was something fundamentally wrong about it too. Not in the way it looked. He wasn't in any way disfigured, but the lines were too hard, too world-worn for a boy barely old enough to shave. The curse had marked him already. How much worse would it be if he went through with the killing?

"Begging your pardon, good sir," the boy said politely, "but how could you possibly? Are you a wizard or perhaps an angel, able to pluck the very thoughts from my head?"

Gabriel choked back a laugh. Trust the kid to be a skeptic. Clearly he'd been a paranoid sod from the beginning of time. "No, I'm no angel. I'm just a man with some years more experience than you who would like to offer you a bit of wisdom."

"And what wisdom would you have me know, sir?" The boy's eyes were still wary, but apparently he had decided to hear him out.

"Let him go. Just let him sleep. Walk out the door and leave this place."

"But sir," the boy protested. "He knows I was here. When they discover the steward, he will know it was I who did him ill."

"He will never suspect such," Gabriel told him. "You've learned your art well. No one will ever know you were there. It will seem that the old man simply died in his sleep, won't it?"

"That's my hope," the boy admitted. "My Lord says the poison will disappear quickly."

"Then there's no need to be afraid of witnesses."

"Mayhap not," the boy conceded. "But I still cannot do as you wish. I have sworn an oath to follow my lord and do his bidding. I'm no longer free to come and go as I please."

"But that oath can be broken by forgiving an enemy, can it not?" Gabriel countered.

The boy's eyes widened. "Aye, it can."

"Then forgive this one. Let that be the end of your oath and leave this place," Gabriel commanded. "I know the oath promises you many things, but in the end, it won't be worth it. All the power and glory and money come to nothing if you lose your very soul, and you will, if you continue down this path. You will lose your soul and everyone you love with it. You're smart and strong and willing. You don't need an oath to give you strength or power. You already have plenty of your own, and right now, the strongest and smartest thing you can do is to let him go and walk away."

In that instant, the two memories shimmered simultaneously in front of Gabriel, the original of the boy walking in the room and the new one where he simply continued down the hall. Then the two merged into a bright and consuming white light.

WHITE. THE first thing Gabriel noticed when he came to awareness was white. It was several beats before his brain caught up enough to identify what he was looking at—a white industrial ceiling tile. The sounds came next—the beeps and whirs and mechanical clunks. Those sounds had only ever meant one thing in his memory. He was in a hospital. Why was he there? How did he get there? The last thing he remembered was that asshole firing at Lucas.

Lucas. Where was Lucas?

He scrambled to push himself up and look around, but the damn machines had him tied. He reached blindly for the wires that restrained him, but before he could pull them out, a familiar voice said, "Hey, look who's awake."

Gabriel jerked his head around and immediately regretted the movement as the room tilted dizzyingly around him.

"Easy there, Shadow," Moose said as he unfolded his large frame from the too-small, vinyl-covered chair and lumbered over. "You've been out for a while now. Don't push it."

"How long?" Gabriel demanded.

Moose didn't insult either of them by pretending he didn't know what Gabriel meant. "Nearly a week now. You gave us a scare.

You came through surgery fine, but no one was quite sure why you wouldn't wake up. Your vitals were fine, so the docs decided your body must just have needed the rest and you would wake up on your own time. Looks like they were right."

"Surgery?" Why had he needed surgery? What the hell had happened that he didn't remember, and why couldn't he remember?

"The bastard missed your heart," Moose said by way of explanation. "Not that he knew or cared. The damn idiot was firing blind, already half-dead. You're either the luckiest son of a bitch alive or you have a guardian angel, 'cause that bullet played ping-pong all through your chest and didn't hit a damn thing vital. Tore things up a bit, though. You lost a lot of blood."

That probably explained it.

"Lucas? Is he okay?"

"He's fine," Moose replied. "He took a hit too, but it was a through and through. We've barely gotten him to leave your bedside since they turned him loose. He's going to be pissed he wasn't here, but I bullied him into going home to eat and sleep. I promised him I'd call if anything changed. I probably should go call him. He threatened everything short of handing me my balls on a platter if I didn't. He's a spitfire, that one."

Lucas? His Lucas. His sweet, innocent do-gooder had threatened Moose. For a minute it didn't seem possible, until he remembered Lucas was the same man who walked fearlessly into the room when he was out of his head in a berserker rage and talked him down. Trained federal agents gave him a wide berth in that state, but Lucas didn't bat an eye. Gabriel had nearly killed him, and he still walked straight to him. The kid had courage in spades. And God, he loved him for it.

Wait. Did he say love? For most of his life, he wasn't even sure he knew the meaning of the word, much less that he was capable of feeling it. More than one therapist had proclaimed he wasn't. They were obviously wrong, because there wasn't a doubt in his mind that he loved Lucas—more than he had ever loved anyone or anything in his entire life—and he was never letting the kid get away from him.

"What about the others?" he asked Moose. "The boy—" What was his name? Dammit, why did his brain feel like it was full of holes? "—Eric, and the girl. Are they okay?"

"Physically at least," Moose said wearily. "They're fine, but they've been through a lot. The docs say it's going to take a while before they're really back to themselves. They've found others too, at least four more."

A nurse passing in the hallway came to a dead stop, did a double take, and charged into the room. "Mr. Ingram, you're back with us. *Someone* was supposed to call the nurses' station when you woke up." Moose hung his head and shuffled like a schoolboy. Gabriel laughed before he could stop himself. The nurse ignored them both and continued, "It's good to see you awake. You gave us quite a scare there, for a while. Let me check your vitals, and I'll go let the doctor know you're awake."

"I'm going to go call Lucas," Moose said quickly. He came up with his cell phone and headed for the door while the nurse poked and prodded. "There's no signal back here. You have to go to the lobby to get a signal. Be back in a few."

It didn't take the nurse long to finish her examination and check his vitals and bandages. She went to the little computer built into a cabinet on the other side of the room and entered some information. Then she turned and smiled at him. "I'm going to find Dr. Carver. I'll be back as soon as I can. It shouldn't take long."

True to her word, she reappeared within moments with a lab-coated man Gabriel assumed to be Dr. Carver. He was a nondescript man of average build with salt-and-pepper hair, chocolate skin, and dark eyes. A big smile broke out on his face at the sight of Gabriel. "Hello, Mr. Ingram," he said cheerfully. "I can't tell you how glad I am to finally meet you properly." He put out his hand and gently shook Gabriel's, paying no mind to the proliferation of wires and tubes. "You've been quite a puzzle for the neurology department. Not many people are out for a week who have a perfectly normal CAT scan. You're the first I've ever seen, actually."

Gabriel made an attempt at a shrug. "I've always been a bit different."

"You've made my job interesting, that's for sure." The doctor turned and examined the display of numbers on the machine next to his bed. "Your oxygen looks good, and your heart rate is pretty good, but your blood pressure is a little elevated. Are you in pain?"

"Some. Nothing too bad," Gabriel said dismissively. The pain was nagging a bit at the back of his mind, but it was the least of his concerns.

"I can get you something more for pain, if you like," the doctor offered.

Gabriel shook his head. He had just come back around. The last thing he needed was some damn pain meds that would inevitably fog his brain and take him right back under. "Not yet. I just woke up, and that would only knock me back out."

"Okay," the doctor conceded, "but I'll leave an order with the nurses. Let them know if you need something. Don't try to stick it out too long. You don't need to put unnecessary strain on your system. Just because that bullet missed the major organs doesn't mean you're not still banged up internally."

"Got it," Gabriel told him.

The doctor pulled down the bed coverings and examined the bandages swathing Gabriel's chest. After a brief conversation with the nurse, which Gabriel mostly ignored, the two of them unwrapped the bandages so the doctor could examine the incision.

"Looks good," the doctor said when he had finished the examination and the nurse had cleaned and rewrapped the wound. "You're healing up quite well."

"So does that mean I can get out of here soon?" Gabriel asked.

"We'll see," the doctor hedged. "Given the unusually long time it took for you to come around, I want to keep an eye on you for a day or two more. I'm considering rerunning the CAT scan tomorrow, for comparison. If that comes out clear again, then we can talk about options for release."

"Again?" Gabriel said, and suddenly the significance of what the doctor had been saying earlier came into focus. "Wait a minute. Did you just say I had a perfectly normal CAT scan when they brought me in?"

"Yes, amazingly so."

"Completely normal," Gabriel pressed. "What about signs of previous damage?"

"There were none." Dr. Carver peered at him quizzically. "Should there have been?"

"I was told several years ago that I had some abnormal formation that could have been a birth anomaly or previously undiagnosed damage."

The doctor's frown deepened. "I'll take another look at your previous scan and check again when we rerun them in the morning, but I don't remember seeing anything, and no one else has mentioned that to me. With as many of the neurological staff as we had looking in on your scans, I'm fairly sure someone would have mentioned it. When were the earlier scans done?"

"Ten, maybe fifteen years ago."

Dr. Carver's face cleared. "It was probably just a shadow or an unclear spot on the older scan that someone misread. It happens more often than people realize."

"That makes sense," Gabriel mused. It did make sense, but Gabriel thought it was more than that. Could that damn oath have actually altered his physical body, even his brain? Who was he kidding? Of course it could. It had given him the birthmark, hadn't it? That brought another thought to mind. If it had changed his brain, had it also changed the birthmark?

His first impulse was to get up and find a mirror to look, but the damn tubes still tethered him to the bed.

"Do you have any more questions for me before I go?" the doctor asked.

Did you happen to see whether I still have the sword-shaped birthmark on my shoulder? Gabriel bit back what would undoubtedly seem to be a ridiculous question. "Any chance I can get rid of all these tubes?" He waved his hand over his arms and chest, encompassing both the monitors and IVs.

"Not until you no longer need the IV antibiotics and I'm satisfied you're stable."

Gabriel grumbled but accepted it.

"Anything else?"

"No. Thank you."

"I'll make arrangements for that scan and check on you in the morning." Dr. Carver slipped out the door without waiting for a reply.

Gabriel dropped his head back on the pillow and cursed the fact that he was already feeling tired despite having been awake for no more than an hour, if he'd even managed that. He closed his eyes. He'd just rest them till Moose got back.

CHAPTER TWENTY-FIVE

LUCAS PACED the floor in the living room. Maybe he should just go back to the hospital. When he first got home, he had been exhausted. He fell fully clothed into bed and slept hard for several hours. As much as he hated to admit it, Moose was right. The sleep helped. He awoke feeling like a new man. Then he went through the tedious task of taking a shower without wetting his bandages. He had a waterproof bandage, which made it a little easier, but he still had to be careful. Infection was a very real possibility, not to mention it still hurt like a son of a bitch.

Lucas knew he was extremely lucky. The bullet had hit the outer edge of his abdomen, low near his flank, meaning it damaged nothing but skin and fatty tissue. That was about as lucky as you could get in terms of gunshot wounds, but any gunshot wound was serious, and it wasn't a scratch by any means. He'd bear the scar for the rest of his life, as if he needed a physical reminder.

Showering and cleaning his wound was exhausting, but at least it gave him something to do. Once he went through that ritual and downed his medications—he was hurting from all the moving in the shower, but he skipped the pain pill to avoid the loopy feeling it gave him—there was nothing to do. All he could do was worry and wonder.

He should be working on the piles of homework he had waiting for him. Gabriel, being a professor, would likely consider his schoolwork a priority, but he couldn't concentrate on anything at the moment. He inevitably went back to worrying about Gabriel. The doctors said he'd be fine eventually, but no one could say why he hadn't woken up. If they didn't know why he was still unconscious, how could they possibly know he would be okay? Anything could happen.

Lucas clenched his hands into fists and continued to pace. Moose had told him not to come back until the evening, and Lucas knew he was trying to help, but Moose didn't understand that Lucas needed to be there. He needed it like he needed food. The thought reminded Lucas he hadn't taken time to eat, but his appetite was all but nonexistent. Still he had to eat or the antibiotic would make him sick. Resigned, Lucas headed for the kitchen.

"Hey Eric, I'm going to scrounge up some lunch. You want anything?" he called.

"No thanks," Eric replied from his perch on the corner of the sofa in the living room. Lucas wasn't surprised. Eric seemed to have even less appetite than he did. It was disconcerting. The whole time they had been looking for Eric, Lucas was convinced if they could just get him home, everything would be fine.

But Eric was nothing like himself. He hadn't left the house since Lucas was released from the hospital. The doctors had said he was physically fine. He was a bit underweight and had cuts and bruises galore, but he was miraculously healthy and whole. He was in better shape than Lucas, but he still seemed a shadow of himself. Lucas had enough training on the effects of trauma and sexual abuse to know that wasn't unusual. Physical healing came quickly. Mental and emotional healing could take years, if he ever fully healed. For all Lucas's professional knowledge, it still unnerved him.

He shook off his frustration, reminded himself sternly that these things took time, and made himself a sandwich. After a moment's thought, he made a second one. Being around other people who were eating always made him hungry. Maybe it would do the same for Eric. And even if Eric didn't want it, Lucas could always leave it near him for later. It couldn't hurt.

Lucas took his sandwich into the living room and settled himself in the opposite corner of the sofa from Eric, who didn't like people getting too close. That was about as close as he would comfortably allow Lucas to sit. Eric never argued or told Lucas to leave, but Lucas knew him better than anyone else on the planet. He could see it written in every line of his body, and he had no desire to make anything worse.

"I know you said you weren't hungry, but I brought an extra sandwich anyway," he told Eric. "It's yours if you want it."

Eric flashed him a small smile. The smile didn't quite reach his eyes, but even so, Lucas was relieved he was trying. "Thanks. Maybe I will try to eat something, after all."

Lucas passed the sandwich over with slow, deliberate movements, careful not to startle Eric. Eric took the sandwich without comment. Lucas turned back to his own sandwich and pointedly didn't watch. They ate in companionable silence. That, at least, was familiar. Quiet wasn't bad. Lucas could deal with that.

When he had finished the first few bites of his sandwich, he glanced at the sketch pad that Eric had pushed between them to make room to eat. The sketch was barely begun, but already it had taken on the recognizable shape of a face. "What are you working on?"

Eric swallowed and took a long drink from his bottle of water. "It's a portrait of this girl I met."

"Do I know her?"

Eric shook his head. "I met her… there. I wish I knew what happened to her."

"We could probably find out," Lucas said. "Moose might know. Or if not I'm sure Agent Parrish would. What's her name?"

"They called her Chyna, but her real name was Monique. She really helped me out. I probably wouldn't have made it past the first day."

"She sounds great. Let me check with Moose and see if he knows anything." Not to mention it was the perfect way for Lucas to check in on Gabriel without seeming like he was checking in on Gabriel. Just as he picked up his phone from the charger, it rang and Moose's number flashed on the screen.

Lucas's heart shot into his throat. "What's wrong?" he demanded as soon as he clicked the button to answer.

"Nothing's wrong," Moose replied. "Calm down, kid. He's fine. He's better than fine, actually. He's awake."

"He's awake," Lucas echoed, staggered.

"Awake and talking and as ornery as ever. His memory is a little shaky, but he's pretty intact," Moose continued.

Lucas breathed a sigh of relief. Since the doctors hadn't had any idea what caused Gabriel's prolonged unconsciousness, they also didn't know what to expect in regard to his mental status when he finally woke up. There was no damage as far as they could see on any of the numerous scans they'd run, but there was also nothing they could see to cause him to be out for as long as he had been.

"I'll be there as soon as I can," Lucas said. He had already set the remnants of his sandwich aside and was reaching for his keys. Then a horrible thought occurred to him. "Wait. You said his memory was shaky. Does he remember me?" The possibility that Gabriel wouldn't remember him was almost too horrible to contemplate, but they hadn't known each other very long. What would he do if the man he loved didn't even remember him?

"Of course he remembers you," Moose assured him. "He woke up asking for you."

The knot of anxiety in Lucas's chest melted, only to be followed by a crushing wave of regret. Dammit. He should've been there. Gabriel shouldn't have had to look for him. His face should have been the first thing Gabriel saw when he woke up. He should have never let Moose talk him into leaving. Never mind that he was exhausted. He should have been there for Gabriel.

"Hey, kid, you still there?" Moose's voice broke into his thoughts. "Did I lose you?"

"No, no. I'm still here, just…. You know what? Never mind. I'm on my way." Lucas hung up the phone before Moose could ask any more questions.

"What's up?" Eric asked as he watched Lucas push to his feet and gather up his essentials.

"Gabriel's awake."

"Hey, man, that's great," Eric said, his face lighting up with real pleasure.

That was easily the most animation Lucas had seen in Eric's face since he came home, but he didn't have time to dwell on it. "I've got to go. Moose says he's asking for me. You're welcome to come along, if you'd like."

Eric shook his head. "No, not today. He probably doesn't need a bunch of strangers crowding around when he just woke up, anyway."

Eric was reluctant to do much of anything these days. Particularly anything that involved being out of the house. That didn't stop Lucas from trying, though. "Maybe tomorrow?"

Eric nodded. "Maybe tomorrow."

IT WAS all Lucas could do not to run down the hospital hallway. His wound ached so much that he just about managed to limp along with great care, but he still wanted to run. He wanted to see Gabriel. Part of him seriously regretted forgoing that pain pill, but the other part knew that if he had taken it, he never would have heard his phone when Moose called. No matter how much he hurt right then, he couldn't regret being awake for that call.

He rounded the corner into the hallway where Gabriel's room was located and nearly plowed into Moose. Moose stood with one shoulder resting against the wall and typed into his phone with practiced ease. He looked up, startled, when Lucas came to a sudden halt, and whatever he had been about to say morphed into a genuine smile.

"Easy there, kid. I know you want to see him, but it won't do you any good to end up in the hospital bed next to him."

"How is he?" Lucas demanded. "Is he—" He bit his lip, not sure how to phrase the question. "Himself?" he said finally. The doctors had warned them that, even though the scans looked good, there was no way to tell what effect the prolonged period of unconsciousness might have.

"As far as I can tell," Moose said matter-of-factly. "He knew me immediately, and he remembered you, but he had some trouble remembering your roommate's name and the name of the girl we found with him."

That wasn't particularly concerning. Given the amount of stress Gabriel had been under at the time he met those two, the fact that he remembered them at all was encouraging.

"Physically he looks better than you," Moose continued. It was teasing, but only partly. Lucas could hear the real concern that lay beneath the teasing.

"I'm fine," Lucas replied. Moose raised an eyebrow, and it was so much like Gabriel that Lucas responded automatically. "Okay, so maybe I shouldn't have skipped that last pain pill, but I couldn't take the chance that I'd be asleep when he woke up. As it turned out, I was right. I wouldn't have heard your call."

"He's not going to like that you're hurting," Moose predicted.

"Probably not," Lucas agreed, "but I'll gladly take that lecture to get to see him. Don't worry. It will be better once I can sit down. I promise."

"Okay, then," Moose agreed. He pushed open the door to Gabriel's room. "Go park your butt in the chair. And you let me know if it doesn't ease. I'll go find the nurse. This is a hospital. Surely they can find a damn pain pill."

Lucas heard him, but he couldn't move. He was frozen in the doorway as his eyes bored into Gabriel's.

"What's wrong, kid?" Gabriel asked. He pushed up on his elbows, and his brows knit in concern. "Are you hurting?"

"Not anymore," Lucas choked. "You're back. You're really back." And then he ran before he could stop himself, flung himself over the low rails, heedless of Gabriel's bandages or his own, wrapped his arms around Gabriel's neck, and clung as hard as he dared.

The tears he'd been holding back burst forth. "You wouldn't wake up, and no one knew why. We were beginning to think you might not ever."

That was the fear that had plagued Lucas for days, the one he hadn't dared let himself voice. He was terrified Gabriel had somehow miraculously survived the bullet, only to linger in an interminable coma. There were fates worse than death, and he wouldn't wish that on his worst enemy—let alone the man he loved.

That was another realization he'd come to over the last few days. He loved Gabriel, really loved him. It wasn't just some student crush or sex-crazed lust born out of a stressful situation. Gabriel was the love of his life, and he vowed that if he ever got him back, he would never let him go.

"Hey, it's okay," Gabriel said gently and ran a hand over Lucas's head and back. "I'm here now. I'm right here. I've got you."

When the worst of the storm had passed, Lucas pushed himself back to standing and dropped into the chair Moose had conveniently positioned behind him. "Don't ever do that to me again," Lucas said fiercely.

"Don't plan—" Gabriel caught sight of Lucas's neck. He reached out and tentatively brushed his fingers over a fading bruise. "Oh my God. I did that, didn't I?"

"Not consciously," Lucas said.

"Is that supposed to be some kind of excuse?" Gabriel demanded. "How can you even stand to be near me? I tried to kill you."

"No, you didn't," Lucas insisted. "When you did that, you thought I was an enemy combatant. As soon as you realized it was me, you stopped."

"This time," Gabriel said bitterly. "That doesn't mean you should give me a chance to try again. I told you before. I'm nothing but a killer. You'd do well to stay far, far away."

"You are no such thing." Lucas vaulted back to his feet, without regard to the sharp catch in his muscles. "Have you killed? Yes, absolutely. And I'm very glad you did. Castillo might well have killed me if you hadn't, but you've never consciously hurt me. Even in the midst of a homicidal rage, the minute you realized it was me, you stopped."

"He's right, Shadow," Moose said quietly. "I don't know how he did it, but he stopped you. I was listening on the comms. The kid did what I've seen trained operatives fail to do."

Lucas shook his head. "It wasn't anything I did. You recognized me. I knew you would. You did the first time too."

"First time?" Gabriel echoed. "How many times have you let me get away with doing this now?"

"The night after the first time they located Castillo, when he ran. I was frustrated and rattling and getting on your nerves. You grabbed me, and for a minute, there was this look on your face like you could've snapped my neck without a thought. But you caught yourself. You stopped. You always stop, and you always will."

"You willing to stake your life on that?"

Lucas laughed. "It's a little late to be asking that question now. I've been putting my life in your hands for weeks now. I've trusted you with more than my life. I've even trusted you with my heart."

Gabriel stared at him, stunned. "You really mean that. How could you possibly feel that way about someone like me?"

"You saved my life, for a start," Lucas said. "You rescued my best friend from a human trafficking ring, and you believed me when nobody else would. You're a good man, Gabriel Ingram, and one day you're going to believe that even if I have to spend the rest of my life proving it to you."

"That's a long time," Gabriel responded wryly. "You may get tired of me long before then."

"I doubt that," Lucas said. "Haven't you figured out yet that I love you and I'm not planning on going anywhere?"

GABRIEL STARED at him, stunned. In all his life, no one had ever said those words to him. It should have been unbelievable, but it wasn't— not coming from Lucas. Lucas, with his big heart, actually did love him. What's more, Gabriel loved Lucas just as much. He never thought he could feel that emotion, but Lucas had brought it out.

"I love you too," he said abruptly. The words felt awkward and foreign, but he meant them with every cell in his body.

Lucas lit up like the stars in the night sky. "Good. Now that we've got that settled, I can't wait for you to get out of here so we can actually date properly like a normal couple."

Normal. That was another one of those words that never applied to him, but right then, at that moment, even weak and hooked up to any number of machines, Gabriel thought it was possible. He had battled his demons and survived. For the first time in his life, he could finally be normal. He could live an ordinary life with the man he loved, and that was a miracle all its own.

EPILOGUE

GABRIEL FIDGETED in the stifling heat of the crowded auditorium and tried to keep his expression neutral. For the love of anything holy, who decided that holding graduation in June and requiring formal academic regalia was a good idea? It was a subtle form of torture. But Lucas liked him in it, and this was Lucas's graduation. For that reason alone, he wouldn't have missed it for the world, heat and academic torture devices be damned.

So much in his life had changed in the past year and a half—most of it due to the stubborn blond whirlwind who had managed to worm his way into his life and his heart. With Lucas he had finally found the normal life he'd been searching for. At least as normal as he would probably ever be. Dates got interrupted by emergency calls from distraught foster parents or equally fractious teenage foster children. Once or twice he found himself sheltering a kid who had nowhere else to go. Lucas was on a campaign to convince him to be licensed as a foster parent himself. Him, of all people.

A year ago the thought would have been utterly ridiculous, but things had changed. For one, by some miracle, the rage he had fought his entire life was gone. Since the moment he first woke up in the hospital, it had just disappeared, as though the curse that had followed him from birth was suddenly shattered. Even weirder, his birthmark had vanished. He woke up into the light to find all of the darkness that always plagued him had dissipated.

For the first time, he was able to live as a normal man with a normal life and normal emotions. He could laugh and love without the constant battle to contain the rage and the need to kill. It was at once a staggering shock and a miraculous freedom, but it was one he loved getting used to. He might never understand exactly what happened during that final battle with Castillo, but he knew with certainty that it had saved him as much as it had Eric and the others.

Gabriel flicked his eyes over the audience and searched for Eric's distinctive rainbow-colored spiked hair. He found it toward the back of the sea of people, and unless he missed his guess, Moose flanked him on one side, and the bouncer from Sparks was on the other. Good. Eric still struggled with many aftereffects of his kidnapping, and discomfort with crowds was one of them. Gabriel hadn't been entirely sure Eric would make it at all, however much both he and Lucas wanted him to. He had to hand it to Eric. The guy had courage in spades.

It was Eric who finally convinced Lucas to move in with Gabriel after graduation. They all knew it was what Lucas wanted, but Lucas, compassionate do-gooder that he was, couldn't bring himself to leave Eric. Instead Lucas spent the past year shuttling between his apartment and Gabriel's house, trying to be everything for everyone. Gabriel tried for months to convince Lucas that continuing to do so just wasn't sustainable. He even went so far as to offer to move Eric into one of his guest rooms, if that would help, since Lucas was no longer using it, but Lucas was nothing if not stubborn. He was adamant that Eric had already lost far too much, and there was no way he was going to let him lose anything else—not his roommate and not his home.

Until Eric finally confessed he wanted to leave. There were too many ghosts in town. It was where he met Damien and the whole horrible nightmare started. He needed to get away from the places and the memories, to start somewhere fresh. Gabriel privately thought that was a very wise decision. Sometimes you really did need to start over again, but Lucas was devastated.

Eric's kidnapping was the longest the two of them had been apart since they were children, and Lucas couldn't bear the idea of Eric being gone again. But eventually Lucas came around. Monique, who was such a help to him in those first awful days of captivity, was located in Ohio the week after Eric came home, and the two had been in touch ever since. Monique had found a place for herself in a small town in Connecticut that had an excellent LGBT community center and mentoring program, and invited Eric to join her. He decided to take her up on it. He and Lucas gave notice on their apartment, and late next week, they would get them all moved out.

Lucas had a new job to look forward to as well. He had been hired by a nonprofit counseling center in a neighboring town. They had several adult therapists and a play therapist who specialized in young children, but Lucas was to become their adolescent specialist. Gabriel couldn't think of anyone better for the job. But first they had the milestone of graduation to celebrate.

The graduates from the school of social work were announced, and Gabriel turned his attention back to the proceedings. From below the raised platform where he and the other faculty were seated, Lucas looked up, found him, and met his gaze with a grin and a wink that very nearly made Gabriel lose his composure. The naughty little minx knew exactly what he was doing too. Gabriel raised an eyebrow, but Lucas wasn't in the least cowed. Instead his grin broadened.

Then Lucas climbed the steps to the stage as his name was called. In the crowd, Gabriel saw Moose rise to his feet, put two fingers in his mouth, and let out an ear-piercing whistle. Beside him Eric winced but held his ground. Lucas caught sight of them and burst out laughing. Then he turned back and shot Gabriel a smile meant for him alone, full of the promise of things to come. Awareness zinged through Gabriel. It made his efforts to stay somber and solemn for the occasion even harder, but he wouldn't have it any other way.

Exclusive Excerpt

Lochlann

ORDER OF THE BLACK KNIGHTS

By Andrea Speed

Violence has been Lochlann O'Connor's companion since he was born into a family of old-school Irish terrorists. From there, he is recruited into Alpha, a secret government agency dedicated to fighting terrorism—with extreme prejudice. Lochlann's bravery, efficiency, ruthlessness—and the natural dead eye that lets him hit anything that moves—quickly make him one of the shadowy organization's most valued operatives.

Cas Vega joins Alpha because it's marginally better than a prison sentence. He's a former drug cartel assassin—or at least that's his story. But Lochlann is suspicious. Despite an irrational and overwhelming attraction to Cas, Lochlann has questions, and they soon lead to a deeper and deadlier mystery. What is Alpha's true purpose, and why does it seem they want to eliminate Lochlann?

Lochlann and Cas must work together to get to the bottom of Alpha's scheme and escape it, and all while Cas keeps secrets that could cost him his life if they're revealed. But it's not an alliance that can last. Duty turns the men into enemies, even while fate compels them into each other's arms. Before they can contemplate which will prevail, they must figure out how to survive.

Coming Soon to
www.dreamspinnerpress.com

PROLOGUE

1963

KLAXONS SCREAMED as Lochlann raced through the darkened corridors, searching out the base intruders. He had a stitch in his side from the bullet wound, but Lochlann was pretty sure it was nothing serious. It just bled like a motherfucker.

It was supposed to be an undercover CIA base, disguised as a sugar processing plant. In fact it was a working plant, but it functioned mainly as cover, in spite of the tidy profit it raked in. People loved their sugar.

Still, if anyone bothered to check, they'd discover that security for a simple factory was a bit overboard. Also the physical security was cutting-edge technology. It was there, buried within an adjunct storage room—a secret cluster of offices and hallways where the CIA did its business in this country. No, they weren't supposed to be there, but that was a separate argument.

Lochlann had run what felt like the entire length of the base, and saw no signs of any interlopers. He was about to double back when he came up to the sealed doors that led out to the storage area and saw a small spot of blood on the floor. He was pretty sure Wilson tagged one before he was shot dead.

Lochlann tried to pass through the doors quietly, but it made some noise, and he was greeted with a hail of bullets. Lochlann shot back blindly and darted inside to duck behind a collection of crates. He was sure he was hit again as he felt a wasplike sting on his arm, but he didn't have time to deal with it. What was an extra bullet anyway? As long as it didn't slow him down, he didn't care.

All Lochlann needed was a glimpse of them. He could hit anything he saw, so all he needed was a hint, a shadow in his vision.

Bullets hit the crates, and splinters flew, causing him to duck. He did not need a sliver in the eye.

The smell of gunpowder finally overpowered the strange scent of cooked sugar that permeated the entire grounds of the plant. At first Lochlann had liked it, but then he hated it. If he never had to smell it again, it'd be too soon.

Finally the men had to stop to reload, and that's when Lochlann made his move. His Beretta in hand, Lochlann stepped out from behind the crates and scanned the room. He caught a glimpse of a shadow behind some large bags of sugar and shot once. He caught the man in the chest, and the bullet left a puff of sugar behind as it cut through them. A second man reared up behind some other crates, and Lochlann shot him in the head before he could fire a single shot.

He caught sight of a man in the shadows, and he almost hesitated, but muscle memory kicked in and he shot him before he even realized what he'd done. Still the man sort of looked like that guy he saw in that bar—that "special" bar he accidentally came across while walking back to his apartment a few nights earlier. Lochlann had taken a different way, because he liked to mix it up just to make sure he wasn't followed. And seeing that bar put a jolt through him. He knew they existed—he even went to one once—but seeing one always terrified him. Like just being in the vicinity of one made him guilty, showed the world he preferred the companionship of men. Lochlann knew he'd lose his job if his superiors had any idea, so he kept to himself and never went out anywhere. But he recalled glancing inside the bar and catching the eyes of a dark-haired, dark-eyed man who was so beautiful… and so tempting.

He hadn't been able to run away fast enough.

Lochlann wondered if it was the same man—if it was coincidence or something else—but he didn't bother to go see if the man was indeed a match. He simply scanned the darkened room, looking for any more gunmen, but it seemed like he got them all. Score one for him.

Lochlann was halfway across the room when he realized how light-headed he was. It was almost pleasant, except it got worse, and he looked down at his arm. The bullet had passed right through it, which he sort of suspected. But then it had gone through his torso and put another hole in his side. You'd think he should have felt that, but no, somehow he hadn't.

He collapsed to his knees on the poured-concrete floor, which hurt, but distantly, as though he were already removed from his body. Lochlann tried to stop himself from falling on his face, but his arm didn't work quite right, and he did it anyway. Since he still felt removed from himself, it didn't hurt like it should have.

Lochlann was cold and numb, but weirdly enough, it didn't seem so bad. He was suddenly aware he wasn't alone in the room, but he wasn't sure what he could do about it. "Here we are again, Lochlann," a deep, familiar voice said. "You never learn, do you?"

Lochlann looked up to see a man in an anachronistic gray robe, his face half-shadowed by his hood. His eyes were like polished stones, his lips thin and taut. He could have been fifty or five hundred or any number in between. But just seeing him gave Lochlann a cold shock down his spine and through his body, as though a ghost had passed over his grave.

He didn't understand it or what he could have been doing there. But when he went to push himself up, he found he was looking down at his body on the floor. "You're dying," the man said. "Are you really surprised, Brute?"

Lochlann wasn't, although he wasn't sure why the costumed old man was there, or why he instinctively hated him. Until it felt like something snapped in his mind, a dam broke, and he suddenly remembered…

…everything.

Lochlann remembered standing in the ruins of his village, up to his ankles in mud and blood, the cottages smoking ruins, the bodies already beset by flies and dogs. He was gone hardly three days on a hunt, and it didn't seem possible that his home could be wiped out so fast. He briefly considered burying the dead before he discovered it wasn't just some of his village that was slaughtered. It was all of them—from the oldest man trampled by horses to a baby ripped in half like a loaf of bread. The cruelty of this senseless act was bottomless.

There was a survivor—the old witch woman who lived in the forest—who told him of strangers from the sea who slaughtered everything in their path. If they had known of her, out there in her isolation, they'd have probably have killed her, but they were unaware and never found her.

From then on Lochlann made it his mission to hunt the bastards down to make them pay for what they did. But he was one man—and a young, impetuous man at that. He didn't have the strength or the ability to do it, no matter how hard he tried. He lurked at the seaside, hoping to take passage on a boat and travel to their lands. But his reputation preceded him, and most captains wouldn't let him on their craft. One night, in the shadows of a tavern, he encountered a man named Moriel. "They call you the Brute, do they not?" The old man in the hooded robe seemed grimly amused, and his eyes were as hard and cold as marble.

Lochlann shrugged. He was a little drunk, but not so soused he didn't sense what the man was going to ask him. He'd been approached by people before who wanted him to kill for them. "I'm not for hire."

"Even if I knew where the men you are hunting were? And could take you to them?"

Lochlann glared at him and grabbed him by the collar of his rough-hewn robe. "How could you—" He got no further. The man pushed him back with more force than he ever could have anticipated, and when Lochlann hit the ground, he was someplace else. *They* were someplace else.

For a second Lochlann thought it was the drink. He genuinely tried to believe that, but he wasn't drunk enough to deny the feeling of smooth stone under his hand or the smell of scented smoke in the air, replacing the gut-clenching stench of sea salt and dead fish. They'd gone from the alley behind the tavern to some sort of throne room, or perhaps a cave. He wasn't sure; the lighting was sparse. "You're a wizard." Lochlann hadn't really believed in such things. The old woman hadn't been a witch. That was just old wives' tales. But there was no other explanation, was there? His mind reeled, and he desperately wished he was drunker.

"My name is Moriel, and I have a proposition for you. Swear an oath to serve me, and I will give you the revenge you desperately seek. You will never want for anything again. In this life and all others."

"All others?" Lochlann repeated. That felt like a trap, but he couldn't quite suss it out. "What does the oath require?"

"A signature in blood. Nothing else."

That seemed wrong. But if he were in fact a wizard, he could give him the men who had gotten away. They would finally pay for their crimes. It wasn't like Lochlann had anything else. His family was dead. His village was dead. He was an orphan in the world, with no one to miss him or mourn him when he was gone. He might as well be dead already. "What's in it for you?"

Moriel smiled, but it was a nasty little smirk, as cold and sharp as a knife. "To gain the throne I require loyal knights. Once you get your revenge, I expect you to serve me."

"And do what?"

"What you do so well, Brute. I've seen your work. You are an efficient killer. No wasted effort with you. That would be quite useful."

Lochlann didn't like that at all. If he was indeed a wizard, there was no way he was good. But Lochlann was hardly good either. He'd killed a dozen men. His hands might as well be permanently stained red. Yes, he did it for revenge, to make them pay for their crimes, but it didn't bring back the dead. It didn't replace a single wall. It just gave him a hollow feeling when it didn't give him the feeling of triumph he so badly wanted. It seemed like vengeance was a hole that simply got bigger and could never be filled, no matter how many bodies you threw in it. "Is this oath forever?"

Moriel made a small noise in his throat. He was in front of a low table with a quill pen and a piece of parchment on it, lit only by a small red candle. The table hadn't been there before, but Lochlann never saw him set it up. Were they even in the same room? "That's up to you, isn't it? Always there will be one person, one enemy you can spare to break the contract."

"How will I know this person?"

"You won't. So choose wisely."

That sounded insane. It *was* insane. But Lochlann had nothing to lose. He was barely a person—more of a nasty fairy tale told to scare bad children. He would die bloody, or drunk. Possibly both. There was no way he could make his life worse.

Lochlann pulled out his short sword and ran it across his left forearm, opening a cut. He put the sword on the table, picked up the quill, dipped it in his wound, and made a mark on the paper. At first it didn't look like anything was written on the paper, but as soon as his blood touched it, the parchment filled with words and runes, arcane symbols that might mean something to men much smarter than him. By the time he put the pen down, Lochlann felt a tingling in his left arm. He looked down to find the wound had not only healed, but there appeared to be a red mark in its place that looked for all the world like a broken sword.

"Wise choice, Lochlann," Moriel said.

But even though he felt powerful, Lochlann was sure it was a mistake. But too late.

"What the hell...?" Lochlann, suddenly back in the storage area of the sugar plant, watched himself bleeding out on the floor. That couldn't have been real, right? Except it was. He remembered everything, including dying a dozen times, maybe more. Each time killing for a cause, whether it be as high-minded as protecting a nation's political interest or as basic as want of money. It was a cruel joke repeated over and over again until it became nothing but a rote tragedy. "I killed him?"

Moriel pointed to the dead body in the shadows. "You always do."

"Stop this," Lochlann demanded. "You got what you wanted. Free me from my oath."

Moriel folded his hands in front of him like a peaceful monk. "The power to break this contract is yours alone. Make better choices and free yourself."

Lochlann snarled at the wizard and lunged for him, but it was pointless. He was not physically there. In fact maybe it was all some bizarre hallucination kicked up by his dying, desperate brain.

Except Lochlann knew it wasn't. And even though he knew he would live again, he didn't want to.

But no matter what Moriel claimed, that power was out of Lochlann's hands.

RK STAUNTON rebelled against having a Christmas birthday in favor of making an unexpected debut in early fall instead, and she's been doing the unexpected ever since. This tendency has resulted in many adventures, including a ten-year stint as a guide in that strange urban jungle called middle school. While entertaining, that expedition ultimately proved too harrowing. After finally making her escape, she turned to a quieter life masquerading as a crazy cat lady living in a small town in the southeastern US.

RK has lived with a menagerie of characters inside her head for as long as she can remember. In a desperate bid to preserve her sanity, she has begun to transcribe the tales they tell her. This endeavor has proven to be fun, occasionally profitable, and cheaper than therapy. It has also fueled raging addictions to caffeine and chocolate on top of her lifelong addiction to books, but everyone is entitled to a vice or three, right?

On the rare occasions when the characters release RK from her duties as scribe, she enjoys chasing dragonflies and volunteering with orphan care charities. RK considers the Internet her second home. She can often be hanging out there at one of her many favorite haunts.

Website: www.rkstaunton.com
Facebook: www.facebook.com/rkstaunton
Twitter: @rk_staunton

ORDER OF THE BLACK KNIGHTS

He struck an unholy bargain,
and now he's paying the price...
again, and again, and again...

GIDEON

Ashe Barker

Order of theBlack Knights

Gideon Maybury enjoys a life of wealth and privilege, not to mention the advantages his position offers him in his career as a merchant banker and his less public life as a high-class, skilled, and very well-paid assassin for Her Majesty's government. When his brother dies unexpectedly, he becomes the Duke of Westmoreland.

Michael Mathison has hated Gideon since they were at university together. He's convinced Gideon had a hand in the death of Michael's college lover, Christopher, and that he had something to do with the death of his own brother. So he gets a job as Gideon's driver, enabling him to investigate the circumstances surrounding the death of the elder Maybury sibling. At first his suspicions seem to be confirmed, but clues emerge that suggest all is not as it appears at Maybury Hall.

As the mystery deepens, so does the attraction between the two implacable enemies, as does the feeling that they have met before— under dark and terrible circumstances. Each has reasons not to trust the other, but neither is averse to a bit of kinky play. Gideon and Michael end up owing each other their lives, and it results in consequences neither could have imagined.

www.dreamspinnerpress.com

Wealth and power were promised.
Hell was given. Can he give up
everything to break free?

MATTHIAS

Alexis Duran

Order of the Black Knights

From Louisiana swamp rat to revivalist huckster to skilled con artist, Matthias Krall clawed his way out of poverty using his natural gifts of grift and manipulation to become the leader of an exclusive retreat center. Exploiting the guise of spiritual guru, Matthias seduces the rich and powerful into turning over their lives and fortunes to his control. But wealth and a small cadre of loyal followers can't protect Matthias from the betrayal he knows is imminent. Everyone wants what Matthias has, except for one man who wants to destroy it. Dylan Connelly is a reporter who's determined to prove the charismatic recluse is not only a fraud but a murderer.

Irresistibly drawn to Dylan despite the warnings in his gut, Matthias lures Dylan to his island retreat, determined to destroy his enemy once and for all.

www.dreamspinnerpress.com

ORDER OF THE BLACK KNIGHTS
Will he kill the one who can save him... again?
VESPAR
Thianna Durston

Order of the Black Knights

Special-ops-turned-professional-killer Vespar McKauley is hired to take out Marcolm Rogers, son of his employer's worst enemy. But Marc isn't like any hit he's ever done. He's just twenty-one, he goes to a private university studying English Lit, and for fun, he plays computer games with his friends. No drugs, no partying, no crime. The day Vespar bumps into Marc and looks into his azure eyes, the world drops out from under him.

With his father in the Chicago crime syndicate, Marc and his mom have stayed out of the limelight, hiding from those who might harm them. He figures he's safe at a small liberal arts university, all the way across the country. But midway through his senior year, he feels eyes on him and the shadows encroaching. Just as he's about to run, he meets Vespar and experiences an instant attraction. When Vespar tells him he's in danger and offers to protect him, Marc wants to believe him. But he's been hunted before, and this time he isn't sure he'll get away. Especially when he finds out he is Vespar's target.

www.dreamspinnerpress.com

ORDER OF THE BLACK KNIGHTS

From the depths
of despair, a
hero shall rise.

JAEGER
Evelise Archer

Order of the Black Knights

US Marshal Jaeger Tripp is assigned to the Federal Witness Protection Program. The hurt and destruction he's seen—along with protecting criminals who are only cooperating with the authorities to keep themselves out of jail—have left him with a bleak and jaded view of both life and people. His current assignment is Wren O'Riley, a computer wizard who witnessed a high-profile cartel hit.

To Jaeger, Wren is the same as any other job. He must protect him long enough to get him to testify at trial, and his personal feelings have no place in his work and must be set aside. But that's easier said than done. On the run and fighting for their lives, Jaeger and Wren can't help but grow closer. And Jaeger can't help seeing beyond Wren's nerdy exterior to a man who might be just what Jaeger needs to settle his soul and capture his heart—if they survive long enough to get that chance.

www.dreamspinnerpress.com

www.ingramcontent.com/pod-product-compliance
Lightning Source LLC
Chambersburg PA
CBHW070114260626
47160CB00004B/1460